Dance
with a Devil

by

Iona Morrison

A Blue Cove Mystery

Dance with a Devil

Cover Art by *Debbie Taylor*

The Wild Rose Press, Inc.
PO Box 708
Adams Basin, NY 14410-0708
Visit us at www.thewildrosepress.com

Publishing History
First Fantasy Rose Edition, 2017
Print ISBN 978-1-5092-1216-3
Digital ISBN 978-1-5092-1217-0

A Blue Cove Mystery
Published in the United States of America

Dedication

Dedicated to Rob, the love of my life
and to my three sons, John, Tim, and James.
Each one has been a constant source of joy
and encouragement to me.

Chapter 1

Someone was watching her. The terrifying thought hit Jessie as she rounded the corner, starting the incline back to her cottage. She wiped the droplets of sweat running down her cheek with the back of her hand. The moon had slipped from sight, leaving the overcast sky darker than normal. Something wasn't kosher. A shiver racked her sweaty body. Panicked, she stifled the scream forcing its way up her throat. He was closing in fast. Yes, it was a man. Where was he? She searched the area as she ran but couldn't see anything. Her heart beat rapidly. Faster, she had to run faster. A stitch hit her side, sending sharp pains vibrating through her, stealing her breath. *Don't stop! Keep moving,* her mind screamed! She ran, her feet pummeling the ground, propelling her forward. Tree branches, whipped by the wind like twiggy fingers, reached out to grab her, clawing at her again and again. She looked over her shoulder, stumbled slightly; he was gaining ground.

The inky darkness hiding her pursuer offered her a sliver of hope. The moon eased its way from behind the clouds to cast its pale glow on two runners on the path ahead, and then it slipped behind the clouds for the second time. With sides burning, she pushed with her last energy to catch up with them. She kept pace with the couple and knew the minute he had veered off from his pursuit. The terror subsided.

Jessie ran back to her cottage, only stopping once she was safely inside with the door locked. Bending over, she grabbed her sides, panting for air. *Now, what?* She closed the curtains, double checking windows and doors. Exhaling a hiss of air, she gasped for another breath. *Calm down!* A wave of panic seized her again. The sweat dripped down her face until she wiped it with a towel. Inhaling deeply, she waited for her heart rate to slow. Her eyes took in the familiar setting from the blue-gray walls to the sun-washed floral chairs. It all felt surreal.

Pushing Matt's number, she got his voicemail. *"Hey, Matt, this is Jessie. I need you to call me as soon as possible. Something happened tonight. You need to know about it. Please call me when you get this."* A tinge of anger bubbled up to the surface, pushing aside her fear for a moment. She was mad at him but didn't want to be.

It was probably just her imagination, but Matt had been a little more remote since Katie's brother Liam was in town and talking about moving to Blue Cove. It seemed like days since they had last talked, at least without Liam hanging around. Matt didn't like him. A frown crossed Jessie's face. She couldn't blame him really; Liam managed to show up every time they went out together. He had to be finagling information from Katie, which meant she couldn't talk freely with her friend anymore. His constant pursuit was beginning to take its toll on her. Worse yet, Jessie had to keep the peace between the two men, who squared off every time they saw each other. It was turning into a full-time job. She was sick of being in the middle of it. Besides being ready to pull her hair out, she would like to give

Liam a piece of her mind. She had tried to be diplomatic. He didn't seem to get the message, no matter what she said to him. Matt didn't think she was saying enough, and she thought it would be nice if Matt lent a hand. Stalemate. Frowning at the phone in her hand, which was still silent, she had no clue what to do next.

She set the phone down a bit more firmly than she had intended. Case in point, normally, if Matt saw it was her, he would have answered immediately or at least phoned her right back. Silence. The clock edged its way toward the ten-minute mark since she had called him. If the darn phone didn't ring soon, she would call Dylan.

"Finally," she grabbed the ringing phone.

"Hi, sweetheart, I got your message. I'm on my way to your place right now. You can tell me everything when I get there."

"Sure, I can wait." Anger flashed in her eyes. "Waiting on you is all I've been doing," she muttered under her breath.

"Sorry, Jess, I can't hear you. I must have a bad connection. We'll talk. I'm almost there."

"Whatever. Thanks, Matt." Irritation punctuated her words. What was wrong with her? Her expression soured. If it hadn't been for those runners, she wouldn't be here to talk to him at all.

Jessie heard Katie outside the door, and she knew without looking that Liam would be there too. She slapped her hand on her forehead. Great. Liam would be here again when Matt arrived.

Jessie unlocked the door and opened it. "Hi, what are you two up to?" Trying to sound cordial, she

3

motioned them in. She could hear her voice tremble.

"We're out for a walk on this nice evening, the first one warm enough to be outside in a while. It'll snow again, you can count on it. You have to get outside when the weather permits. Plus, my big brother wanted to stop by and say hi." Katie winked at her.

Jessie clutched her hands at her sides. "It's nice weather, for sure. I ran outside for the first time in weeks. Felt great." Small talk wasn't helping. She needed Matt.

"I can see." Katie pointed at her running clothes. "I haven't seen you in that get-up for a while."

"I've been working out at the gym mostly, which I plan to do for the foreseeable future." She clasped her clammy hands behind her back. "I was just talking to Matt. He's on his way here." She looked directly at Liam willing him to leave. "We need to talk privately over a case." She hoped he could take a hint but probably not. Liam appeared content to stand there looking way too comfortable.

Katie grabbed his hand. "I hope it's not another big case. Come on, brother. We need to let them talk."

Liam shook off Katie's hand. He placed his arm on Jessie's shoulder. "You seem a little rattled. Is there something wrong? Do you need to talk? Can I help?"

She shook her head. "I'm fine. Matt's the one I need to discuss this with." Darn, she never could hide her emotions.

Jessie heard the light rap on the door. Matt walked in and was not happy. She could see it in his eyes. Stuck in the middle again.

****

Matt leaned against the doorframe, his eyes

4

narrowed. Jessie's clothes were damp with perspiration, she was twisting her hair around her finger—not a good sign. Something was wrong. Liam's arm around her didn't help either. He frowned; his hand curled into a fist.

"Hi, Matt, we were just leaving. Jessie said she needed to talk to you." Katie grabbed Liam's hand for the second time.

"Matt." Liam lifted his chin. "I was trying to get our girl Jessie to tell me what has her so upset." He dropped Katie's hand again.

"Liam," Matt nodded coolly at him, "I'm sure she'll talk when she's ready. Did you find a place yet?"

"Not yet. I'm looking for a storefront to set up my practice. If I decide this is where I want to settle in. I have to make sure the conditions are right for it." He looked pointedly at Jessie. "I think I might maintain my practice in the city and come out here on the weekends to help Katie." Liam finally moved when Katie tugged on his hand a third time.

"That might be a practical thing to do. I'm sure you'll figure it out." Matt took Liam's place beside Jessie. He put his arm around her and drew her close to his side.

Katie pulled her brother out the door with her. "I'll stop by tomorrow, Jessie. You know how I need to know what's going on. It's my job." She chuckled. "Jeremy should be here in a couple of weeks, and we need to double."

"Sounds good," she said distractedly. Jessie walked out from under Matt's arm to shut the door. She locked it and turned the deadbolt.

Matt watched her do both. "What's up?" He eased

into his favorite chair, stretching out his legs

She sat on the couch across from him playing with the fringe on the pillows while she told him about what had happened to her during her run. "I know it wasn't my imagination," Jessie clutched a pillow to her chest. "He was real, and he was after me, but I don't know why."

His mind went into overdrive. What had he been thinking? Liam was the least of their problems. There was a hitman out there. The FBI had been tracking him since Palm Springs. Was it possible the man the FBI called "The Hunter" was in the area? "I know it wasn't your imagination, Jess. I don't know where my head has been."

"I don't understand, what do you mean?" She pursed her lips.

"I'll let you know as soon as I have it figured out myself." He looked away from her and leaned his head in his hands.

Her head tilted; she watched him closely. "Who do you think might have chased me? If I hadn't come upon those runners, who knows what might have happened. I'm scared, Matt."

He moved over beside her on the couch, pulling her in protectively to his side. "I'm not sure," his voice sounded gruff to his ears. "I'm thankful you saw the runners ahead of you in time. I'll talk with Maxwell. It's possible," Matt took her hand, "this might be a residual left over from the Palm Springs case. They're all about to go to trial over the next several weeks." He felt her relax against him.

Her eyes narrowed as she glanced sideways at him. "Where have you been? I'm not talking about location either. You've seemed distant to me. I know Liam has been a little underfoot lately." She pressed her lips together shaking her head. "Trust me, I'm not encouraging him. He's a friend from my past and it's bugging me, too. I hope he'll give up soon. But you two together are driving me crazy." She gave him an angry look. "You could, at least, lend a hand in keeping him in his place."

"A little underfoot, hell, he's always here or wherever we are. It's too contrived to be accidental. Liam's arrival hasn't allowed us to have a moment alone, and it's driving me nuts." Matt massaged his temples. "What do you expect from me, Jess? He's your friend. If I lend a hand, it might be to punch him in the face. He knows you're my girl. I've made that clear, yet he's still all over you."

"He's not all over me." She glanced at his skeptical face. "Okay, maybe a little." She looked briefly away. "I've tried to tell him to back off, but he's still hanging around, I just think you could do more…never mind…I don't want to fight."

"I don't want to either. We need to concentrate on what just happened to you. But, the Liam issue isn't going away either. We'll have to come up with something."

She crinkled her nose. "Agreed." She smiled tentatively at him. "Who do you think might have chased me? More importantly, why was he chasing me? I was scared, and I still am."

"I don't have a clue. What do you want to do?"

"Maybe I'll stay at the Inn. I feel uncomfortable knowing he could still be in the area."

"Is Liam still staying there?" Matt's brows rose.

"Yes. Don't you trust me?" She frowned at him again.

"Sweetheart, I trust you completely. I don't trust him," he said under his breath.

"I can't even go see to my friend. He's always hanging around. I know he pumps Katie for the information I've shared with her, or how else would he know where we are all the time." She started to pace.

"Concentrate, Jess." He grabbed her hand, making her stand still. "Why don't you put some things together and you can stay at my place? I have an empty room. I promise to be on my best behavior." He winked at her. "Or I can sleep in your extra room, whichever you prefer."

"Do you mind staying here? I have to be at the store early tomorrow for another delivery."

"That's fine. I've got a bag packed in my car. I've been traveling back and forth to Rocky Pointe during the investigation. I'll grab it and be right back."

She stood at the door watching him. "Hurry, I don't like what I'm sensing."

He walked toward his car, calling Tom Maxwell on his way. "Hey, Tom, this is Matt."

"How's it going, Matt?"

"We may have the beginning of a little situation brewing here. Jessie was being followed tonight." Matt repeated what Jessie had told him. "I'm wondering if maybe there's been some movement or a location shift with the guy you've been tracking."

"It's possible. He turned up missing a couple of days ago according to our surveillance team. I guess he could be in your area. It wouldn't have given him much time to get there, though."

"Damn, not the news I wanted to hear." Matt opened the trunk of the car.

"He's elusive, a mystery man if you know what I mean. My people didn't even know he was gone for a couple of days. Truthfully, from what you've told me so far, it doesn't sound like his MO." Tom paused. "Do you think it's possible you have a predator in the area?"

"Anything is possible, I guess. I didn't think it sounded like his calling card, but I don't like the sound of the alternative either. Have you heard of anything?"

"Not specifically, but I'll check into it for you. I vaguely remember hearing something about the murder of a few women last summer. My team wasn't handling it, so I didn't give it much attention at the time. In the meantime, tell her not to go out alone after dark. No running alone through the woods, for sure, until you have an idea about what you're dealing with. Maybe she should run with someone." Tom cleared his throat and chuckled slightly. "Someone like you, perhaps. I know how much you love to run." He laughed outright.

"Damn, you sound too cheery about me suffering."

"Hey, I'd be happy to volunteer for the job. I wouldn't mind running with her. No sir, I wouldn't mind it at all." Tom chuckled again. "We all have to stay in shape at the Bureau. Unlike you small town cops, we can't afford to get soft around the middle."

"As if I'd ever let that happen. Call me if you pick up the Hunter's trail. Don't be a stranger, Tom. Talk to you later." Matt grinned. Tom sure liked to bait him.

"Okay."

Matt got his bag out of the trunk and walked backed to the cottage. Damn, he couldn't believe they'd lost the guy. Not good, not good at all.

Chapter 2

The minute he walked in, Jessie locked the door behind him. He placed his bag on the back of the couch and took her hand. "We'll figure this out together, sweetheart."

"I know." She led him into the kitchen. "I haven't eaten yet." She opened the refrigerator door and stared blankly inside. "Do you want something?"

"Why don't you watch some TV or take a shower, and I'll make dinner. What sounds good to you?" He watched her fidget with the bread wrapper.

"I don't know. I guess whatever sounds good to you." She chewed on her bottom lip.

"I'll surprise you, how's that?" He saw her nod as she left the room. She walked back over to check the door again and then disappeared into her room. Jessie had been through a lot since moving to Blue Cove, and the one thing she needed to be able to count on was him. He had been absent too much lately. Liam had him off his own game. Enough said. It stops now.

The table was set, and everything was ready. Matt added a pair of candles for ambiance and dimmed the kitchen light. The oven-grilled chicken breasts lay on a bed of salad greens with tomatoes and green onions. Matt topped the salad with sweet dried cranberries, candied walnuts, and a honey mustard vinaigrette. He observed her check the door again on her way back to the kitchen. Darn, she was pretty, freshly scrubbed, wet hair, and all. She was also troubled.

Jessie sat in the chair across from where he stood. "This is lovely. Thank you."

"You don't have to keep checking it, Jess. The door is going to remain locked. I promise."

"I know." Her voice was barely audible; she stared down at the table. "It makes me think I'm still in control." She inhaled slowly. "Wow, this smells good. I guess I'm hungry after all."

"I figured I owed you something special. I've been gone a lot lately." He lit the candles and sat down across from her. The fear he had seen on her face could save her life, but he didn't want it to paralyze her.

"Yes, I believe you do." She glanced at him and smiled. "I can't believe you just threw this together. It's a little intimidating to go with a man who can cook better than I can. But, I suppose it does come with some great advantages too." She placed her napkin on her lap and took a sip of wine.

"It's not hard to do when you enjoy cooking and are standing in a well-stocked kitchen. You had the chicken already." He gazed into her eyes. "Jess, we'll get through this. We've hit a rough patch, that's all, sweetheart."

"Why can't it just be simple? Life is always complicated." She sighed.

"What do you mean?" Matt glanced at her.

"We just got through a case, and now this. Why Liam after all these years? Why now? I can't deal with this all at once."

"It seems to be the way life dishes it out. It comes at you all at once. We can muddle through this with

Liam. Although, I can't promise you I won't deck him eventually. I told you once when it comes to you, Jess, all bets are off." He reached across the small table for her hand. "Can you tell me what you were thinking when you felt the guy closing in?"

"I was terrified. That was my first emotion. The clouds obscured the moon, so it was dark, and I couldn't see where he was coming from." She extricated her hand and wrapped her arms around herself. He could hear the echo of remembered panic in her voice. "He had murder on his mind."

Matt knew better than to ask her how she knew. Whatever her talent was, he had learned to trust it. He pressed his lips together, watching her over the rim of his wine glass. "Jess, I don't think you should be running alone. I'll run with you from now on. When it's warm enough, I'll be running out there with you until we know what we're dealing with. I know how much it means to you to jog outside."

"Thank you." She glanced at him and shut her eyes. "I wouldn't want to run through that area again if there were the remotest possibility he could still be there." She shuddered.

"I don't want you or Katie going out alone at night. I don't want to cause a panic, but the same is true for any woman staying at the Inn. I'll talk to Katie about how to explain it to her guests without causing a panic." He rested his chin on his hand.

"What are you thinking?" she asked.

"I'm not sure. I'll check out some police logs in the vicinity to see if there has been anything in the surrounding area." He frowned. "I would feel better if I knew I was doing everything I could to keep people in

Blue Cove safe."

She stood and started to clear the table. "I know you'll do everything you can."

"Jess, leave those. Finish your wine and watch a little TV. I'll do the dishes after you go to bed." He turned her gently around, pointed her in the direction of the living room, and gave her a soft nudge. "I'll be right there, I'm going to put the food away first."

He watched her move to the couch. She sat down, wrapping herself in the throw that was draped over the back of the sofa. *Murder on his mind. Damn, another mess.* "Can I get you anything?" He turned off the kitchen light.

She rubbed her eyes and yawned. "No, I'm good." She glanced over at him. "Come and join me." She patted the couch beside her.

He carried his wine glass and sat down right where she had patted. She leaned into his side, resting her head against his shoulder. "What are we watching?" He put his arm around her and held her close.

"I don't know." She looked bewildered. "I have no clue."

"Do you mind?" He grabbed the remote from her hand. Kicking off his shoes, he put his feet on her coffee table. "Is this okay?"

"Go ahead and make yourself at home. I'm just glad you're here, and I'm not alone." She turned to him with a slight smile.

"Don't mind if I do." He winked at her, turning to one of the police shows he liked to watch. This time, he was the one who couldn't concentrate on the story. The sensation of her against his side took over his thinking. And every time she looked at him, their lips would meet. He had missed her and moments like this the last few weeks. Damn Liam. Matt would have liked to kick it up a notch, but this incident was nagging at him, and she was a wreck. He reached into his pocket and pulled out his glasses. "Jess, do you mind if I look something up on your computer?"

"No." She sat forward and stretched. "Go ahead. I think I'll go to bed. She gave him a quick kiss and walked to her room. "Thank you for staying here. I'm a bit overwhelmed right now."

"I understand. Call if you need me." He opened her computer and began his search. Matt sat there for a while taking notes. His frown deepened. "Hell," he said under his breath. Had anyone put all this information together? Probably, but they should have warned other local authorities. He poured over police logs up and down the east coast through several states and looked for an APB sent to the different jurisdictions. He needed to check their stack when he got to work in the morning. He would run this by Tom Maxwell and a few others, but this was trouble.

It was late when he finally turned off the computer. On his way to bed, Matt paused at her closed door. She was mumbling and talking. A quick check on her told him she was sound asleep.

****

Her first scream came at one in the morning. He knew the exact time because he jumped up, looked at the clock, and banged his knee trying to pull on his pants on the way to the door. He went cursing under his breath. When she screamed again, it was unlike anything he had ever heard. It sent chills racing through him. Matt crashed through her door—gun drawn—not knowing what he would find. She was sitting up in bed, wild-eyed and unaware that he was even in the room.

"Jess, Jess," he gently called to her. She screamed again with that same blood-curdling sound, clearly seeing something.

He sat on the bed beside her. She thrashed wildly, her arms smacking him more than once. He rubbed the spot when she belted him again. She packed a punch. Grabbing her hands, he held them and spoke softly to her. "Jess, it's me. You're okay, sweetheart. You're safe." He rambled on, not knowing what to say. "Come on, Jess, I don't know what's happening. Tell me, sweetheart, what are you seeing?" He repeated it several times trying to get through to her.

"Matt." She freed her hands, her eyes clearing. "It was awful. He killed someone right here in our woods. I know…I saw it. Please, help me. I saw it. I could have been her." She sobbed, and he knew they needed to comb through the woods. Right now! Adrenaline rising, he stood, knowing it would have to wait until daylight. Had she seen it in real time, or had it already happened?

"Don't leave me." She held on to his arm.

"I'm not going anywhere, Jess. I need my phone." He saw hers on the table. Matt picked it up and called Dylan. He put his free arm around her, patting her shoulder.

"Jess, what's the matter?" Dylan answered his phone, sounding groggy.

"It's Matt. I'm using her phone," He explained what had happened. "We'll need to go into the woods as soon as it gets light enough to see without destroying evidence. I'll call in our crime unit. You can meet me here as soon as the sun comes up."

Jessie still had his arm in a death grip. He placed his hand over hers. "I'm not going anywhere, Jess. I'll stay right here beside you." Matt sat with his back resting against the headboard. He stretched his legs out the length of the bed. He held her hand and talked softly to her until he felt her relax against him. "We'll get through this together." She shivered, and he tucked the blanket tighter around her as she snuggled into his side. He was going to attain sainthood for all the times she wiggled against him during the night, and he let her rest. She slept; he watched the clock and her sleep.

****

The knock on the door and the sound of Dylan's voice finally awakened him. "I'll be right there," Matt called out. He watched Jessie stir. "Jess, Dylan's here." He extracted himself from her grip. "I need to open the door." He caught the shadow that crossed her face. The fear was once again her eyes. Damn. "What time do you need to get to your store for the delivery?"

She stretched. "Eight-thirty." She stood, groaning as she walked into the bathroom and closed the door.

"As soon as you're ready, I want you to tell us again what you saw," Matt called to her. He opened the door for Dylan.

"You look like hell." Dylan sounded grim.

"It wasn't a good night. I swear, Dylan, at one point I thought the guy was in her room the way she screamed. I've never heard anything like it." Matt shook his head.

"What are we looking for?" Dylan looked amazingly well rested.

"I want Jessie to describe it to you, but I think I'm safe in saying a woman's body."

Chapter 3

Jessie could hear Matt and Dylan talking in the living room. Running the brush through her hair, she gathered it into a ponytail. The dark circles under her eyes were a reminder of last night. She didn't want to go to the store alone. If only there were a way to erase the night from her mind as easily as she could conceal her tired look. She dabbed on concealer. The scene was firmly entrenched, playing like a movie reel in her mind with no escape. She was spooked.

Joining the two guys, she sat down next to Matt on the couch. "Good morning." She smiled slightly at Dylan.

"Jess, I want you to tell Dylan about your dream." He took hold of her hand.

"I saw a young woman running where I had been earlier in the evening when I first felt him watching me." She nearly stumbled over the words. It was hard to describe. "I was fortunate there were two runners up ahead on the path, but...there wasn't anyone for her." She squeezed the pillow to her chest, her heart rate picking up with the memory. "He came out of the woods and grabbed her." Moisture filled her eyes; her voice softened. "He dragged her kicking and screaming deep into the dense wooded area. He, he attacked her, ripping her clothes off and punching her." Jessie shut her eyes and exhaled slowly. "He stabbed her over and over with a big knife. I could hear the awful sounds she made." She took a deep breath. "I can still hear it. I saw her eyes. They were filled with fear, pain, and then a sad resigned look replaced the fear, as if she knew she was dying. He seemed to get high off it." Tears ran down Jessie's cheeks. "I believe I saw it as it happened. I tried, but I never saw his face, only her eyes." Jessie took the tissue Matt handed her. "And yet…something, he seemed…familiar."

"Damn, Jess, I don't know how you handle this stuff. I guess we'd better check it out." Dylan stood shaking his head. "I'll take a couple of the guys, and we'll start searching the area."

"Dylan, it's right where the path makes a curve and starts the uphill climb toward the Inn," Jessie explained to him.

He nodded. "We'll start there."

"Jess, I'm sending Gary to be with you this morning until your store opens up. I don't want you to have to go into your store alone."

"Thank you. I was kind of hoping for that." She took a deep breath. Bless Matt for reading her. She gave him a grateful smile.

"He'll meet you there. Wait for him before you go in." He walked with her to her car. "I'll call you and let you know."

"I hope you don't find anything and that I'm totally wrong." She looked at him. Yeah, they'd find something. He knew it too.

"I hope we don't, either." He kissed her and shut the car door.

****

Matt caught up with the others at the base of the

small incline. "We'll need to fan out to begin our search." Dylan nodded at him. "Be slow and methodical first time through. We don't want to destroy any evidence or overlook anything." They moved off in different directions, searching the ground closely.

Kip squatted down suddenly. "Chief, look at this." He pointed to marks on the ground. "Drag marks?" He went a little farther and bent down. "It appears someone put their heels on the ground right here and was fighting all the way."

Matt bent down beside Kip to observe where he was pointing. "You're right. Follow them, and I'll search around this area with you."

They walked deeper into the heavily wooded area. Matt spotted a running shoe and another one a little farther into the woods. The laces were still tied. The further they went, the more Matt knew Jessie had seen it happen as it unfolded. The feeling of death was in the area. The air was oppressive and silent. He knew what came next.

Matt noticed the leg before Kip. "Call the others in; we've found the crime scene." He knew a good portion of the people in town. He didn't want to have to tell anyone that his or her loved one wouldn't be home. Hell, it was his job. Matt walked over to the body, and what he saw turned his stomach. Jessie was right. It had been vicious. This perp was sick. No one should ever have to go through what she had. The girl's battered face was unrecognizable. Her naked body lay in an awkward position with her dark brown ponytail stuffed into her mouth. In contrast, her hands were folded with care over her naked body as if she lay in repose. Nothing could cover the stab wounds or the look of fear on her face.

"She fought back. If I don't miss my guess, there's a lot of DNA under these nails." Matt looked at her hands and nails without touching them.

"So many stab wounds," Marcy's voice broke. "This was fueled by a hate-filled rage." Marcy photographed the body and the surrounding area.

"Are you okay?" Matt could see her gulping. Hell, it was hard for him. "Do you want someone else to finish taking the photos?"

"I'll be all right, but I'm mad as hell at what he's done to her." She looked over at Matt. "We have to nail this guy."

Matt got out the notes he had taken. He compared them to what he was seeing. He meticulously wrote detailed notes on the report, not wanting to miss anything.

They spent the better part of the day, into the late afternoon, processing the crime scene. It was an area thick with trees and undergrowth. It was too early in the year for some of the trees to have their leaves yet, but the pine trees made a dark canopy that more than made up for it. They had shielded the madness and witnessed a brutal murder. Too bad they couldn't talk.

Kip and Dylan found the victim's clothes scattered around the area. The sun was making its descent in the sky when Dave Lewis, the coroner, finally bagged the body and took her from the scene.

"If I never see something like this again it will be too soon for me. It was awful." Dylan leaned against the trunk of the large tree and massaged his temples. "We're dealing with one sick perp."

Matt stood next to Dylan. "It fits the MO I was

reading about in some of the crime scenes from surrounding areas."

"What made you think to do that?" Dylan's brow rose.

"After what happened to Jess while running last night, I called Tom. He mentioned the idea of a predator, which got me thinking. I decided to check it out."

"What did you find? Are we looking at several victims in multiple locations?" Dylan's muscles in his face tightened. "Were there any similarities to our murder victim?"

"There seemed to be several areas hit in the larger New England area. A few towns had only one murder victim, and a few towns had a couple. Her hands folded the way they were is a dead giveaway. We're dealing with the same suspect or a damn good copycat. I'm sure of it." Matt folded his arms across his chest. "All the evidence is here including some not in the public record. Every police report I read mentioned the hand placement. I went down the list of his MO from the other crime scenes, and all of it was at our crime scene."

"What do we do next?" Dylan crossed his arms.

"We need to contact the other jurisdictions where a similar murder took place and talk to them, compare notes to the smallest detail. I might have Frank bring his dog to town, just in case our perp decides he wants to stay around. I'll put in a call to Tom Maxwell, too." Matt rubbed a hand over his dark stubble.

"We have a lot of wooded areas just like this around Blue Cove." Dylan pushed away from the trunk of the old maple tree.

"I know, too many for my peace of mind." Matt walked beside him. "How do you warn women not to go out alone without causing a panic? I think it's something we're going to need to do and catch him before he does it again."

"How would we know if he's left the area?" Dylan grabbed a pine cone off the ground and pitched it.

"I guess if no one else is murdered here, it could mean he's moved on." Matt stopped. "One trend I noticed was, in the beginning, the murders were few and far between, but the last several he has ratcheted up his pace. It looks like our perp likes it, which scares the hell out of me."

"Are you going to tell Jessie?"

"Of course, she needs to know. I'm sure she does already."

****

It was almost time to close the store, only fifteen minutes to go. Five was closing time until the summer hours started in June. It had been a long day, and Matt hadn't called yet, which meant he was busy with a crime scene. There were still a few customers in the store when she shut the doors opening into Java Joe's and locked them. The bell rang, and a disheveled man rushed in the door. His eyes had a wild look about them as his gaze darted from Jessie to those in the store. Jessie grabbed a hammer that she kept under the counter and moved toward him. She would use it if she needed to. He muttered a few expletives and turned to leave. He bumped into Reba, who was walking in the door, shoving her out of the way.

"Well, I never," Reba yelled after him. "You are a rude young man."

Jessie reached her hand out to steady Reba. "He was higher than a kite." Jessie locked the door and flipped the sign around to the closed side. She assured those still shopping that they could finish. He was not going to come back in if she could stop him. She was still a little jumpy.

"Did Sadie get home okay? I enjoyed meeting her." Reba smiled at her. "She has the sight like you do, my girl. That's where you get it. You're spunky like her, too."

"I know," Jessie, sighed softly. "She enjoyed her time here, and she liked meeting you, too. She would love to live here."

"Oh, I would like it if she moved to Blue Cove." Reba watched Jessie ring up the last few customers and let them out.

"Do you want to sit for a few minutes?" Jessie read a text that had just come in. "Matt told me Dylan was dropping him off, and he will need a ride home. I have to wait for him."

"I'll stay with you, dear." Reba sat, placing her purse on the table beside her. "Something bad is happening in our town. I awakened at little after one, and I knew something awful had happened." She shook her head, her eyes narrowed. "Whatever it was left me feeling desolate and sleepless for a few hours. You have to be careful. Matt and you both have to be alert. This case will come at you from a couple of directions. I saw darkness, and you, my dear girl, are kind and intuitive. You scare people who mean to do harm because you know they are there. I know you've had to learn things quickly. Everything has come your way so fast since you moved here, but it's for a good reason you are in

23

the middle of all of this. I can't say why as of yet, but we'll know soon enough. If you need me, you know you can always call."

"I know." Jessie yawned and smiled at her. "I guess I didn't sleep so well myself last night."

"I had a feeling you hadn't. Jessie, promise me you'll be careful. Someone is watching you."

Jessie nodded. "I'll do my best."

"We'll talk more." She stood. "I see your handsome fella getting out of the car. You two have a lot to talk about, and you don't need me. I'll let you both walk me to my car, though." Her smile faded. "I suddenly don't want to walk there alone."

"I didn't want to drive home alone either. So I'm happy Matt's here, and we will be happy to walk you to your car." She went to open the door for Matt.

"Hello, ladies." He dropped a kiss on Jessie's cheek. "I've come to escort you both safely home."

Jessie put on her jacket and took hold of Reba's arm as they stepped out the door. Matt shut off the lights and made sure he locked the door. Once Reba was safely in the car, Jessie leaned down to whisper in her ear before she shut the door. "We'll follow you home and make sure you get safely to your house. I know you're feeling the same way I am." She kissed her cheek.

Chapter 4

Matt escorted Reba up to the door and then returned to the car. "I think she's still upset about the guy who shoved her. She mentioned it several times and made me promise to look after you."

"He was definitely a strange customer." She looked at him. "Let me have it. I know you're trying to think of the best way to tell me. You found her didn't you, and it was dreadful." Jessie's voice got soft.

"Yes, on both counts. I've never worked a worse crime scene." He pulled away from the curb.

"What are we up against?" She inhaled a sharp breath.

"After you went to bed last night, I did some research on police reports up and down the coast. This guy has been very busy. The evidence, in this case, fits the reports I read last night."

"A serial killer?" Her mouth tightened into a grim line.

"There's a high probability of it. He's been in the New England area for the past several months, but it started in Florida a couple of years ago."

"I knew he was coming at me with murder on his mind." She shivered, fighting down that memory of terror and the bile rising in her throat. "I was fortunate that there were people ahead of me, which scared him off. She didn't have anyone…" Her voice trailed off.

"I think you can see why I said no running alone after dark." He stopped at a light on Main Street.

"I believe I was a random choice. I happened to run by where he had decided to wait for his victim."

"When I think of what could have happened to you, it makes me sick." Matt's jaw clenched.

"I was thinking today that I need to take another self-defense class." She frowned into the darkness. "What if I had needed to defend myself against someone like that guy who came into my store? If I keep finding myself in the center of these things, it's time for me to be able to defend myself. To do a little damage to those who mean to hurt me." She gave him a smile, trying to make it light. "At the very least, I want to go down fighting."

"I was thinking the same thing myself. You are doing more and more work for us. You need to be able to fight."

She rubbed the nape of her neck. "Was she young?"

He nodded his head. "As far as I could tell; her face was swollen, cut, and bruised. I hope we have an ID on her soon." Matt parked in front of her cottage. He turned to her. "The thing is, I'm not sure that he's gone from the area, and he's got the taste for it. The number of victims attributed to him has increased in the last couple of months. If he's still here, no female out alone is safe."

"Is there any pattern in his preference or choice of victims?" Jessie turned to look at him.

Matt noticed the reporter instincts coming out in the way she had asked the question. "It seems they were all young from what I could tell; as far as the hair color, age, or height, that didn't seem to matter."

"I already know the answer, but"—she wrung her hands in her lap, trying to shut out the images that wanted to surface—"did she suffer?" She gulped.

"Yes." He drew a deep breath. "I have to be honest with you, Jess, it was awful. He is one sick perp. The sooner we can catch this guy the better."

"Reba was awakened after one this morning. She knew something was going on. She made the statement to me that it was going to come at us from two fronts. I wonder what she means." Jessie stared out the window.

He opened the car door. "Let's go in, and I'll tell you my theory on the subject." He grabbed his bag from the back seat.

He locked the door behind him, sat down on the couch, and gently tugged her into his lap. "I've been very thankful all day you got away from him. Days like this always remind me you never know from one moment to the next. You've got to live life while you've got it." He kissed her cheek and held her tight. "As far as a second front goes, who knows what that might be? It could be our hitman or something entirely different. I guess we'll know soon enough. For now, I want to concentrate on what I know is happening."

She nodded at him. "Are you hungry?"

"Yes, I ordered a pizza. It should be here soon. I told him to deliver it by six-thirty."

"Wow, how efficient of you." She smiled at him. "When did you have time to order it?"

"I ordered it on my way to pick you up." He gave her a lopsided grin. "Hands-free. I figured it was a perfect time. Besides, having a lot of calls to make tonight, I didn't want you to have to cook, either."

"Thank you." She kissed him.

The rapping at the door brought Matt back into the present moment. Bummer, he had liked where that kiss was going. "I think our dinner is here."

Jessie stood, and Matt went to answer the door. It was the pizza delivery guy, along with Katie and Liam. Matt folded his arms across his chest.

"I didn't see your car, Matt," Katie smiled at him. "We didn't mean to interrupt dinner. I wanted to ask Jessie something, and when Liam heard I was coming here, he wanted to tag along. Since you're here, I'll ask you. You're a better source."

"Are you hungry?" Jessie carried the pizza into the kitchen.

"No, we just ate but go ahead while it's hot." Katie followed her. "I could use something to drink."

Jessie handed her a glass and the pitcher of tea. "Do you want a beer, Liam?"

"Sure, sounds good."

"They're in the fridge, help yourself." She pointed at the refrigerator with her chin.

Katie stood beside Matt. "Why were all the police in the area today? I figure you, Mr. Police Chief, should know the answer to my question." Her pointed finger jabbed his chest a couple of times.

"I was going to come up to the Inn and talk to you about it tonight. You saved me a trip." Matt told them what had happened to Jessie. He told them about the murder, leaving out most of the details. "Until we know the guy is no longer in the area, or he's been caught, it would be best not to go out at night alone. We have to warn your female guests as well."

"Can you do that?" Katie frowned. "I have

28

absolutely no clue how to go about it."

"I'd be happy to. As soon as dinner is over, Jessie and I will walk up your way. Maybe you can get them all together, or at least those that aren't out for the evening."

Katie nodded. "I can't believe it happened right here in our woods." She hunched her shoulders. "Do they know who it is yet?"

"No." Matt's answer was brisk.

"Look, Jess, why don't you come up to the Inn and stay? There is no need for you to be alone." Liam walked over to stand by Jessie.

"Matt stayed here last night, and he's staying tonight. I was the one he first chased, and I saw him kill her." Jessie reached to get another glass out of the cabinet.

"What do you mean you saw it?" Liam looked shocked.

"I saw it. Ask Katie later; she can explain it to you."

"A lot of weird stuff has happened to her since she moved here. I'll tell you, but you'll never believe it." Katie chuckled at her brother's expression. "My friend is no ordinary person."

"Yes, I am." Jessie rolled her eyes at Katie.

"No, sweetheart, you really aren't." Matt chuckled when Jessie sucker punched him. He grabbed her hand and held tight so she couldn't do it again.

"No, Jessie, you're not." Katie's voice got louder. "No one else I know hangs out with ghosts, hears people talking in their heads, and dreams weird dreams like you."

"I don't hang out with ghosts…besides, I don't try

to do these things. I'm as normal as you."

"If you're as normal as Katie, then we are in trouble." Liam chuckled and then winced when Katie smacked him.

"In all seriousness, Liam, I'll tell you what I'm going to tell the men tonight. Don't let your sister go out anytime at night without an escort. Don't let her walk down here alone. Until this guy is caught, or we know he's no longer in the area, it's better to be safe than sorry."

"You've got it. I've never seen it from this side before." He looked thoughtful. "I'm the one who is defending them in court. This should be interesting."

"You can walk me home, Liam. I need to get the guests ready for Matt." Katie gave her brother a look. "See you both in a little while. Come on, Liam." She grabbed him by the elbow when he didn't move. "I forever have to wait for you. Let them eat their dinner in peace." She pulled him toward the door.

"I guess that means I have to go. If you need anything, Jessie, you know where to find me."

"She won't." Matt was abrupt. He looked at Jessie when they closed the door. "What?"

She sighed. "I think you were a little rude."

"You asked me to lend a hand, I gave you one." He grinned. "I'm a man. I'm not about to talk to him for twenty minutes on the subject of why he won't be needed by you. I don't dance around the issue. If you want it done your way, do it yourself."

"My, my, aren't we testy." But she smiled. He was so predictable sometimes.

"Yes, I am." He sounded a bit defensive. "It's been a hell of a day working the crime scene. As if that's not enough, I wanted to punch Liam for liking you. How can I fault a man for the same affliction I have?" He sat down and took a slice of pizza. "Let's eat before it gets too cold."

****

"Whoa, that was grueling." Jessie's soft voice broke into Matt's pensive mood. The night was dark and chilly as they walked back from the Inn.

"It's never fun to deal with something as horrific as murder." He grabbed her hand. "You said something this morning that's been bothering me. You said the killer seemed familiar." She nodded at him. "In what way?"

"That's the strange part. I don't know. I couldn't see him, and yet I've seen him before. I know it." She glanced at him. "I can't explain it, I'm sorry. It's just something deep in me knows he's familiar. I saw it in the way he moved and his purpose resonated with me. I've seen it before."

"Do you think he would know who you are?" He stopped and turned her toward him.

"I don't know. It would seem likely if I recognized him without seeing him, he would recognize me if he saw me. But, how much of me he saw I don't know, for when I sensed him coming after me, I was running pretty fast to get away."

"If you think of anything about him that was familiar let me know."

"Of course, you know I will." She started walking again, all at once feeling vulnerable standing there. Was he even now watching them, or was he miles away? "I wish I knew where he was."

"You and me both, sweetheart." Matt unlocked the

door and held it open for her. He followed her in.

"I'll remember it at some point, and I'll tell you when I do." He nodded and sat down on the couch with the remote.

****

The man hadn't expected to see that vision of loveliness from his past right in front of him, almost his for the taking. It had almost stopped him dead in his tracks when Jessie looked over her shoulder as if she knew he was there. Her face, awash in the brief moonlight—he felt the thrill of that moment still. He had settled for the next one to come along. She was cute enough, but it wasn't the same. Now, what to do? Should he stay or leave to find another? Seeing Jessie's face there was so unexpected, but it made his decision easy. She was as stunning as he had remembered her. Yes, he would definitely stay. He might simply have to find a reason to work his way into her life, a little reminiscing with an old friend. There were infinite possibilities. Life was looking up—it sure was looking up.

Chapter 5

Who was it? Her mind couldn't let it go, not even in the safe comfort of her store. He was there, skipping along the edges of her memory, teasing her, but refusing to come into view. She needed to know who he was. It could possibly save another woman's life. Thoughts raced through her mind all night, too, keeping her from sleep. Matt seemed to have no problem, though; she could hear him snoring off and on through the night. She turned on the light over the counter.

The killer could be anybody, someone she had passed on the street or smiled at when she walked into the store. Anybody. It could make it difficult to narrow down. *Think Jessie, what made him familiar to you?* Her brows furrowed in concentration. Earlier, she had read on the Internet about a man who had murdered several women: a deacon in a church, and no one had suspected him. The murders had been carried out over several years. Shocked church members described him as a nice guy, a decent family man, and a civic leader. How could they not see the dark side of him? There are warning signs, always some warning sign. How many times had she heard them uttered by a close friend, usually remembered after the fact? A church was a good place to hide and live a double life, she guessed. Pastor Rick had done it. Still, you would think he would feel some sense of guilt or remorse. Obviously, he didn't.

Matt had tried to explain to her last night that the mechanism for guilt didn't work for a serial killer the same way it worked for most people. The killer detached what he was doing from his everyday life. She shook her head at the memory of their discussion. She still didn't understand it.

What turned an ordinary person into a serial killer anyway? She had asked Matt. He told her a few things, but she wanted more information. Most were men, Matt had told her, and it was rare if it were a woman, but there had been a few. The FBI defined a serial killer as a person who had murdered at least two or more people over a period of time with a usual cooling off period in between. The murders were a form of psychological gratification, which might include an element of anger, thrill, or financial gain. She shuddered at the thought of someone getting pleasure out of killing another human being. One site she had visited said that the victims might have something in common like race, sex, appearance, or age, and the murders were committed in a similar manner. It wasn't the same as a crime of passion or a rampage. She had read about a few of those too. This felt more sinister to her: planned, premeditated, and almost an obsession. She knew what she had seen, and this guy liked it. She had to do something…she couldn't wait too long…he would strike again.

Had he seen her and recognized her, too? That was a scary thought. She pushed her hair behind her ears and got to work opening the box of new books sitting on the counter. They wouldn't put themselves away. Jessie carried a few of the books to arrange on the display table at the front of the store. She watched several people as they walked by the store. A man stopped suddenly, turned, and made eye contact with her. He smiled. Jessie diverted her eyes away for a moment. When she looked again, he was gone. Would she suspect everyone now? Yes, she needed to be cautious and on guard, but she also had to remain who she was, or he would be the winner.

****

So far, Dave Lewis hadn't been able to identify their Jane Doe. Matt had Gary checking out any new missing person reports filed in the past few hours. It was probably too soon, but it was hard not to do something. Matt turned his chair to look out the window.

Jess certainly attracted the male population, good and bad. He couldn't do anything about it. What was he going to do about Liam? He couldn't keep snapping at the man. Liam was a nuisance, but Matt couldn't fault Liam's attraction to Jessie. He understood it completely. She was a beautiful woman. It was about time he figured out a better way to handle the situation. He couldn't afford to be jealous every time another man got near her. Jessie didn't like it, and he didn't either.

"Matt, you're wanted on line one," Dylan called out to him.

Matt turned his chair around. "Thanks." He pushed line one. "This is Chief Parker how can I help you?"

"I have an ID for you on our young victim."

"I'm ready, Dave, give it to me." He opened the file and erased Jane Doe on the top line.

"Her name is Emma Wilson. She was twenty-three and visiting her grandparents in town while her parents are out of the country. My assistant told me he had met her at a mutual friend's house a couple of days ago."

"Wilson? Any relation to Dick and Amanda Wilson?" Matt clicked the pen in his hand off and on.

"Yes."

Matt had a sinking feeling. "Damn. I'll take care of notifying them. They're two fine people. This will devastate them."

"I've done everything I can to make her look presentable if you want to bring them by to confirm her identity."

"Thanks, Dave. I'll bring them by sometime today." He stood up and walked toward Dylan's office. "Dave has identified our victim. We have a call to make."

"Who are we looking at?" Dylan asked him.

"Amanda and Dick Wilson's granddaughter."

Dylan exhaled and swore under his breath. "I hate this. It shouldn't happen to anyone's kid or grandkid."

"Her parents are out of the country, and we'll need to track them down. In the meantime, this is our job so let's get it done."

They pulled up in front of the Wilson's home fifteen minutes later. Dick opened the door immediately and called out to them as they walked up the sidewalk. "Amanda and I were going to come to see you and fill out a missing person report. Our granddaughter didn't come home last night. We were hoping she'd lost track of time and met up with some friends. But, she hasn't called, and that's not like her." He motioned them into the house, and Matt saw the fear he was trying to hide. Hating it. For this moment, hating his job. "Why are you here?" Dick paused to look at them. "You're here to talk about her, aren't you?"

"I'm sorry to say we are." Matt sighed. "Why don't you sit down, Dick, and call Amanda in here, too."

The fear in Dick's eyes grew. He sat in the chair after calling for his wife to join them. Matt watched him take out his handkerchief to wipe the moisture from his eyes.

"Hi, Matt," Amanda smiled at him as she walked in, wiping floury hands on her apron. "I hope your parents are doing well."

"Amanda dear, sit." Dick's voice trembled. "They have some news about Emma, and I don't think it's good."

****

Matt looked absently up at the ceiling. He couldn't erase the look on the faces of the Wilson's after they had identified Emma's body. Life was such a mixed bag of highs and lows. He would take Jessie by to see them. They would need lots of support. He didn't know if they could recover from it. It was bad enough to lose a child or grandchild as it was, but the brutality of her death made it worse. He was going to nail this guy no matter what it took. He tapped his pencil on the open file. Everybody has a weak spot, what was his? With the help of Dick Wilson, Matt was able to notify her parents traveling abroad for their anniversary, which was another tough moment in his day.

Matt picked up his phone and called the person he wanted to talk to most. "Hi, sweetheart, how's your day?" Her voice sounded wonderful to him.

"I'm glad you called. Is everything okay?"

"It's been hard." He stared out the window.

"I can imagine. I couldn't stop thinking about her.

We've got to do all we can to stop this guy." He heard the quiver in her voice.

"I know. Let's talk at dinner. I have an idea for some alone time, are you in?" He doodled on his notepad.

"Of course."

"I'll have Dylan drop me off at the store, and we'll go from there. It's been a rough day, and I don't want to add Liam into the mix if that's okay."

"Fine by me. See you in a little bit."

Matt liked the idea of talking things over with her. She had a perspective he didn't always see. Plus, she was nice to look at. No rocket science involved, he wanted to be with her not just once in a while, but all the time. After a day like today, it made him want it even more.

He closed the file and put it in his briefcase to work on later. He made a few calls and stopped by Dylan's office to remind him he needed a ride to Jessie's store and not to leave without him.

****

Jessie locked up after her last customer left. Reaching up, she turned the sign around to Closed and shut off the light. A car drove by the shop slowly. She hid beside a bookshelf near the front of the store and watched as the car turned around and drove slowly by the store again. Maybe they were looking for someone else, but when she saw the car drive by a third time, she was anxious.

Chapter 6

"Matt, please hurry," she whispered into the dark store. She watched the car pull off the road on its next pass and stop in front of the church. Was it a man or a woman driving? She couldn't tell. It had to be a man. She frowned. For some crazy reason, she attracted men who wanted to harm her—like bees drawn to honey. Or it sure seemed so. What was the make of the car? She squinted trying to see a few of the car's details. It was too dark to see much; she couldn't even make out the color. Dark color. Was it black, blue, or dark green? If he would pull up just a little nearer to the light, maybe she could see something. Another item to put on her agenda; she had to learn to tell the make and models of cars by their shape and size.

"Okay then, if you're not going to pull forward, stay right where you are," she murmured softly. "That's right, don't go anywhere." She fixed her gaze on the car idling across the street willing him to stay put. If only Matt were here to check it out. He would know the make of the car. No such luck. As soon as Dylan pulled in front of the store in his cruiser to let Matt off, the other car drove away. She tried to see the license plate, but it had happened too quickly for her to catch a single letter or number.

She opened the door. "Hey, you didn't happen to see the car that passed you as you were pulling up, did you?"

Matt walked toward her. "Nope, I didn't notice it." He grabbed her hand and pulled her out the door. "Are you ready? Give me the key. I'll lock it for you, sweetheart." He turned toward her, frowning. "Why? What about the car?"

She explained what had happened. "I couldn't tell the model, and it was too dark to see the color. I think I need to learn about cars next." She smiled. "I'll fit that in right after my self-defense classes."

He opened the car door for her. "I don't like the idea of someone casing your store. Keep your eyes open as I'm driving." He shut her door and got in. He turned the engine over. "Let me know if you see it again." He leaned across the seat and kissed her. "So far my plan is working like a charm."

"What plan is that?"

"No, Liam."

She smiled, but this Liam jealousy was getting old. "Where are we headed?"

"I've decided to always make it a surprise so you don't let it slip to Katie, who can, in turn, let Liam know. Maybe he'll stay away for a while." Matt frowned. "That is unless, of course, he was the guy watching the store."

"Why would you say that? Of course, it's not Liam." She shook her head, frowning at him.

"And you know this for sure, because?" He looked at her, his brows rising in challenge.

"It just can't be; that's all." *What a silly thing to think!* "He's a friend." She frowned a bit and looked down at her hands in her lap. Another lecture was coming. She could feel it.

"The chief was *my* friend, remember? People are not always what they seem." He glanced over at her. "I'm not saying it's Liam, but never rule anyone out until you know for sure." He pulled the car out onto Main Street. "You know that to be true in your line of work. I'm not telling you anything new." He stopped at the stop sign. "You even said it yourself, why Liam? Why did he turn up now? Until you can answer the question definitively, you can't rule him out."

"I know in theory and in practice, you're right. But, I can't wrap my head around it. I've known him for years." She let her breath out in a gusty sigh. She would feel it if he was, surely. "He's a flirt, but I can't believe he's evil."

"I'm not asking you to. I'm reminding you of the first rule of any investigation. Everyone is a potential suspect until ruled out. How does he always know we're together? Is Katie telling him, or is he watching you? You can't rule him in or out."

"I get it, and I'll keep my eyes open." She folded her hands in her lap and turned her head away from him.

"That's all I'm asking you to do." He pulled onto the highway. "I learned it the hard way. My refusal to believe the evidence in front of my eyes almost cost you your life. I'm not willing to risk that again for anyone."

"May I ask you something?" She tilted her head to glance at him for a moment.

"Fire away." He grinned at her.

"What made you think of him? Is he a suspect?"

"He's new to the area, and everyone is a potential suspect, but it doesn't mean he's guilty of anything other than being annoying." He was smiling, but his eyes were serious. "All I'm trying to do is remind you not to rule anyone out—or in, for that matter—until you know for sure. Be cautious and play it safe. That's your best possible defense."

"I can do that."

****

He wasn't sure that she could. Matt glanced over at her again. Jessie was loyal to her friends, and it would be hard for her to be suspicious of any of them. She was too quiet. "Are you all right?"

"Yes. I'm thinking about what you said." Her tone was subdued.

"And?" He had to pull it out of her.

"I'm not sure I could ever suspect my friends. I don't know how you were able to suspect Anderson's involvement in the Harvest Club." She rubbed her hands together.

"It was you who told me to go with my gut, even if no one else suspected him." His lips thinned, and he frowned. "I had Collins watching you the morning of the funeral just in case. My one mistake was that I didn't believe Anderson would attempt anything with so many people nearby. Joe got concerned when he could no longer see you. He called me, and his call saved your life." He glanced at her, wanting her to understand. "You can do anything you have to do to keep yourself safe and prevent another murder. Even suspect your friends." She wasn't going to hear him, and he suppressed a sigh. "Don't forget our victim in all of this."

"You're right, of course. If it becomes necessary, I can and will do it. It's thinking about it when you have no facts to go on that makes it hard."

After driving thirty minutes, Matt turned off the highway and followed the road back about a quarter of a mile. Tucked back in the trees, the restaurant looked like a part of the landscape with its weathered wooden exterior. He parked the car. It would be up to him to pay close attention to those around her. Friend or not. He studied her profile briefly before getting out of the car. "Let's eat. I'm starving," he said, opening her door. "Jess, I don't want you to worry about this. I just want you to be smart. Your intuition will tell you what's true."

****

The Hideaway was off the beaten path. The architect had designed it to look as if it was a natural part of the woods. Trees lined the road all the way to the restaurant, and the building had very few windows in the front. Hand in hand, they crossed over an arched wooden footbridge with a creek running underneath it on their way to the two large wooden doors. Once inside, the maître d' escorted them to their table with a beautiful view of the ocean. The back of the restaurant was almost all windows. It was lovely.

Jessie loved the simple décor: understated, but elegant, nothing that would take away from the beautiful views beyond the windows. Chamber music played softly in the background, and the lights were dim, very romantic. She sighed inwardly. It was perfect. He had done it again.

"This place is great. I've driven up and down this highway numerous times on my way to and from New York, and I never saw the sign until tonight." She smiled at him and looked at the menu the waiter had handed to her. He was so thoughtful about his choices of where to take her. She liked that about him. "If the food is as good as the ambiance, it should be fantastic." It was hard to choose. She scanned the menu, smiling. It all sounded good. "How did you find such a special place?"

"Dylan told me about it. He said it had great food." Matt opened his menu. "I said I wanted to be alone with my girl." He grinned at her. "And he said this was the place to go."

They both settled on the same thing: a wood-fired grilled chicken breast basted with olive oil and the house's special herbs, garlic mashed potatoes, and a house salad with a creamy parmesan dressing. The waiter poured the light chardonnay into their glasses.

He looked over his wine glass at her. "Jess, I'm not trying to cast doubts just on Liam. The same is true for anyone who suddenly comes back into your life from your past right now. Be smart, sweetheart, that's all."

"I know you're right, and I'll pay attention." She smiled and sipped her wine. "But, I still think the only thing Liam is guilty of is being a pest." He surely had been. Matt was to be excused for being annoyed. She touched his hand. He looked tired to her. "Was it a hard day?"

"Very. We got an ID on our victim. There was plenty of DNA but no match in the system, other than stored DNA from the other crime scenes. All that means is our perp lived a clean life up to the point he started killing women. If we catch him, his DNA will convict him." He paused as the waiter placed their salads in front of them. "We had to notify her grandparents. The Wilsons are great folks and friends

44

of my parents. She was staying with them." He shook his head and frowned. "Emma was only twenty-three. Today was one of those days when I hate my job."

"I understand." And she did. She placed the napkin on her lap.

"Then you know why I needed to be with you tonight. Without Liam." He took a bite of his salad. "I have a short fuse."

She nodded. "So how are we going to get this guy?"

"I want you to do a story on Emma." His gaze met hers and held it. "If you don't mind, I would like to take you by to meet the Wilsons. They're going to need a lot of support. I think you might be able to help them. See if one of those support groups meets locally, and tell them about it."

"I already know of a chapter in town. They will do all they can to support the Wilsons." They would surely need it. She couldn't even imagine how they were coping. "I'll call the Blue Cove chapter tomorrow, and they will contact them right away." She took a sip of her wine.

"Here's where it gets hard. I think our perp is going to stick around because he knows you're here now. I know you don't want to hear it, but it's my gut feeling. It might have started out random. I'm not sure if that's still true." He turned sharply when a waiter dropped an empty tray, and it clattered to the ground.

"You're right, but I don't want to think about it." He really was nervous. And it was…infectious. She fidgeted with her napkin. "I guess we need to have some kind of plan."

"What's this? You *guess* we should have some

45

kind of plan." His eyebrows rose. "That's not my girl—she always has to have a plan. What's up?" He scrutinized her face.

"I don't like to even think about it." She shuddered. "I saw what he did, don't forget, and he was high on it."

"I know this won't be easy, but we'll do it together." It was his turn to reach for her hand. "We have to be smart and not play into his plans. I want to sneak Frank and Radar into town quietly. I want the element of surprise to be on our side." He sat forward in the chair and spoke more softly. "The thing is, I can't sit by and do nothing, waiting for him to strike again."

"I know." She sighed, stroking his hand and gazing into his eyes. "We have to do something." She leaned forward, closer to him. "I'll do anything I can to help. I don't want to add to your concern." She waited for the waiter to set their plates in front of them and leave.

The first bite was great. "This chicken is delicious." She took another bite, closed her eyes, and savored the taste. It was moist, juicy, and bursting with flavors. When she opened her eyes again, Matt was smiling at her.

"I'm glad you're enjoying it."

"Oh, I am." She smiled at him back at him. "Good food and even better company—what more could a woman ask for?"

"That my dear is a loaded question." He leaned closer to her. "If we were someplace private, I could show you a few other things that a woman could ask for."

Jessie felt flushed. She knew without a mirror to tell her that she was blushing.

"That sounds like an interesting proposition." She

gave him a flirtatious smile.

"I'd be happy to show you personally anytime, sweetheart." He chuckled, teasing her.

"I wouldn't want to put you out; although, it could be fun." She leaned closer to him.

"I'd make it fun, trust me." He held her gaze.

"It's a little too public here to take you up on your interesting challenge." She smiled, fanning her face. "I think a change of subjects is in order, so I'll throw it out there. I know you're right."

"I can see the conversation is getting a little too hot for you." He grinned when she nodded. "I'm right about what?"

"He is going to be watching for me to trip up, and I need to be on guard. I have no clue what I'm looking for. He may seem familiar, but he's still vague."

"I have every confidence in you. You're unlike anyone I've ever known. I'm sure you'll know him when you see him or feel him. I'm counting on you, sweetheart."

"No pressure at all." She frowned. What would happen if it didn't work this time? If she couldn't sense him? He could sneak up on her. She didn't even want to think about that possibility. It would be too awful. The sudden chill made her reach for her sweater. How had she gotten into this mess?

****

The restaurant had several walking paths that led to the ocean, with benches placed along the way. After they had finished dinner, he took Jessie's hand, and they strolled together down toward the beach. A cloudless night left the air slightly chilly, but the stars were out in force. The silvery glow of the moonlight reflected off the water, giving the evening its perfect final touch.

"Here's another beautiful night for the records." He held her hand more tightly, pulling her closer to his side.

"I don't think it could have been any better than if you had special ordered this night just for us." She gazed into his eyes.

"Do you know how nice it is to have this time alone with you?" He motioned for her to sit then sat beside her.

This was all he needed right now, to be with her, to feel how alive she was in every way. Maybe if he sat here long enough, it could erase from his mind the awful sight of Emma which had shadowed his every waking moment today. It could have been Jessie. He was happy it wasn't—and felt guilty for the thought. Not that he wanted it to be Emma. No one should have to go through what Emma had. Damn, he had to get this guy. He didn't want to see another devastated face on his watch. He realized he'd been sitting there silently. Some lover! He smiled to himself. Jessie knew him well enough to know he wasn't up for much conversation tonight. He liked that about her. He felt her shiver and pulled her closer.

"You'll get him, Matt. I know you will. We'll do this together." Her voice was soft but firm. He shuddered. He knew she was right. Her believing it made him feel he could do anything.

Chapter 7

She heard Matt moving around in the kitchen and could smell the coffee. She finished her morning grooming quickly and made her way to the kitchen. "Good morning." She smiled at him. "Did you sleep well?"

"I've slept better. I couldn't shut my mind off." He placed a bagel in front of her and filled her coffee cup.

"Thanks, Matt." She buttered her bagel. "I thought maybe we should change things up a bit."

"What do you mean?" He sat down across from her.

"We should stay a couple of nights at your place, and then we'll change again. That way, we aren't so predictable. It will make it a little more convenient for you some days, too." She sipped her coffee. "I packed some clothes, so we can switch out tonight if you want."

"Great. I need to take care of some things at home." His phone alerted him to a text message. "Are you ready to take off? A flood of calls has come into the station. I need to do some catch-up."

She poured her coffee into her to-go cup and wrapped her bagel in a napkin. "I'll get my suitcase, and I'm ready." She hurried to her room for her bag, grabbed her laptop, and met him at the door.

"Let me carry something for you." He grinned as

she tried to juggle it all while holding her coffee cup and bagel.

"Thanks." She followed him out the door and turned to lock it. It would be good to stay with him for a day or two. His house was safer and wasn't so close to where it all had happened.

"I made several calls to other police and sheriff's departments, looking for confirmation and information. The return calls are starting to come in now. It looks like my day is full." He put her things in the trunk once she opened it, then reached for her keys. She dropped them in his hand.

"Hopefully, someone will have a key piece of information you need." She clicked her seatbelt on.

"One can hope." He backed out of the parking space and drove past the Inn to the highway. "Watch for the car you saw last night. If you see it, give me a call right away. I mean it, Jess, right away. You won't bother me." He glanced at her. "I know how your mind works."

"Not so much anymore. I won't mess around with this. I saw what he did, remember."

"I remember! I can't forget that you were almost his victim either." He pulled up in front of the store. "Do you want me to go in and check it out with you?"

"Please, if you don't mind." When could she stop being afraid?

Matt jumped out of the car and walked around to her door. He checked the outside of the building as she walked beside him, her heart beating a bit too fast. Taking the key from her hand, he entered the store first and carefully checked it over. "I think you're good to go." He smiled at her.

"Thanks, I have to admit I'm still afraid of this guy."

"I know, sweetheart." He gave her a kiss. "Call me if you see the car or anything else strange. I'll try to call you before I leave to come get you, if I don't forget. Don't go out without me."

"How can I? You have my car."

He kissed her again and left.

****

She got busy with her morning routine. A quick glance at her watch told her she still had an hour before the store opened. First, on her agenda was to tackle the box of books from her distributor, the ones delivered yesterday. There should be several books on the New York Times Best Seller List in that box. It was a treat for her to open because she knew she could count on them to sell. Customers would be looking for them. Jessie grabbed a stack of several different books after opening the box and carried them to the front of the store. She would have to shift some of the books on the display table to the shelves to make room for them. When she finished, a glance at her watch told it was almost time to open the store. The display table looked great, and the store was ready for another day.

Jessie opened the doors between her store and the coffee shop first. Molly waved at her and motioned for her to wait a minute.

"Can you believe someone was murdered in our woods?" She spoke softly so only Jessie would hear. "Kenny told me all the guys were talking about it. He said it was pretty awful."

"Matt said it was, too."

"Kenny won't let me go out alone, so I'm stuck

here until he is off work."

"You can always come over here and relax when your day is done." Jessie pointed to all the books. "I have a little bit of reading material to keep you busy." She liked Molly. It would be nice to have some catch-up time with her.

"Thanks." She grinned. "I'll let Kenny know I'll be at your store." Molly glanced over at the counter. "I've got to get back to work; the customers are starting to line up."

Jessie unlocked her front door, and her day began. She watched the people coming in and leaving. Everything and everyone seemed normal to her. She had made a smart move earlier, putting several books from the bestseller list on the table where they were easy to see. Ten books from that table had sold by noon. Her sales got an enormous boost when a busload of tourists stopped at the coffee shop, and several found their way through the doors into her business. She barely had time to take a breath, what with all the questions, requests, and sales.

She was talking to a customer when the first feeling hit her. He was near. Her gaze shot around the room, pausing at every male in the store. She could sense he was watching her. Jessie rubbed her tingling arms as she walked to the front of the store to help a customer. She automatically looked at the church. He was somewhere over there, probably in the woods behind the church, and he could see her. Matt needed to know. She pulled her phone out of her pocket and bumped into a woman who was reaching for a book. "I'm sorry, let me get that for you." Jessie's hand shook as she handed her the book. She moved away from the window and called.

The phone rang several times with no answer. Pick up, Matt. Please, pick up. Where was he? He always carried his phone at work. *"Matt, this is Jessie. Call me as soon as you get this."* Another customer called to her, and she was off to find another book. Her store was hopping. It seemed everyone wanted her attention all at once. If she got a lull, she would call Matt again.

****

Plain weird. She was standing at the window looking directly at him. Did she know he was there? How could she? He shook his head and tried to clear his thoughts. This was definitely a different Jessie than he remembered. She had always been pretty, but her strength and confidence were new. It fascinated him. What would happen if he got too close? Intrigued, he had to find out. It would make the dance exciting, stimulating, and a challenge to his skills. The right moment would present itself soon enough, and Jessie would be his for the taking. She had bewitched him. He adjusted his binoculars. There she stood, looking his way again. "Yes, my dear girl, I'm here, and you know it. We are going to have such fun. Should I make it quick and easy? I think not. You are a fine wine, I want to savor, sip slowly, and appreciate all your charms. I will, my dear Jessie, I will take pleasure in every moment we are about to share together." He chuckled. Yes, he was going to like this dance very much indeed.

****

Jessie could sense him out there watching her again. He knew her. She was sure of it. Who was he? A customer tapped her on the shoulder, and she jumped.

"I'm sorry I didn't mean to startle you. Do you

have this book?" She handed her a piece of paper with the name written on it. My friend said it's a must read."

"I have it right over here with several other books written by her. She is one of my favorite authors, and you'll love this book." She smiled as she led the woman to the shelf. "I have an autographed copy if you would like one." Jessie pulled it off the shelf when she nodded. They walked to the counter, where Jessie rang up the purchase. She put the book in a bag with one of her special bookmarks.

"Thank you. I love your store." She picked up her bag. "This is one of my favorite towns on our trip so far. It looks like a lovely to place to live. A lot safer than the city; although, I suppose every place has its problems."

"It is a great place to live but not without its problems. Such is life." Jessie smiled at her, suppressing a shiver. What would the woman say if she told her that a wanted killer was watching from across the street? "I appreciate your business." Jessie glanced at her watch as Molly came through the door with two cups of coffee and a white bakery bag. That late already? The day had flown by.

"I've come bearing gifts." Molly set the cups on the counter.

"Is that what I think it is? A scone perhaps?" Jessie opened the bag as Molly nodded. "I do enjoy these. I guess you know that by now."

"It's a no-brainer." Molly headed for one of the empty chairs with a table beside it. "Whew, it has been crazy busy all day. I need to sit down."

"I know. My store was busy too. I'm sure it was a great day for my business." She sat down in the chair beside Molly until she had to get up to ring up the last customers and lock up. Relief flooded her when she finally turned the key and locked the door. She stood at the window for a moment. He was gone—along with the sickening feeling.

What she needed now was a nice chat with Molly. Matt hadn't called her back, which was so unlike him. The threat seemed to be over for now. She would tell him when he picked her up.

"How is married life?" Jessie sat down in the chair across from Molly.

"So far, so good. I like it." Molly giggled and blushed. "I think I may be pregnant. I know we haven't been married long." She tilted her head back, and her smile broadened. "I haven't told Kenny yet. I'm waiting for the perfect moment—after I know for sure." Molly glanced at Jessie. "Please don't say anything to anyone."

"I won't. You must be thrilled." Jessie hugged her. It was easy to see; it was written all over her face how she felt.

"I'm a little scared about what my folks will say. But when I imagine a little dark curly-headed boy or girl with Kenny's dimples, I fall hopelessly in love with the idea."

"For now, I offer you my quiet congratulations, but when you find out for sure, I'll be the one standing up and cheering for you." Jessie grabbed Molly's hand. "I'm happy for you, Molly." Jessie enjoyed her time with Molly. She was fun to be with, and for a moment, it let her forget about *him*. "You and Kenny must have a fun time together."

"We do. Speaking of Kenny, I wonder where he is.

I thought he would be here by now."

"Unless I miss my guess, he just pulled up in front of the store." At least, she hoped it was Kenny. She stood to get a better view of the car.

Chapter 8

Jessie locked the door after Molly left. She straightened her display table, picked up the remaining trash, and cleaned the surfaces as she went. She glanced across the street at the church. Something was going on over there tonight. Cars were entering the parking lot. It must be the book club night. The wind blowing through the trees cast eerie dancing shadows among the headstones in the graveyard. The partially hidden moon with dark clouds streaking through it set a perfect scene for a spooky beginning to a book. She looked at the church and to the dark woods beyond, and a sudden chill moved down her back, taking her by surprise. He had been watching her today. Up on the hill behind the church, he had been there—skulking in the woods like some kind of madman. Where was a ghost when you needed one? Jessie sighed.

Shutting off the main lights in the store, she sat down in the leather wingback chair to wait for Matt. She saw the lights as the car pulled into the space in front of the store. Her heart started to race. It wasn't Matt. She slipped to the floor, not wanting him to see her. Whoever it was drove off a few minutes later. She made her way to the bookshelf on the other side of the store to hide. From there, she could watch the street and be out of view. There the car was again, on the other side of the street in front of the church. She closed her eyes trying to block out everything. No thoughts, no feelings, or impressions, there was nothing, only a strange notion that the person in the car was not him, but someone equally dangerous. She called Matt again.

Her breathing was shallow and rapid; her mouth went dry. She eyed her bottle of water across the room. A sip of water would help, but she couldn't move now. The ringing phone startled her.

"Hi, Jess, I just noticed you called earlier."

"Where are you?" She interrupted him, her voice sounded shrill to her.

"I'm just leaving the station. What's wrong?"

The car door swung open, and a large foot planted itself on the street. "Please hurry, there's someone coming."

"What the hell, Jess."

"I can't talk now. Hurry." Shutting off the phone, she took a deep breath and waited. She wrapped her arms around herself and squeezed deeper into the darkness. She heard the car door slam. She couldn't see his face; an oversized hood shielded it from view. He was crossing the street, heading toward her store. Her heart pounded in her ears, and then she heard the door jiggle. She pressed against the wall as a light danced along the interior of the store and held her breath. "Please hurry, Matt," she whispered.

"Hey you, what are you doing over there? You need to move along. The store is closed for the night," a man's voice called out loudly. She exhaled her breath slowly. Someone was looking out for her.

"I just wanted to check the times on the door. I decided to peek while I was here. It looks like a nice little store," the man's deep voice answered back. "You don't need to be worried about me. I'm no robber." He chuckled. "I'll check back again tomorrow at opening time."

Listening intently, she could hear him chatting with the man as he walked away. She poked her head out when she heard the car door open and watched as he lifted his foot back into the car, closed the door, and drove off. The other man stood in the street and waved his arms. She didn't know who had called out to him, but she was so glad he had. She calmed herself, taking deep breaths.

She couldn't spend her life hiding behind things or waiting for Matt to check out her store. A good plan was what she needed. First thing in the morning, she was signing up for those darn lessons in self-defense. Maybe she would start to follow his advice and carry her gun. She wasn't about to go down without a fight. She wouldn't be stupid either. Matt could help whenever he was around.

When she finally stepped out from behind the post, she saw a police cruiser stopped in front of the church and a man talking to the officer. He pointed over at her store. He pulled his car up in front of the store and got out. She opened the door when she saw who it was.

"Jessie, what are you doing in there?" Kip looked surprised to see her.

"The store closed about thirty minutes ago, and I was waiting for Matt to get here to pick me up."

"It's a good thing Lawrence Thompson saw that man and scared him off."

"You're telling me," Jessie smiled and waved at Mr. Thompson. "Thank you," she called out to him.

Lawrence crossed the street. "You have Reba to

59

thank. She wouldn't let up until we drove to the church. Wouldn't you know it; there he was just as she had seen him. His story didn't seem to add up to me, as I was telling this nice young officer."

"Let's go inside, and you can tell me what happened." Kip opened the door, and they followed him inside. "I don't think you should be standing out here in case he drives back around."

Next to join the group was Liam. "Is everything all right?" Liam looked at her.

"Now it is. What are you doing here?" Jessie frowned. His timing was awful, as usual.

"I was driving around checking out the town when I saw the police car in front of your store. I wanted to make sure you were okay."

"I would think checking out the town might be better in the daylight." Her remark sounded snide even to her. She didn't buy his story. Matt's arrival came next. The minute he walked through the door, he frowned when he saw Liam.

"What happened, Kip? Jess?" Matt looked directly at her, his tone irritated.

"I was just about to find out," Kip answered.

Jessie started the story, telling about the car and the man. Lawrence finished it with Reba making him drive to the church to find the man looking in Jessie's window with a flashlight.

"Did you see the man?" Kip directed the question at Lawrence when Jessie shook her head no.

"I never saw his face." Lawrence shook his head. "He had a big hood pulled down to hide it from view. I would say he was about the same height as you, young man." Lawrence pointed at Liam. "No offense, he just seemed to be about your height is all."

"None taken, sir," Liam smiled at Lawrence. "I'm just over six foot, and there are quite a few of us around. I think Matt and even you might come in right at that height."

"It was the same car I saw the other night."

Lawrence ran his hand through his hair. "I'm sorry; I didn't even think to look at his car. I was so concerned about getting him away from Jessie's store. Reba knew she was still in the store and wanted him gone."

"I'm not sure how I know, but he's not the murderer you're looking for, Matt. I can tell." The words tumbled out before she could stop them. "He's dangerous, too, but he's not the killer." She tilted her head and glanced at Matt.

Matt saw the perplexed look on Liam's face. "Don't ask, you'll just be more confused."

"I'll leave her in your capable hands, Chief Parker, and take Reba home, if you don't mind." Lawrence glanced from Jessie to Matt with a smile.

"That's fine, Lawrence, and thanks for coming along when you did. Who knows what he might have done."

"See you, Jessie. I'll fill Reba in on all the details. You can chat with her tomorrow."

"Goodbye, and thanks again." Lawrence nodded and left the store.

"I'll be on my way too, Chief." Kip headed for the door. "Not much that we can do tonight."

Liam walked out with them. "Jessie, if you need me for anything, just let Katie know."

"I will, but I'm sure Matt can take care of it." She got in the car.

He spoke as soon as he shut the car door. "What aren't you telling me, Jess?" Matt turned to face her.

"What makes you think that I'm not telling you something?" She sounded unconvincing, even to herself.

"Because I've been around you long enough to know. Out with it."

"I had a super busy day in the store. A bus tour came in." She stopped abruptly and grabbed his hand. "I called you earlier and even left you a voicemail. Why didn't you answer me?"

"I forgot my phone when I went to check out a vandalism call. I was in a hurry. I didn't notice the missed call when I got back, or I would have called you earlier instead of when I did. What are you trying to tell me?" He looked through his messages and played hers.

"He was out there watching me from the woods behind the church. I could feel him." She sucked in a breath, remembering the sick feeling in her stomach. "He was aware I knew he was there. It was like some kind of sadistic dance, mind to mind. It felt similar, but not the same as with Irwin." She patted his hand. "Even if I had gotten you, you couldn't have gotten here in time. He knew what was going on."

"Damn, Jess, why is it that you attract all the weird perps for miles around?"

"I wouldn't say that exactly." She crossed her arms and met his gaze. "Well, I mean there have been a few, I guess."

"A few? I would say it was more than a few. Since you've been here, there have been several strange folks."

"I don't think that's my fault. I mean, I didn't put

up a sign telling them to follow me here, now did I?" She let the sarcasm she felt color her voice.

He grinned and softened his tone. "You look pretty, by the way."

"Oh no, you don't. You're not going to flatter your way out of this. You started this, and you may as well own up to it and say what you want to say."

"What can you tell me about this other person in the car? Is there something I need to know?"

"I didn't get much with him. He's dangerous, but right now, he's observing, not acting. Will he act later? I have no way of knowing." She reached over and touched his hand again.

"What am I supposed to do with that?" He grumbled.

"You asked, and I told you, so don't get all bent out of shape. I know what it is you're really itching to ask and have been dancing around." She clamped her lips together to keep from smiling at his expression. "I have no idea what Liam was doing here. He just showed up when it was all over. I didn't completely believe his story of how he came to be there either. Does that mean anything? Probably not, but I thought I should tell you anyway. Now you can be civil again."

Matt grinned. "That bad, huh?"

"Pretty much…"

"How about I make it up to you with a nice quiet dinner? I'll make it, and you can put your feet up and watch TV."

"Bribery…" She smiled at him. "I think I can live with that." A sudden shiver ran down her back. Kip's cruiser idled in front of them with lights still flashing, people were leaving the church, and she was safe with

Matt. Still she knew the man was nearby. She glanced around, her hand in a white-knuckled grip on the armrest. Where was he?

Chapter 9

Walking out of the church, the man pulled his coat tight around him to ward off the chilly night air. It had gone off without a hitch. He had made it through the whole evening without messing up once. How he loved a good joke, and this whole evening had been one. The man picked up the pace and wrapped his scarf around his face when he saw the cop car in front of the store across the street. Hurry, he needed to hurry. His steps quickened. The chill cut right through him. Skirting through the woods, keeping away from the streetlights, he made his way back to the motel where he was staying. It wasn't much, but he didn't need much at this point. Light flooded the room when he flipped the switch. He laid his coat carefully across the back of the chair.

He had mingled among the church folks as if he was one of them, playing the part of the new man in town to perfection. A smile spread across his face. What a performance he had given. His acting was superb. Long fingers ran through his ink black hair after shedding his disguise. A glance at the mirror showed a perfect pair of turquoise eyes looking back at him, now lit with amusement. "You have eyes like Elvis," the girls used to tell him. Early on, he had figured out how to use them to his advantage. Why mess with perfection? He looked again at his reflection on his way to his paper spread out on the table. One more article for his collection. He was infamous; they called him an evil monster, detestable, and lots of other names, but his favorite was "the devil."

He chuckled. The devil went to church tonight. Yes sir, those good folks had fawned over him until he almost laughed at what a fraud he was. He picked up the scissors, cutting with care another article about himself for his scrapbook. If only they knew. They would have fled in terror. It suited him that no one knew, of course, but it might have been fun to see their reaction. The devil loved the challenge of hiding in plain sight.

The folks in the little towns he passed through were so eager to please and talk to him. In no time at all, he had them eating out of his hands. Tonight was no different; a strategic question here and there, and they fell all over themselves, anxious to tell him all about their wonderful church secretary. She worked at the church part time, and she owned the cute little bookstore across the street. He had found out in no time. She was an investigative reporter who had moved here from New York. Yes sir, Jessie had been very active since her move to Blue Cove. A heroine in this town, she had been busy rescuing kids, saving the police chief, and outmaneuvering people trying to harm her. No wonder she had enticed him the minute he saw her. He wanted this dance—with her. It was an obsession. She represented his greatest challenge to date.

He had played several roles in the last few years, but never had he gone into a church. Only someone as fine as her could tempt him to enter the church doors ever again. He had spent most of his adult life avoiding those places, for more reasons than he could count. The image it conjured up made him laugh. A frown replaced it as another image crossed his mind. The vein in his neck throbbed, his jaw clenched, and his brows lowered as memories he wanted to forget marched through his mind. All the years he had spent years running from his past, but, still, it seemed to rear its ugly head again. The man slammed his fist on the table.

The monster pushed back from the table, tipping over the chair, which hit the floor with a thud. He grabbed his jacket and keys. Only one thing would appease the demons. The devil drove out of Blue Cove and began his search.

****

"You've been quiet. Is everything all right, Jess?" He pulled into the garage beside his pickup and car. He was glad he had opted for the three-car garage for just such an occasion.

"I could feel him close by when we were sitting in front of the store. I don't want him around, but I don't want him to hurt anyone else either."

"I know it's hard." He could see how much it was bothering her. "I'm wrestling with the same emotions. He's lingering around town because of you. Frank will be here in a couple of days," he said soothingly. "He's working another case and will get here as soon as he can break away. In the meantime, I need you to think of people from your past who might be capable of something like this."

"I can't imagine anyone I've ever known being capable of anything like this." Her voice sounded tight to him, tense. "I mean, you always meet a pest or two, or your occasional strange bird along the way. Kids and teens can always be strange. Bobby Angel tormented me for a year but then moved on to Lisa. He grew up to be charming and quite popular. Liam had a few friends that were a pain, too."

"I don't think you need to go so far back. How about starting with your days in New York?"

"I'll think about it. Maybe something will ring a bell." She followed him into the house. "Every time I walk into your house it impresses me all over again." She placed her purse on the polished granite of the kitchen counter.

He took her suitcase and computer into the guest bedroom. "Here's your home for a couple of days. Thanks for doing this, Jess. It will give me a chance to catch up around here."

"I don't mind. I love your house, and hey, if you're cooking, I'm all in." She tilted her head back, smiling at him.

She was finally relaxing a bit. "You're a good sport, Jess. Most people would have left a long time ago, after experiencing what you have the past few months." And thank heavens she hadn't! "You haven't even been here a year. I'm sorry, sweetheart." He lifted her chin up and gazed into her eyes. "I hope someday soon Blue Cove will be all you wanted when you moved here." He ran his finger across her lips. "Jess, you know how I feel about you." He bent his head and kissed her. He ended it abruptly, took her hand, and led her to his recliner. He handed her the remote. "Now relax. That's an order." He smiled. "Dinner will be ready soon."

****

Jessie couldn't contain her smile. He had a way of shaking up and settling her world all at the same time. She turned on the TV to watch the news. It didn't take long for her mind to drift as questions flooded in. How did she know him, or better yet, how did he know her? Jessie got out of the chair. Drawn to the window, she looked out into the night. The clouds had lifted, and the moon was shining brightly over the cove, mesmerizing her as the light danced across the water. She held her breath when she saw another shimmering light moving in the gardens on Matt's property. What was it? Dancing back and forth playfully, the light dimmed until Jessie could see the form of a person. A woman. "Who are you?" Turning as if she had heard her question, the woman looked at Jessie; "Emma," Jessie whispered. They stood still staring at each other for what seemed an eternity. Every sound faded away as Jessie's gaze locked on Emma's face. Tears spilled from Jessie's eyes and ran down her cheeks. She was overwhelmed with the sadness she saw. "I'm so sorry. You had your whole life ahead of you. We will get him, Emma, rest easy." Jessie watched her move away into the shadows, and then she was gone.

"What the hell, Jess? Why are you crying?" Matt pulled her into his arms. "You didn't even hear me call. What is it, sweetheart?"

"I saw her, Matt, right out there in your garden. She was so sad that it breaks my heart to think of it."

"Who did you see, Jess?" His hand rubbed up and down her back.

"It was Emma." She shuddered. "Emma was there. Oh, no, it's happening again."

"Are you sure it was her?"

"You do realize who you're talking to?" She managed to smile through her tears. "It was Emma. I'm not sure why she was here or if I'll ever see her again. We have to get him, Matt. We have to!"

Chapter 10

Dick had gone to get Amanda from the bedroom. Jessie watched Matt head for a chair. He sat down, stretching out his long legs. He looked good. She fanned her face as she walked to the fireplace and stopped to look at the pictures on the mantel. Emma's smiling face was there in various stages of her life. Her chocolate brown hair and smiling hazel eyes were recognizable features in each picture and a beautiful part of who she was. "She was lovely," Jessie turned and spoke softly to Matt.

"She was just as sweet as she was pretty." Amanda walked up beside her. "She was seven here and missing her front teeth, as you can see." Amanda laughed. "She was our spunky little firecracker, so full of life." Her lips quivered; tears welled in her eyes. She pointed to a picture off to the side. "This was taken right before she came to visit. She had it done for her fiancé. Her high school sweetheart had asked her to marry him at Christmas. Her engagement ring was beautiful." She sighed.

"I'm so sorry, Amanda. He must be devastated."

"He is. We all are. I feel like I'm just going through the motions of living right now." She wiped her eyes with a tissue.

"I can't imagine how you'll even begin to recover from something so awful." Jessie touched Amanda's shoulder softly.

"After we grieve, we will because Emma would want us to. It won't be easy. I know I will fight as hard as I can for the rights of victims and their families. No one should have to go through this hell." Amanda dusted the top of the frame with her apron. "My son and daughter-in-law will be here sometime today. They are on their way back from Europe. I can't imagine how they are doing. Meredith was so excited about planning Emma's wedding. Now it will be her funeral. I'm afraid it will be a long, long flight for them." Amanda shuddered.

"It's not much consolation, but you can't get a better person for the job of finding the guy than Matt." Jessie glanced his way and saw he was watching her. "He's the best, and he won't stop until they have him in prison or dead."

"We have confidence in him. He's good, and we know it." The tissue in her hand wiped more tears rolling down her cheeks. Jessie touched Amanda's shoulder and held back her own tears.

"I want to do a story about Emma. It may help to stir up the public's memory. It could trigger a thought about something they might have heard or seen. Also, I think it's important to put a human face and life to Emma. Murder touches not only the victim but their families as well, and I don't want her to become just another statistic. Would you and Dick be willing to tell me some special memories of her? I'll ask her parents as well."

Amanda and Dick were more than ready to talk. They told Jessie one story after another. They laughed and cried, and Jessie did the same, right alongside them.

"Jessie, be sure to come back with Matt and meet my son and his wife," Amanda told her as they were leaving. "You are welcome here anytime."

"Thank you, I will." She hugged Amanda briefly. "I know they'll have things to share about their daughter. We want to get this guy." Jessie smiled at them and closed the door behind her.

****

"You're something." Matt glanced at her when he got in the car. "You handled yourself like a pro in there. You amaze me every time. I never know what to say to folks. Their sadness seems to overtake me, and I get angry. Not at them, of course, but it still comes out as if I'm angry." She grabbed his arm as they walked to the car.

"You think about the suspect and how to get him. I think about the victim and about keeping their memory alive. We make a pretty good team." She smiled at him when he opened the door, and she got in the car.

"Yeah, we make a damn good team." He grinned at her and fastened his seatbelt. Then, his expression became serious. "Do you think you'll see Emma again?"

"I kind of hope not. It was way too sad. But I never know. I guess I'll cross that bridge if and when I get to it." She looked over the notes she had taken during her time at the Wilsons. "Emma seemed like such a nice person. I would have liked her, I think." Jessie paused to write something on the paper. "I feel bad for her fiancé."

"I can't imagine how he feels. I know how I felt when I realized it could have been you. It makes me wonder why I ever involved you in any of this mess."

"You didn't." She looked up at him, surprised. "If anything, I involved you when Gina first appeared to me. We seem to muddle through it well enough." She smiled. "I believe we should try to help people any way we can. This seems to be our way."

"Well, getting this perp off the street might save a few lives, and I would like to do that."

"I agree," She touched his hand as he started the car. "So what is our plan? How are we going to get him?"

"I'm thinking about it. A lot of ideas are popping in my head." He looked over at her when he stopped at the light. "Right now, though, I'm hungry, and I want to eat. How about it, are you up for going out for dinner? It's getting late."

"Sure, that's fine by me." She winked at him. "Neither one of us will have to cook. Sounds perfect."

"Any place in particular?"

"You're the one driving. Surprise me."

"I can do that, sweetheart. I'm full of surprises." He drove out of Blue Cove and turned on Old Homestead Road. Down the road a few miles were several homes on acre parcels. Intermingled were a couple of small businesses and a restaurant too. "You haven't been here yet, have you?"

"No." She shook her head.

"Great home-cooked tasting meals and the best pie ever. I think you'll like it." He got out and opened her door.

"It smells delicious," she said as he held the entry door for her. It was a classic diner. From what era, she wondered. The fifties?

"Sit anywhere. I'll be with you in a minute," the

waitress called out to them.

They sat down in a booth by the window and looked over the menus that were sitting there.

"Are you kids ready to order?" She looked over her glasses at them and took the pencil from behind her ear. She licked the tip and flipped through her order pad. "What do want, hon?" She looked at Jessie.

Jessie smiled. Matt wasn't much of a kid, and neither was she. "I'll have a bowl of chicken noodle soup." Jessie noticed her name tag on her uniform. Franny. It fit, somehow.

"You'll like it, and it comes with the homemade dinner rolls and refills. The best rolls for miles around." She glanced at Matt. "How about you, son?"

"I want today's special."

"You can't go wrong with the chicken and dumplings. Anything to drink for either of you?" She looked back and forth between them.

"Water is fine for me," Matt answered, smiling at her.

"Me too…"

"How old do you think she is?" Matt asked when she had walked away.

"I think she's cute. She looks perfect for the place." Jessie bit her lip to keep from giggling. "Her teased bouffant and blue eye shadow threw me into the sixties."

"I haven't been called a kid in years."

"I think we're young to her, obviously."

Matt grinned at Jessie. "You think?" He frowned, and his face took on a serious look again. He reached across the table and took her hand. "Jess, I'm a little concerned. I know that this guy is staying around Blue

Cove for you. He may try to throw us off the track. It's going to take everything we have to stay on top of this and not give him any opportunity to get at you."

"I don't want to give him anything. What he did to Emma makes me angry." It made her more than angry. They *were* going to get him. "How are we going to trap him?"

"Radar may be able to help us with our search for him once Frank can get here. Keeping our eyes and ears open is paramount."

"What about the one casing the store?"

"That's another area of concern." Matt quit talking when the waitress brought their food. Franny set the basket of rolls on the table with a dish of butter pats and returned to the kitchen to fetch Jessie's deep bowl of steaming soup and Matt's plate of chicken and dumplings. "If you need anything, either one of you, just give me a shout-out, and I'll be right with you. I'll be back for your dessert order when you're done with your meal. Believe me, you don't want to eat here and not have the pie." She gave a throaty chuckle. "It's the best part."

Jessie buttered the roll and took a bite. "Oh my, Franny was right. These are really good."

Matt took a bite and agreed. "Franny?"

"I read her nametag," Jessie smiled at him. "Do you mind if we change the subject while we eat?" He shook his head no.

"So tell me about Liam." Matt looked up briefly from his chicken and dumplings.

"There's not much to tell. I had a crush on him when I was a freshman in high school." She shrugged. "He was on the football team, a senior, and always had a girlfriend. He had some handsome friends who could make their way into my thoughts from time to time." None as good-looking as Matt, but she wasn't about to tell him that! "I was a nuisance to him back then. He tormented Katie, and we pestered him. I think he's just getting back at me now."

"He was a real ladies' man, huh?"

"Pretty much." She made a face. "You know—he was a star running back and his friend, Connor Moore, was the quarterback. He was easy on the eyes too." She smirked because she could see that Matt was getting jealous. "He asked me to the senior prom."

"Did you go with him?"

"Yes, but with the third degree my father put him through, I was surprised he didn't run for his life and stand me up." Jessie laughed. She told him a few more of the stories from her growing up years, laughing her way through one tale after another. Matt found them funny, too, she noticed. It seemed to relax him. Franny stopped by for their pie order. Matt opted for blueberry with a scoop of ice cream, and Jessie wanted the chocolate cream. Both had a cup of coffee to top it off. Franny had been right about the pie. The crust was flaky and melted in her mouth. What was there not to like about chocolate?

"Thanks for the great service," Jessie smiled at Franny.

"You kids come back again soon."

"I'm sure we will."

It was late when Matt pulled the car into the garage. "We can stay at your place tomorrow if you'd like."

"Sweet." She headed for her room but called back

to him. "Thanks for dinner and company. I had a good time."

"I enjoy hearing you laugh. It makes me happy. You haven't had much of a chance to enjoy yourself since being here. I figure we are going to take the chances that fate hands to us. Goodnight, Jess."

"Good night, Chief." She smiled all the way down the hall, imagining his grin.

Chapter 11

Matt watched her walk down the hall and couldn't take his eyes away from the gentle sway of her hips. Her retort brought a smile that turned to a goofy grin plastered on his face; he knew he must look like an idiot standing there. It didn't get any better when she turned back to look at him. Hell, he didn't care. She made him happy. He wanted to follow her and take her in his arms, but tonight she was as skittish as a new colt. All in good time. The grin got broader; the cat and mouse game they were playing was the best part of the chase.

Matt went into his room, grabbed the remote on his way, and stretched out on his bed. He flipped through the stations and stopped on the sports channel. Unexpectedly, the murder scene flashed through his mind. He shuddered. Damn, would he ever get the gruesome scene out of his mind? Emma could have easily been Jessie. He had come too close to losing her. He couldn't imagine his life without her now. She was entrenched in his heart, and he was happy to have her in it. He didn't want to go back...he *couldn't* go back to how it used to be. He raked his hand through his hair. Emma's family hadn't wanted to lose her either. He couldn't sit by and wait for it to happen again.

This perp wasn't about to roll over and stop on his own. Matt was sure of that. What made him tick? How did he know Jessie? Was it from her days in New York or before? Whoever he was, he was obsessed now that he had seen her. Jeremy. He sat up straight. He might know of someone from her past. Matt sent a quick text off to him, but his mind wouldn't shut down. He went through the conversations he'd had with the other police agencies all day. Only the investigating officers at the murder sites—who were now under a gag order—knew all the details. It was important to keep it out of the hands of the press for a while. Matt hoped the murderer would tip them off by bragging about some little detail that the public knew nothing about. He flipped through the channels again. A new subject, he needed a new subject to think about, or he'd never get to sleep. He turned around and punched up his pillows.

What was he going to do about Jess? She was one of his favorite subjects. He wanted her by his side, without the complication of Liam or living in two places. He smiled and laid his head back against the pillows. She was something. He needed to step up his charm campaign, or they might be stuck here for years. He shook his head and reached over to shut off the light. The TV was next.

It had been one hell of a day, and he was tired. He was just beginning to doze off when moans reached his ears. Jessie…He grabbed his pants, pulled them on, and zipped them on the way to the door. His hand was on the doorknob when her moans turned to screams. His only coherent thought was that there had to be a better way to be together than this.

****

Emma was there in Jessie's dreams, smiling and running through the woods. Her ponytail swished behind her as carefree as she was at that moment. The woods were alive with sound, teeming with life and beauty. Suddenly, it became still and dark, the dense fog swirled through the woods swallowing Emma. The nightmare began. Jessie tossed and turned, moaning as she relived the murder. The dark figure danced along the edge of her dream, never showing his face, only the results of his madness. The scene suddenly changed, and Jessie thrashed about as the covers tangled around her. *She saw him again, his dark form standing over a body. The shadows spun the web around him pulling her closer, ever closer. Jessie crept through the swirling mist until she saw a sweet face, but it wasn't Emma's face. Another face looked up at her from the ground with eyes wide open.* Jessie's own screams awakened her. He had killed again. Tears gathered in her eyes, overflowing down her cheeks as she grieved for the young woman she had never met.

She was vaguely aware of Matt opening the door. She heard him walk across the floor and felt his weight on the edge of the bed. He pulled her tenderly into his arms and held her while she cried; his hand rubbing up and down her back; his chin resting on her head. Quiet, not moving, he held her until her crying subsided. A sense of relief filled her with her spent tears.

"Tell me, Jess, what did you see?"

"He killed again." She took the tissue he held out to her and told him about the dream. "Her hair was light, maybe blonde, not dark like Emma's. Oh, Matt," she sobbed. "We have to stop him."

"I know. We'll think of something, sweetheart. It'll be okay, we'll find a way. I promise." He lifted her face, his finger tracing her cheek to her lips.

She touched his hand, stopping its motion. "I keep thinking there is something that I should remember about him. Any detail that will give me his identity." She shook her head. "But it won't come."

"You'll remember in time. It'll come to you." He released her hand and stood up. "Let's get these covers untangled—you're all tied up in them."

"Thank you." She shivered. "I don't know how to erase this from my mind. I keep seeing it, every time I close my eyes."

"Did you recognize the area? Was it familiar?" He studied her face.

"No, I'm not sure if it is even in the area. I don't know all of Blue Cove yet, but I don't think it was here, which might mean he has moved on."

"I wouldn't get my hopes up. He may be taking it out of Blue Cove to throw us off track, but you are his obsession now." He took her hand. "I don't think he'll leave until he's done toying with you, to be blunt." His hand fisted. "We'll get him, don't worry. Do you want me to sit here while you go back to sleep?"

"No, you need your rest too. I'll be okay." She lifted her face to look at him. "I know you'll do your best to find him. He's there at the edge of my mind. Just when I think he's close enough to see him, he moves into the shadows. Why can't I put it together yet? We need to know who he is."

"Don't worry about it, Jess. It would be helpful, but it's not necessary. We have to be smart about it, though, and not let him have a chance at you." He bent down and gave her a quick kiss on the cheek. "Good night, sweetheart. If you need me, call." He shut off the light on his way out the door.

The room seemed empty the minute he closed the door. "Emma," Jessie whispered, "I need your help. He's not going to stop until we get him. I'm not sure what you can do, but there must be some way to get through to me who he is." Jessie propped her head up using the pillows against the headboard. She hadn't done a story about a serial killer that she could remember. Maybe he wasn't a murderer when she knew him. What made him familiar? His actions, his hair color, body shape, what was it? She closed her eyes, trying to remember. Did he use his left hand or right when he was stabbing his victim? Was his clothing familiar to her? She would figure it out. She had to. Jessie shivered as the room turned cold. "Emma, I know you can help us," she whispered. Emma was there, and Jessie knew it.

****

Matt stood outside her closed door. It was getting harder to leave her after her dreams. He sighed inwardly and walked back to his room, where he pulled out his laptop and started looking over the file on Emma's case. There were several murders attributed to the same suspect. Each murder was vicious, similar in pattern, and filled with rage. This perp obviously hated women. Why?

He needed to talk to a criminal profiler. Maybe the conversation could give him some insight. Jessie could go along with him; it might help to stir her memory.

She would keep pushing herself to remember. It was possible a little nudge was all she needed. O'Malley would know of a criminal profiler in New York. There might even be one in his precinct. He'd call first thing in the morning. A trip to the city would do her good. Now, all he had to do was to find a time when she could get away from the store for a little while.

If he didn't miss his guess, another town somewhere in the area would be dealing with a murder shortly.

He read over the file again, several times, hoping that some little detail would jump out at him. There was plenty of incriminating evidence. All they needed was a suspect. One damn break was all he needed, and this perp could be behind bars. He turned off his computer, stretched out on the bed, and let his mind drift toward more pleasant thoughts. He heard the soft knock on his door. "Come in, Jess."

"Do you mind? I don't want to be alone tonight." He patted the bed beside him. It was going to be another long sleepless night.

Chapter 12

Jessie found Matt in the kitchen when she emerged from her room after she showered and dressed.

"I was just about to wake you. I figured you needed to get to the store." Matt smiled at her and poured her a cup of coffee. She looked at the cup and then over at him. "It's decaf, so don't worry. I know your preference by now." He pointed to the second coffee maker on the counter. "Why you even bother to drink it is beyond me." He smiled at her as he said it.

"Thanks. I know it's a little strange, but it works well for me." Her phone alerted her to a text. She paused to read for a moment. "Katie is going nuts. I'd better call and let her know I'm okay. It seems she got an extra key and looked inside when I didn't open the door. She was afraid I had been murdered." Jessie smiled at him. "To know Katie is to love the way her mind works."

"Don't give this safe haven away, or I'll have Liam camping out on my doorstep."

She nodded at him with a smile. "Hi, Katie, it's me. I'm returning your call. And, before you ask, I'm fine, really. I'll be home tonight if you want to stop by. I had a few things to take care of with the case. Besides, you know you can always get me by phone. There's no need for you to worry. Next time, wait a little while before you get wacky. You know I'll get around to calling you back."

"I know, but Liam wouldn't take no for an answer. He had to check for himself. I love my brother, you know that, but he's driving me batty. If I were you, I'd stay away a few more nights, or he'll be hanging out at your door like a lost kitten." Katie giggled. "I'm not kidding; he's so pathetic right now. I hope he finds a place soon, or I'll be ready to move out myself."

"Why did he need to see me?"

"He wanted to tell you Connor Moore will be here this weekend and wants to see you. I'll be making dinner for all of us, including Matt, on Saturday night. Plan to be there, or I'll be driven nuts by my brother."

"Of course, I'll be there. You can let Liam know. I'll tell Matt, and I'll talk to you later when I'm off work."

"Let me know what?" His deep voice startled her.

"Connor Moore will be in town this weekend, and Katie is making dinner for all of us on Saturday night. You're invited of course."

"I should hope so. Wasn't that Connor fella the one you went to the senior prom with?" He watched her nod with a grin. "If I remember correctly, he's the one you said was easy on the eyes. I'm not crazy enough to leave you unescorted on Saturday and let another guy move in on my territory."

"Just so you know, I'm no one's territory, and no one will move in on me unless I let them." She saw him frown. "Having said that,"—she smiled at him and ruffled his hair—"I wouldn't want to go without you anyway."

"Don't you find the timing a little strange?"

"I was going to mention that before you started the

whole jealous thing." She picked up her cup and sipped her coffee. "Look, Matt, I know you've had plenty of girlfriends over the years. You're a lot like Liam in that regard. If I thought about it all the time, it would bug me too. In fact, *I* would be doing the jealous thing." She saw the corners of his lips turn up. "Liam and Connor are from my past. I haven't seen them for years, and you're in my life now. You don't have to worry."

"Trust me, neither do you. I'm just wondering why your past has decided to show up right now when we have a murderer in town who knows you from somewhere in your past."

"I don't know, but I'll keep my eyes and ears open. However, I do know that Liam knows that Katie has a key to my cottage. He also knows where she keeps it. I'm not sure if I like that." She placed her cup back on the counter.

"I sure don't. I'll be your shadow until I can rule those two out and catch the real one."

"I appreciate it. I know our perp's intent on what he's doing, and I admit I have no clue at who I'm looking for."

"I talked to O'Malley this morning about us coming to New York to talk with a criminal profiler. He said he would make an appointment for us as soon as I knew when you could go with me. I think it's something we need to do. He might say something that will give your memory a little nudge. Is there a time when you can leave the store?"

"I hired a woman who will work a few days a week in the morning while I work at the church. I sell some of her creations in my store."

He looked surprised. "I didn't know you had hired

someone."

"She hasn't worked yet. She'll start next week. I still like working at the church, too. I'm not sure how long I'll keep it up, but I'll train the next secretary for them before I leave."

"I'm sure they're glad to have you still working there, even if it's only part-time."

"It seems to me that my coming to the church has brought on several difficulties. They might actually be happy to see me quit."

"I don't believe that for even a minute. I've seen how those people love you. They feel about you the way I do." He smiled warmly at her. "You want to stay here tonight, or at your place?"

"If we don't want Liam to find out about your place, we should stay at mine. It sounds like he's driving Katie nuts with questions about where I am. You don't have to stay with me, though. I should be fine."

"Like hell, I don't! I'm not leaving your side while there's a murderer out there stalking you. We'll stay at your place."

"All right, I'll be happy to have you there with me." She smiled. "Besides, it's my turn to make dinner for you while you take it easy."

"I like the sound of that. When should I set the appointment with the profiler? Frank will be here no later than Wednesday next week. I had a text from him this morning. Does Monday work for you?" He unplugged the coffee pots and started cleaning the counter.

She nodded. "If Audrey can't work, Reba might be able to. I'll be happy to have Frank here with Radar. I want to get this guy in the worst way. Speaking of dogs..." She looked around the room. "I've meant to ask you what happened to your dog. Is he at Dylan's house? I wouldn't mind if you brought him to my place."

"When I was laid up and going through rehab, my brother Jason took care of him. They hit it off really well, and Jason wanted to take Cocoa when he left. Jason's job doesn't keep him away from home as much as mine has lately. I think it was for the best. I still miss him though."

"I'm sure you do." She put on her coat and got her stuff together to carry out to the car. "I'm so glad we have a plan coming together. I now understand why you hate the waiting game. Sometimes things drag so slowly. It seems like he's free, and we are imprisoned, waiting to catch him. I want him off the streets so he can't kill another young woman. I know you want it, too."

"So we keep working the case meticulously, hoping he slips up. We watch, wait, and keep our eyes open." He grabbed her suitcase and computer.

"Why don't we set a trap for him, using me as bait, of course?" She stopped and turned back to look at him when she said it.

His frown was instantaneous. "Don't even think what you're thinking. We are not going there. Do you not remember what happened the last time? It went bad, and Mabry shot Jed while he sat beside you. It could have just as easily been you. Things can go wrong, and this guy isn't to be messed with. You are not going to be bait."

"I guess you're right." She let the subject drop.

Matt looked like he was ready to explode. Later, she'd try again. "We should go." Eventually, he would see it was the only way to save lives.

"After you." He motioned her out the door. "Just so you know, you'll never talk me into it." He scowled. "Don't even try." He locked the door as he closed it. "It's never going to happen while I'm Chief of Police."

He had issued the challenge. She smiled to herself. There was nothing she loved more than a good challenge, and he knew that. Maybe he wanted her to talk him into it.

Chapter 13

He knew Jessie would see it as a challenge to try to change his mind. He frowned, turning his chair to look at the window. Not one of her sweet pleas would work this time. He would stand firm. It was crazy to consider it. All thoughts of a trap were on hold until after they talked to the profiler on Monday.

Kenny popped his head in the door. "Matt, Jeremy is on line one. He said you haven't been answering your mobile phone."

He looked at his phone. "I had it on silent. Thanks, Kenny." He picked up line one. "Hi, Jeremy, did you get my text?"

"I did, and I'll do a little research, but nothing rings a bell right now. This case sounds serious."

"It is. This perp has viciously murdered several young women, including a young woman in Blue Cove. Jessie was almost his victim. Hasn't she told you about any of this?"

"No! She sent a text telling me she wanted me to do some research on a serial killer, and she'd get back to me later with details. She never said any more to me about it."

Matt filled Jeremy in on everything he knew so far. He heard the intake of air on the other end of the line.

"It's never simple with her. I can't believe, having escaped the guy, that she'd even consider baiting him."

Jeremy's tone became serious. "I'll look into it quickly before she tries something stupid."

"Look, I need you to look into a couple of her friends for me. I have to look at anyone from her past who shows up in town right now. I want everything you can get me on Liam Donovan and Connor Moore. Before you say it, I know Liam is Katie's brother, but I have to check him out too." Matt tapped his pencil on the notepad. "I don't like this any better than you, but it's the only way I know to eliminate someone."

"I understand. Katie had better never get wind of it, or I'll catch hell."

"You can blame me. Jessie is racking her brain trying to figure out how she knows the man, but it's not coming to her. He knows her, I'm sure of it. I'm hoping the criminal profiler will say something Monday to give her mind a little nudge."

"Anything else you want to lay on me? I can't believe she never told me this." He sounded totally annoyed. "I'm going to give her the what for."

"The reason might be that having seen the murder of Emma in a dream, another murder somewhere else, and Emma's ghost, her mind is slightly preoccupied."

"You think? I guess I can be patient and wait for her to tell me."

"Plus, someone is casing the store and watching her. He tried to get in the other night. I think she might be on overload."

"I can't imagine why." Matt could hear the sarcasm in Jeremy's voice. "Blue Cove hasn't been a very inviting place for her to live. I think New York might seem like a piece of cake in comparison. Maybe I should talk her into moving back."

"Not if you value your life. Besides, didn't I hear a rumor about you moving here?"

Jeremy chuckled. "I haven't made up my mind on that yet. Katie and I are by no means a sure thing."

"That's not how I've heard it, old man," Matt grinned.

"You can't believe everything you hear."

"In all seriousness, Jeremy, our perp has already marked her as a target. I have to figure out a way to make it as hard as possible for him to get at her."

"Damn, don't let him hurt her."

"We'll be in the city on Monday. Why don't you meet us for lunch?"

"I can do that. I'll have something for you by then. You'd better not tell Jessie we're looking into Liam and Connor. You might find yourself on the outs alongside me. I'll see you Monday." Jeremy hung up.

Matt knew he was walking a tightrope. That was for damn sure.

****

Jessie's morning had been busy thanks to another tour bus that showed up in town. There had been hardly a moment to think. She smiled. A good thing, no doubt. She had just checked out a customer when the bell rang, and the door opened.

"Hey, Blondie," Melinda called out as she walked in the door. Her frizzy red hair was in riotous curls on her shoulders. Her glasses were up on her nose where they belonged. "Dang, that church has been quiet the last several weeks without you there. I hope you're coming back soon. You liven up the place." Melinda ceremoniously paused for a breath and promptly plopped down in one of the leather chairs.

Jessie smiled as she walked toward her. "Howdy, Red," She came to a stop beside the chair. "What's up?"

"I've stopped by to fill you in on some gossip." She cackled. "I'm thinking our Matt had better get serious about courting you, there's some mighty strong competition for you going on."

"What do you mean?" Jessie sat down in the chair beside her and wrapped a piece of her hair around her finger.

"There was this new dude at church the other night asking everyone about you. He was super dreamy, a real hunk of a guy. If you know what I mean." Melinda fanned her face playfully.

Jessie rubbed the nape of her neck, feeling her pulse quicken. *He* had been at the church that night. "Do you remember what he looked like?" She fought to keep her voice normal.

"He was real handsome in a drop-dead gorgeous kind of way. He's a little hard to describe because, as good-looking as he was, something seemed a little off about him. I couldn't tell you what it was because he was about perfect in every way. Hubba, hubba! She slapped her leg and laughed. His hair was reddish blonde and his eyes a deep dark green. I did my share of daydreaming. His build set more than a few hearts all atwitter."

From that moment on, Jessie smiled when she remembered to and tried to listen, but knew she had to call Matt. Right now. "Why don't you take a look around the store, Melinda? You might see something you like." Jessie grabbed her phone and called Matt, filling him in quickly.

"Don't let her leave until I get there. I need to find out if he approached anyone else. This could be our lucky break." Jessie heard the phone click off. He was on his way.

"Do you see something you would like to read? The books on the table here are popular right now. I also have some great series if you're into them." Jessie pointed to the shelf, making small talk. She tried to tamp down her anxious feelings.

"I'm not much of a reader outside of the book we have to read for our ladies' group. I decided to give it try after my friend told me about the book she was reading. She said she really liked it and wrote it down for me." Melinda rummaged through her purse and handed a crumpled piece of paper to Jessie.

Jessie glanced at it. "I have it right here." She found the book and handed it to Melinda. "She is one of my favorite authors, and I'm sure you'll like this one." The cover showed a woman jogging in the woods. Jessie took a deep breath, her hand tense around the book. *Too close for comfort*. He had actually been around her friends. The thought made her feel sick.

"I'll give this reading for pleasure stuff a try." Melinda walked with Jessie to the register.

"I think you'll really like it. I'll bet you'll be back for another one soon." She had scarcely finished ringing up her purchase when Matt walked in the door. Relief filled her.

Matt headed straight for Melinda and began to ply her with questions. Jessie could hear Melinda telling him the same thing she had told her. While Jessie finished checking out another customer, Matt walked out of the store with Melinda without so much as a wave good-bye. Every inch of him was the chief of police now, and he had that look about him. Jessie walked to the front window and watched them cross the street as they made their way to the church. She watched until she could no longer see them. She wished she could follow. She wanted to know what she was up against.

This guy was starting to bug her. He'd come into her world, had been among her friends, and had thrown it in her face. She was mad. He was an arrogant man, which might be one major flaw that could work to their advantage. She had to give this some thought.

Even though her store was busy all afternoon, she saw several cars come and go from the church during the afternoon. Matt must be talking to several parishioners. Interesting. Her brows furrowed as she watched Jared walk to the door carrying his sketchpad. Maybe they would get a good likeness in a composite, and she would know him right away.

He certainly had audacity to show his face among people who knew her. He had to know someone would talk about it. Maybe that was his whole purpose—to work his way into her life through her friends. The bell rang above the door, her signal to get back to work.

Chapter 14

By the time Matt had questioned everyone, he was perplexed. The description kept changing, and only a few of those he questioned agreed on the color of the suspect's eyes. It had been a couple of days since they'd seen him, but at least a handful of them should have agreed on something. Jared was drawing, but Matt didn't hold out much hope.

"How's it going, Matt?" Pastor John stopped at the table where Matt was sitting.

"Okay, I guess. I was hoping we would have a good description by now. Those who talked to him the night he was here can't remember much about his looks other than he was handsome." Matt tapped his pencil on the table.

"It makes me sick to think a murderer was here, walking around in the church as big as you please. Does he have no guilt?" The pastor sat down in the chair across from him.

"Knowing what I do about serial killers, I doubt he felt anything. He was probably pleased that he had fooled everyone." Matt took a sip of coffee

"I often wondered how observant I would be if I were ever faced with needing to remember details. I do those little memory games from time to time. I've noticed when reading news articles that two eye-witnesses can give very different accounts of the same event."

"That's true because things happen so quickly in real time. One person may see one part of the crime being committed or an accident, and the other person sees something else. But, there'll always be some facts that are the same or similar from both witnesses. I'm not finding that here, which has me puzzled." Matt shook his head.

Pastor John started to stand and then sat back down. "There is something...at the time, I thought his eye color didn't seem natural. His eyes were such an intense green that I thought maybe he had on a pair of those colored contacts."

"Is there anything else that you can recall?"

"At one point I thought I saw darker hair near his collar in the back, but I could be mistaken about that."

"A disguise maybe?" Matt looked at John.

"It's possible."

"That might account for the very different descriptions we are getting. Would you mind sitting down with Jared and telling him what you think?"

"I would do anything I could to help catch this monster." The pastor's lips thinned. "I met Emma Wilson a few days before her murder. She was a sweet girl. Her memorial service will be here next Friday when all the family can get here."

Matt watched as Jared listened and sketched. John had remembered quite a few details that others hadn't mentioned. When Jared was done, the man in the composite was a friendly looking man, handsome, and there was something about the man's eyes. Matt wasn't sure what to think.

He made a copy of Jared's sketch to show Jessie.

Maybe this wasn't even their guy.

****

Jessie saw Matt walking across the street and smiled at him as he entered the store. Her last customer had just brought her books to the counter. "I hope you found what you were looking for."

"I did and probably more than I should have." She laughed.

"I understand." She smiled. "Books are one of my major weaknesses. That's why I bought a whole store." Jessie returned her smile as she rang the books up. They talked a few more minutes, and then Jessie followed her to the door, locking it when she left.

"What did you find out?" She turned around to look at Matt who was standing near her.

"Not a whole lot other than most of the church women thought he was handsome, and the men didn't pay attention to what he looked like. I have a sketch." He handed it to her and walked toward the chairs.

Jessie studied it, shaking her head. "He looks familiar, but I'm just not sure why. I couldn't tell you who he is." The more she looked at the sketch, the more convinced she was that she knew him. How did she know him and from when? "Can I keep this?" She held up the copy.

"Yes, study it. Maybe you'll remember something. We've already sent it over the wire. One thing for sure, he's not afraid of capture. He had to know one of your friends would tell you he was asking about you. It was only a matter of time."

"That bothers me. He's so sure of himself. Why is that?" Jessie looked at the sketch again. There was something about his eyes.

"Pastor John thought he might have had on a disguise, which could explain some discrepancies in how people saw him. The thing is, the ladies were all charmed by him, and I do mean charmed." Matt's hand combed through his hair.

"Scary…" She shivered just thinking about it. "He charmed them, and all the while he was filled with rage toward them. What kind of man is this?"

"That is what we hope to discover." Matt sat down. "He's a tall man, I know that for sure. It was the one and only consistent detail in everyone's description of him. Outside of that, nothing stood out to all the people who talked to him that night."

Jessie studied the sketch and then looked at him. "I know why you might have so many ideas of how he looked, but you're not going to like it." She frowned as she sat down in the chair across from him.

"Why is that?" His eyebrows went up when he asked it.

"He's strong, mentally. I could tell it that day he was behind the church. In the dream last night, he pulled me into the dark mist and forced me to look at his next victim. Maybe people see him only the way he wants them to see him. I'll talk to Reba about it. It's only one possibility."

"You're right. I don't like it." He grimaced. "But after Irwin, well, I know everything can't be answered with simple logic."

"I know there are logical answers in every case. But, having said that, I think it's also about good versus evil, and right against wrong. I may be naïve, but I do believe love can win against hate." She scrunched her face. "You have to admit these few cases I've been involved in have not been simple crimes. There's a sinister element to them. Maybe that's why all these strange things are happening to me." She gazed at him, a thoughtful expression on her face.

"I have no clue. You could be right for all I know. What's happening to you definitely challenges all of my neatly packaged theories." He touched her hand.

"That's what I'm saying." Jessie placed her other hand on top of his. "It challenges mine as well. I have always dealt with facts, even though I'm something of an idealist too."

"I don't know why it's happening to you here, but justice is being served. I can't fault that. I do know this perp has been killing women for a while, and I think he met his match with you. With a little luck, we'll catch him soon. I guess what I'm trying to say is, as long as you can handle all of it, sweetheart, I'm grateful for all the help I can get."

"It's safe to say you're getting it, whether you want it or not, and so am I." She stood up. "I'll tidy up, and then we can leave."

Matt's phone rang. "Hey, Dylan, what's up?"

Jessie walked into the backroom, not wanting to hear Matt's conversation. She knew they had found the girl, and what she had seen was all true. She grabbed a tissue, patted her eyes, and wiped her cheeks.

****

He would lay low for a while. Their dance was only in the early stages. Once again, he had appeased the monster inside himself, and all was well. Maybe he would head up to the city and do a little sightseeing while he was in the area. He'd always wanted to visit the Big Apple, take in a show, and dine at a fine restaurant. Now would be a good time. They would find her soon, if they hadn't already. He had made this one easy for them. Like a diamond lying on the ground for anyone to discover.

Maybe he should take a few weeks or longer and just kick back. He'd let them think that he was gone. He needed his head clear for his next dance. Jessie was a different partner. She was stronger than the others were, but he didn't care. He had to have her, and he would.

Shoving his suitcase in the car, he left an envelope with the key and money in the lobby and departed without detection. He smiled as he drove out of town. He would be back. Yes, sir, he would be back. The devil had a dance with a beautiful lady to finish. He could dance and do it well: a real ladies man. He smiled at his image in the rearview mirror. He would make her last dance the best of all. She would die happy.

Chapter 15

"Jess, are you all right?" He clicked his seatbelt on and turned to look at her.

"I knew they would find her eventually but I...I hoped I was wrong. I wanted to believe it didn't happen." Oh, how she had hoped that just this once, she was wrong. She sniffed and reached for her tissue box. "Where did they find her?"

"In a small town up the coast. He laid her in the town square on a park bench and covered her with a blanket. A police officer making his rounds thought it was a drifter sleeping out and went to wake her up. You can guess the rest."

"Yes, I suppose I can." She could barely get the words out.

"We're going to get him, Jess. It may take every resource that we have, but we'll get him."

"I know, but how many more will he kill before we do?" She fixed her eyes on him. "You need to consider setting a trap for him. Using me. We can't just sit by while he continues to murder women."

"I admit I've thought about the idea." His brows furrowed, his voice gruff. "But I'm not going to go any further until we talk to the profiler on Monday. Jess, we have no idea what we're looking at. Even you said he's strong mentally. We can't rush into this until we have all the facts we can gather. We need to know what makes him tick. I don't want you to do anything on your own. Do you understand me?"

"Of course. I wouldn't even try." She turned away and stared through the windshield. "I'm glad you're a least considering it."

"I will exhaust every available avenue before I even consider putting you in jeopardy. We haven't done anywhere near that yet, sweetheart." He glanced at her. "Plus, the other agencies involved would have to see the merit of it."

"Yes, I can understand that it's their case too. I'll try to be patient and give you time. I tend to jump right in and not think about all the details."

"Let's just concentrate on getting through dinner on Saturday with Liam and Connor." He grinned at her. "You know how I'm looking forward to that."

She couldn't hold in the giggle. "I just bet you are."

Matt parked the car. "If it's okay with you, I need to make some calls." He got out and opened her door.

"I'll make dinner while you take care of them."

****

Jessie watched Matt push back from the table. "That was a fine meal, Jess, thanks. I'll help with the dishes. Maybe if we're lucky, we'll get through the night without a visit from Liam." He carried his dish to the sink.

"I can guarantee we will." She smiled at him. "I forgot to tell you. Katie texted me earlier to tell me Liam is on his way to New York to meet up with Connor for the next few days."

Matt turned around, took Jessie in his arms, and playfully danced with her around the room. "That's great news." He swung her around again and then dipped her. He grinned as she laughed. He lifted her up and pulled her tightly to his chest, resting his chin on the top of her head. "I'll keep you safe, love," he whispered in her ear. "I like having you around."

She pulled out of his arms and looked up through her lashes at him. "I never doubted you would, not for a minute." She grabbed her plate off the table and carried it to the sink.

"I talked to Jeremy today." Matt glanced over to see her watching him. "I think he might be a little miffed at you." He put the dishes she handed him into the dishwasher.

She quickly lowered her eyes. "Why's that?"

"You sent him a text but never got back to him with the details. He heard the story from me, which didn't make him very happy. Why didn't you tell him what was happening to you?"

"To be truthful, I forgot I even mentioned anything to him. I haven't exactly been thinking too clearly. I'll send him an email and get back on his good side."

"He's going to meet us for lunch on Monday, so it might be nice if you two were talking." He grinned at her and snapped her playfully with the dishtowel.

"Jeremy might give me a hard time for not telling him, but he would never stay mad at me. We're better friends than that." Jessie cleaned the surface of the stove. "Why did you call him anyway?"

"I wanted him to be thinking of anyone he knew from your past that might be capable of this. Sometimes an outsider can see what we fail to." Matt glanced her way again. "We need all the eyes we can have on this right now."

"He might be able to help, but I doubt it." She shook her head and frowned. "There, we're all done. Why don't you relax? I'll put this away and be right in."

She walked past Matt on her way to the computer. He always chose the floral chair to sit in. She saw him pull his glasses out of his pocket, put them on, and look at his notepad. He looked good sitting there. *Stop drooling, Jessie*. She smiled to herself and began her note to Jeremy.

"There, that's done." She hit "send." "If Jeremy's online, he'll respond, or I should have a call fairly soon." She looked over at Matt then back at the computer screen. "Wow, that was fast. I'm all forgiven. He'll call me later."

****

The next couple of days were busy ones for Matt. He found himself working on a Saturday, which was fine for him, while Jessie stayed occupied at the store. His reprieve from Liam was ending tonight. He frowned and turned his chair to look out the window. He sent a text off to Jeremy, wondering if he'd been able to find out anything about Liam or Connor. It seemed strange that they were here now when all of this was happening. He would like to rule them out as suspects for Jessie's sake.

Matt picked up his ringing phone. "This is Matt."

"I got your text, I was going to call you later, but I figured now must be good for you. I learned a few things of interest."

"Let's hear it."

"Liam is clean, from what I've found so far. He's a lawyer, as you know. He's defended some questionable characters during his career and has been a part of some high-profile cases. Some of the cases he won left a bad taste in a few mouths. I'd say he's made a few enemies."

"Why is he here?"

"He wants out of the rat race. He's well off. The high profile cases paid off in big bonuses, if not friends. He wants to have a quiet practice. At least, that's what he's been spinning. Connor Moore is a different story. He hasn't done as well for himself. Connor's been in trouble with the law. He hit his girlfriend, and she pressed charges. His most recent job was as a bartender at an Irish Pub in the Boston area, until he got in trouble with the law. He lost his job. Liam and Connor met up in New York and had dinner with me because, according to Connor, he had never been there."

"You had dinner with them?"

"I sure did. You can learn a lot in casual conversation." Jeremy chuckled. "Sometimes more than you want to know. In all fairness to Connor, I should add that there are charges against his ex-girlfriend too. She hit him in the head with a mug of beer first."

"Sounds like a happy couple and a damn waste of beer."

"Both men are over six feet tall, which is the size of at least one of your suspects, and neither man has ever married. They were inseparable in high school and have remained good friends."

"Is there anything else?"

"I found this interesting. Connor has been traveling for the past couple of years and doing odd jobs along the way. I talked to a few of the people he worked for, and they found him quite charming—at least the females said that."

"Did you think of anyone else from her reporting days during the process?"

"No, but I'm going over her old stories to see if anything touches a nerve." Matt heard Jeremy take a deep breath. "Jessie and I are all square. I wasn't upset with her, why did you let her believe I was?"

"I wanted her to talk to you. She can't hold all of this stuff in, and you two work together so well. You might be able to get her thinking in the right direction. I'm not sure what to think about what you've told me, but I'm not ruling either of them out yet."

"I don't suppose you can. I'm hoping neither one of them are that dumb though."

"For Jessie's sake, so do I. Call me if you find out anything else."

"I will. I've been reading all the information from the papers and police reports on this creep. He's one sick dude. I hope they catch him soon. I don't want Jessie to have to contend with him."

"I don't either."

"I'll try to have more for you on Monday, but I'll put it on a flash drive and give it to you discreetly."

"Sounds good. I'm meeting Connor tonight, so we'll see how that goes. Catch you later."

****

Jessie was ready and waiting when Matt arrived at the store. She figured she had just enough time to go home and freshen up before Katie expected them. Curiosity is all she felt when she thought about Connor showing up right now. She hadn't seen him since Christmas break, her first year in college. They had all gone out for pizza. Connor was fun, but a little rowdy.

Truthfully, she hadn't thought about him much over the past several years, or Liam, for that matter. So why now?

She locked the door and went out before Matt could come in. "Are you ready for this?" She opened the car door and got in.

"Sure. A man has to know his competition." He grinned at her. "I'm on a fact-finding mission to satisfy my own interests."

"I don't know what to expect, but I'm going to do a little eavesdropping myself. I can't figure out why he's here now."

"Maybe he's just coming to see his old friend and to check out his onetime girlfriend."

"To see his friend, maybe, but to check out his old girlfriend, I doubt. I never was his girlfriend. He was older than I was. I think I was more like his pity date." She chuckled. "He got tired of me following Liam around like a lost puppy dog and took pity on me."

"If that's how he felt, my dear, then he's the one who'll need pity once he sees you now." Matt pulled away from the curb. "But I can't imagine you've changed that much since high school."

"You're sweet." She turned to look at him. "I've wanted to ask you a question for a while. Do you think our guy is gone or might have left the area? I haven't felt him around the last few days."

"He might be out of the area, but don't think for a minute that he's gone for good. That would be underestimating him." He shook his head. "Be thankful for the reprieve and get ready to be a super sleuth tonight. Keep your ears open."

"I will. We need to stop by my place first. I want to

change my clothes." Jessie caught his expression from the corner of her eye. "We have plenty of time, so don't give me that look."

He chuckled. "What look?"

"The look that says you don't want to wait for me to get ready. The one that says you want to get this over with as soon as possible and any extra time will make you crazy."

"That little look said all that to you? Whew, I wasn't even thinking half of that." He grinned, giving her an innocent look. "Okay, well, maybe I might have thought that I didn't want to wait. It's possible that I want to get this night over with, but I never thought anything about going crazy or you driving me there." He laughed, and she rolled her eyes at him.

****

He sat down to wait. She would use all of thirty minutes, he was sure of that. It gave him time to think about Liam and Connor. Liam had enemies, and Connor had traveled for a couple of years. He needed to give that some thought. "Jess, if you don't hurry up we're going to be late for real." He stood up and started to pace.

"I'll be right there. I'm almost ready," she called back to him.

He grabbed his jacket when he heard her bedroom door open and glanced at her as she walked in the room. She was stunning as usual. He almost felt sorry for Liam and Connor, but not quite. She would be on *his* arm tonight, and that was all right with him. "Are you ready, sweetheart?" He held her coat out for her.

"I'm ready." She slipped her arms into the sleeves. "Thanks." She smiled at him. "I heard there is a

Nor'easter setting up for next week. I guess it was naïve to believe this beautiful weather would last until spring officially shows up."

"It's been mild. I guess we're due." He opened the door, holding it for her, and they walked hand in hand to the Inn.

She stopped and looked at him outside. "I'm a little nervous. What if one of these guys is our suspect? I wouldn't know what to think about it. These are my friends. I know people can change, but I can't believe it of them."

"We'll cross that bridge if we come to it." And he really hoped that they didn't have to cross it. He brushed a wisp of hair back from her face. "In the meantime, enjoy your visit. I'll be close by, if not glued to your side."

"I appreciate it, Matt. I like you close by." She smiled up into his face. "It makes everything just about perfect."

They could hear the laughter as they reached the door of the Inn. Matt turned Jessie to face him and kissed her long and sweet. She pulled away, a bemused look on her face.

"What was that for?"

"I wanted you to remember that we're a couple, sweetheart." He grinned at her. "I'll share, but I won't let them touch." He held the door open and whispered as she walked by, "Let's get this over with."

He heard her giggle.

Chapter 16

The Inn was full of guests when they stepped in the door. Liam and Connor were entertaining them with some of the same old stories she had heard for years.

Katie walked over to Matt and Jessie. "As you can see, they're already off and running." She pointed to them. "They just got here a while ago, and already they have this group hanging on their every word. Do you remember when they told stories at the dinner table?" Katie nudged Jessie.

"How could I ever forget? They told some crazy stories. We laughed through every meal when they were together." Jessie smiled. "If I remember correctly, your parents laughed just as hard as we did. I often wondered if anything they said was true."

"Probably not or they'd still be in jail." Katie laughed. "Remember how they would act out the lines from the hot movies, using the accents and all?"

Jessie nodded. "They were good at it. I can remember laughing until my sides hurt." Jessie watched Liam and Connor bantering back and forth while the guests laughed. They still had it.

"I hope you don't hate me when this night is over. If Connor acts anything like my brother, you'll be ready to ship them both off." Katie smiled at Matt. "If I were you, I wouldn't leave her alone with those two. They have no shame when it comes to women."

Matt grinned. "Most men don't, but don't worry I'm glued to her side for the evening."

"Brace yourself..." Katie swatted Matt's arm playfully. "They just saw her and are headed this way. You're about to be annoyed beyond the norm."

"Hey, Jessie!" Liam gave her a kiss on the cheek. You remember Connor?"

"Hi." She smiled at Connor.

"Didn't I tell you she grew up to be a looker?" Liam elbowed Connor in the ribs.

Connor shoved Liam back. "She was when we were young too, but you were just too dumb to notice. She grew up right under your nose, and you couldn't see it. I saw it." He smiled at her and winked. "Hi, back at you." He gave her hug. "Who is this?"

"This is my boyfriend, Matt Parker. He's the chief of police here."

"Nice to meet you, Matt." Connor shook his hand. "You're a smart man to snatch her up and a lucky devil to boot."

"I can't argue with you there, Connor," Matt smiled, but Jessie noticed that it was a bit stiff.

Connor leaned close to Jessie. "Liam's right, you're a looker. As I remember it, you were sweet too. A lot like your Grandma Sadie—feisty when you needed to be." He grinned at her.

"Sadie is certainly feisty." She returned his grin. "And I don't mind being like her."

"I always liked my visits with her."

"Dinner's ready," Katie announced to everyone.

Matt grabbed Jessie's hand and walked with her to the dining room. "This might prove to be an interesting evening after all," he murmured in her ear.

Katie had place cards for everyone. She had seated the old friends together at one end of the two tables in the dining room. Jessie was by Matt, with Katie on her other side. Katie was wising up. Jessie smiled as Matt whispered the same thing in her ear.

The meal was buffet style. Katie had made prime rib cooked to perfection, with roasted new potatoes, and broccoli covered in a light cheese sauce. Salad, homemade dinner rolls, and a chocolate mousse completed the meal. Everything was delicious.

"Katie, it's all wonderful, as usual." Jessie took a bite of her salad. "Do you remember when you experimented on me with your creations?"

"I can't believe you survived them and remained my friend." Katie laughed.

"You've come a long way." Jessie buttered her roll.

"Boy, and how. Connor and I were her guinea pigs on more than one occasion. She made some awful stuff in those days." Liam helped himself to another huge slice of the roast. "I have to admit, you're much better at it now, sis."

Katie rolled her eyes. "Well, don't choke on the compliment, brother."

"Man, Liam, Katie is a wonderful cook." Connor shook his head as he forked up broccoli. "Whatever happened to your smooth way with the ladies, my friend?" His green eyes took on a mischievous look. "I think Jessie's rejection of your advances has messed with your head." He winked at Jessie again.

"Don't go there, Connor, if you value our friendship," Liam growled.

"I'm just joking, my friend, get over it." He took

Katie's hand. "This is a wonderful meal; everyone seems to be enjoying it." Connor looked around the room.

As soon as dinner was over, some of the guests made their way to the main sitting area of the Inn while others went out for the evening. Jessie watched the interaction between Liam and Connor. Growing up, she had always watched them, enamored with Liam back then. He could do no wrong in her eyes. If anything happened, she'd blamed Connor, naturally. The more she watched them now, the less sure she was that she'd had it right back then.

Liam was sulking, and it took her by surprise. Anger etched the lines on his face, and the looks he was sending at Connor made it clear where his ire was directed. How often had Connor cleaned up after Liam and made him look good? Liam needed Connor, not the other way around, as she used to think. She sighed. Memories…As the evening progressed, Connor charmed every woman, working the room like a champion. Liam brooded, a scowl on his face—and then she saw it happen. Liam cornered Connor and ripped into him. How many times had she seen that growing up, and always blamed Connor? Liam kept his voice soft, but she could tell from the look on his face that he was angry. Connor stood with his arms folded, his hands fisted, and a quick flash of anger crossed his face. He turned his back on Liam and walked away.

"Looks like our boys are fighting." Matt sat on the arm of the chair beside her. "Liam is lucky to still be standing. Anywhere else and he might be picking himself up off the floor."

"You're right about that." She smiled crookedly.

"Seeing them this way has made me remember so many things." She told Matt what she had been thinking.

"Connor told him the truth when he said you looked like this back then, and Liam was too dumb to notice."

"Liam never wanted anything until it belonged to someone else." She gave him a sideways look and a smile. "He's only interested in me right now because I'm with you."

"Don't sell yourself short, sweetheart, there is the also the fact that you're easy on the eyes."

"A nice compliment," She smiled at Matt. "Are you trying to earn brownie points?"

"I figure that being on your good side couldn't hurt, especially with those two in the room."

"The truth is, if I suddenly made a play for Liam, he'd run back to the city as fast as his feet could carry him." She studied him thoughtfully. "He's not into commitment."

Matt put his arm around her shoulder. "We won't put your theory to the test. He may be ready to settle down now, and is living with a few regrets." He squeezed her shoulder. "You know, sweetheart, men do grow up, even though we're slow to catch on."

"I'm sure that's true, but what I've seen so far…makes me wonder."

Matt shrugged. "Connor seems like a nice fella."

"He always was. He used to have some great conversations with Sadie. She liked him."

"Sadie is a good judge of character."

"Yes, but we all change. He seems a little harder around the edges. Although, from the way he's working the room, he can still charm the ladies."

"Here they go with their movie impersonations. It looks like it's the one we always heard when we were kids." Katie pulled up the footrest to sit on.

"What movie would that be," Matt asked?

"So I Married an Axe Murderer," both girls said together and then laughed.

"We must have heard them do this a hundred times, but I still laugh every time." Katie chuckled at one of the lines.

"I've never heard of the movie."

"It was from the nineteen-nineties. These two love it." Katie glanced over at the two of them carrying on. "They latched on to it in their pre-teen years and never let it go."

"They were crazy about it...I can't tell you how many times they had us laughing. Most of the comical lines they memorized, and then they'd go over and over them." Jessie listened and laughed along with the others. She laughed harder when she heard Matt laughing.

"Hey, sis, can we turn on some music?" Liam smiled when she nodded. He turned around to the other guests. "Let's do some dancing." They moved a few pieces of furniture.

Jessie looked at Matt. "This is the other thing they always did—dance. They are both good at it and love to show their moves. Now that I think about it, these two always loved to show off." Jessie smiled, and Katie nodded.

"It looks like I'm going to have to share you. I can see Connor headed this way. Remember to keep your ears open, sweetheart."

"I will." Jessie stood up when Connor asked her to

dance.

"Jess, remember to save me a slow dance, sweetheart."

"You can count on it." She turned to flash him a smile.

Connor led her into the makeshift dance area. "So, you like that cop, huh?"

"Very much." She glanced over at Matt. He was watching her.

"The last I'd heard you were working in New York. How'd you end up here?" Connor turned her.

"I had a lot of reasons why I wanted to leave the city, but the biggest drawing card here was Katie. I don't regret it."

"The way I hear it, you've become somewhat of the town heroine," Connor grinned at her.

"Not really." She made a face. "Let's leave it at that. I've had an interesting life since moving here."

"I can't believe our little Jessie grew up to play and work with a cop." He shook his head, his eyes intent above his smile. "I didn't see that coming when I took you to the prom."

Jessie didn't like the way he kept saying *cop*. "Do you have an issue with the police, Connor? You sound disgusted every time you say the word 'cop.'" She glared at him. "Matt is a great guy and respected in this community."

"Sorry, I'm just angry at a few right now." He forced a smile. "It has nothing to do with you or him. I lost my job when my girlfriend, who is my ex now, tried to hit me in the head with a glass mug filled with beer. I swung, trying to keep her from slamming it into my skull and hit her instead. They arrested me on assault charges and did nothing to her until several patrons testified that she had started it."

"Cool, defusing an escalating situation is always the first plan of action for a police officer called to the scene. In your case, they separated you and your girlfriend." She stood up straight. "Next, they process the crime scene, talk to the witnesses, and determine guilt. It's what they always do. It may seem unfair at the time, but you have to remember they're coming into the scene cold, and it's your word against hers."

His expression was downright angry now. "I liked my job, and she screwed that up for me."

"Well, I doubt she took that mug of beer and hit you with it because you were sweet to her. It takes two to have a fight." She chuckled, trying to ease the tension. "It's hard to fight alone."

"How'd you get so smart?" His smile was still forced. "I guess you're going to tell me to quit feeling sorry for myself next."

"The thought had entered my mind…" She smiled at him sweetly. "Either that or you need to quit saying things that make the girls want to hit you with whatever is in their hands."

"Not to change the subject, but do you know who we saw when we were in New York?"

"Not a clue."

"We saw one of your old boyfriends, Jake Perry. He said to tell you hello, by the way. He's in the city on vacation. When we were in Times Square, we ran into Bobby Angel, unbelievably. He was touring, just like us. He also said to tell you hi."

"Gosh, I haven't seen them in years. I hardly knew Bobby, but Jake and I went together for a while in high school."

"It was like old home week, right in the middle of the huge city."

The music ended, and he walked her back to Matt. "Our Jessie is a tough one; you won't find any sympathy here." Connor handed her off to Matt.

"What was that all about?" Matt raised his eyebrows.

"I refused to take his side for his assault charge. He wanted to blame it all on his ex-girlfriend. You know me." She lifted her chin. "I don't like it when a man blames it all on the woman. He had to have said something that made her pick up that mug and swing it at his head."

"My sweet little hothead, we men bring out the warrior in you." He chuckled. "Are you sure you're a real blonde and not hiding red hair under there somewhere?"

She watched Connor dancing with Katie and Liam dancing with a guest from the Inn. "I'm not sure about Connor, he's changed."

"Well then, sweetheart, I'll keep my eye on him." He followed her gaze. "By the way, the next dance is mine."

She took his hand. "Of course, the only thing he might be guilty of is being a jerk. I guess only time will tell."

"You know, Jess, most guys aren't that complex. We don't analyze all of our feelings. We tend to say what we think. And what you see is what you get. I'm not saying we're always smart, but I *can* say that it doesn't take much to make us happy." He gazed at her. "Take me, for example. I know that I like being with you, you make me happy, and life is better with you in it. It's simple, really."

"I like being with you too." She looked up through her lashes at him. "If the last few cases have taught me anything, though, it's that men can abuse power and not be what they seem at all. They can be greedy, cruel, and have no regard for human life. But, then, so can women."

"It can be a real dilemma. We all have the potential to go either way. Figure out what determines the call and you could understand the mind of a criminal." He pulled her close as the music started—nice and slow. "Right now I would rather dance with my girl."

Chapter 17

They walked down the path to her cottage, hand in hand. "I enjoyed the evening, and Katie made a fine meal. I couldn't eat like that every night." Matt patted his stomach. "She is an excellent cook."

"She wasn't always, believe me, but she's great now, which probably means anyone can learn something new."

"I did find one thing quite odd though." He stopped to look at her.

"Oh, what was that?" She glanced over at him.

"Liam never asked you to dance, not even once. I find that strange. Don't you?"

"I never thought about it." She blinked. He was right, that *was* strange. "Maybe Katie told him to quit bugging me, or maybe he was too upset with Connor, or embarrassed."

"I don't think being embarrassed is something he experiences often. He's comfortable in his own skin. Maybe too comfortable. I find it a little hard to believe he didn't ask you or even cut in when I was dancing with you. He's been such a pest. I didn't think anything could deter him." He frowned. "So why now? It gives me something to think about."

"I'll leave the thinking for you tonight. If you come up with anything, let me know." She started walking and pulled him along. "Come on, I'm getting cold." She shivered and suddenly felt uneasy. She wanted to get inside, quick.

"Okay, sweetheart, let's get you in where it's warm." He unlocked the door and held it open for her.

"Lock the door." Her voice sounded strange to her ears.

"I always do. Why the sudden reminder? What's up?" He studied her face, making her nervous.

"I felt like…like we were a target, standing there. I guess I'm getting paranoid." She lowered her head.

"As I've said before, any feelings you get, I want to know about them. They've been spot-on, and I don't want to take any chances." He lifted her chin and gazed into her eyes. "I know this is hard for you, but let's take this seriously."

"I don't like it. I never know when one of these feelings is going creep up on me. I don't think our killer is back, but I just don't know."

"It could be the person casing your business, or anyone for that matter, so we'll play it safe and try not to make ourselves a target. Sound good?"

"Okay." Her voice was barely audible, even to herself. "I know I should be used to this by now, but I'm not. It's as simple as that." She went over to her desk, turned on her computer, and walked into her bedroom. "I'll be right with you," she called out to him.

Was it possible that either Liam or Connor was involved in some way? She shook her head. It was too far-fetched to believe. Sure, they both had some anger issues, but that didn't make them murderers, did it? If suspecting her friends wasn't enough, what was Jake Perry doing in New York? Just another strange coincidence, or was it something more? She grabbed her sweater and walked back to her computer.

"Are you all right?" Matt glanced at her.

"Yeah, I'm just chilly." She looked at her computer screen. "Did I tell you that Connor told me they ran into my old boyfriend, Jake Perry, in New York?"

"No." He looked up from his case file again.

"It's like old home week or something. I haven't seen any of these guys in years, and suddenly, here they are." She scrolled through her emails. "We might need to add Jake to the list of possible suspects."

"Why is that?" His brows furrowed.

"He's from my past, and he suddenly shows up not too far away. Not that I believe any of them could be our vicious killer, but how can I possibly know for sure?"

"I'm doing my best to eliminate them as I become aware of them. Don't worry about it, Jess, we'll know more soon enough." Matt held her gaze.

"The thing is, Matt, I know that I knew this guy. There isn't a doubt in my mind. I have to consider everyone until I can figure out what made him so blasted familiar."

"I get it. More important right now is why you felt we were a target standing outside just now. Any ideas?"

"I don't know, but I know that we were."

"We'll go with that for now. If we are in someone's crosshairs, it's better to be a moving target versus one that is standing still."

"What are you saying?"

"Let's not make it easy. Keep moving, changing things up, my place, your place, out of town, in town. I'm sure you get the picture."

"I get it, and I don't like it. I was getting used to

having my life back, and I don't want to give up my freedom." She let her breath out in a gusty sigh. "I'm not the criminal, but I'm the one altering my life again."

"No, sweetheart, you're not a criminal, and I don't want to curtail your activities at all, but we do need to play it smart." He reached for her hand. "After Monday's meeting with the profiler, maybe we'll at least understand the kind of man we're looking for."

****

"I'm on overload." Jessie walked out the door and into the cool New York Monday. "That's a lot of information to digest."

"We have all the way home to talk about it, and I think we're going to need all the time that we have." Matt grabbed her hand as they walked toward the parking lot. "Hey, Jess, the restaurant where we are meeting Jeremy is only a few blocks down. Maybe we should just walk. It might be simpler than looking for a parking place."

"I don't mind walking. It might help to clear my head." She glanced over at him. "I used to walk here all the time. I never drove my car in the city—only on my way out of it." She smiled at him. "Then, I was watching the city skyline sink out of sight from my rearview mirror."

"Did you like living here?"

"In the beginning, I did. It was so exciting. There's always something going on here, some super great places to eat, and the Broadway shows are the best. I went to a few concerts in the park."

"So why leave?"

"It's big, crowded, and expensive. I was tired of the hassle. When Katie moved to Blue Cove, it seemed like the perfect opportunity to me." A man walking by slammed into her, nearly knocking her to the ground. He kept going without saying anything. She turned to say something to him, but he had already blended into the crowd.

"Are you okay?" Matt grabbed her around the waist trying to steady her.

"Oh, and there's that. Sometimes, the folks here can be a little rude. Are we almost to the restaurant?" The chilly wind stunned her. She pulled the collar of her coat up around her neck.

"It should be somewhere in the middle of the next block." He glanced at her. "Are you cold?"

"Yes, the wind is freezing." She stuffed her hands into her coat pockets. "I have a lot to process from this morning's meeting, but I learned a lot."

"I know what you mean, sweetheart, but I'm glad we took the time to come. I want to run some of this by Jeremy and see what he has to say."

"Sounds like a good idea." She shivered again. This time, she realized it was more than the cold air. She looked quickly over her shoulder, her eyes darting over the crowd.

****

He couldn't believe his good fortune. Here, in a city of millions, he saw her—walking out of the police station just as he arrived. And she was stunning, a real knockout. He held his breath, watching her walk down the steps. The Internet was a marvelous tool. Thank you to the inventor. He did a quick bow. A little research here, a name search there, and he now knew quite a bit about her. He grinned. This devil was lucky all right; he had come here to ask questions about her, at this exact moment, and lo and behold, there she was, coming out the door.

It must be all his clean living, or better yet, his upright church life. He chuckled. A chance meeting on this day—no way—it was all a part of their dance. The first moment he'd seen her, their lives had intersected, and their tango began. He rubbed his hands together. It was a cosmic collision of sorts. The questions could wait.

He followed them, hanging back in the crowd, his hood pulled up to hide his features. He shoved his hands into his pockets and tried to blend in. The busy streets could work to his advantage. From the shadows, he watched. Her hair bounced on her shoulders, mesmerizing him. Up and down it sprang, like spun gold in the sunlight. She turned around suddenly looking back to where he was standing. He ducked into a doorway out of sight. *Interesting*. He trailed behind her until she turned around again. She knew he was near. It enticed him. The excitement danced like flames over his senses. She was strong, a challenge to his skills, and he was hooked. He shadowed her until they disappeared into the restaurant. From a hiding place outside, he waited, imagining several pleasant scenarios.

He licked his lips.

Chapter 18

"Is everything all right, Jess?" Matt took hold of her arm.

"Sure, why?" She glanced at Matt.

"I don't know, maybe it's because Jeremy has asked you a couple of questions and you never responded. You looked right through him." He frowned, studying her face. "It seems a little strange, even for you."

"Our guy was following us. He's here in the city, and he was following us." Her voice was breathy and got higher in pitch with each word.

"That explains a lot." He took hold of her hand. "Was he the one that almost ran you over on our way here?" Matt's free hand fisted at his side.

"I'm not sure if that was him, but he was following us, I know that for sure. This is where he's been hiding for the last several days. Now it makes Jake Perry being here even stranger."

"Who is Jake Perry?" Jeremy asked her. She didn't answer.

"An old boyfriend from many years ago," Matt answered for her.

"Jake was such a quiet and nice guy that it's hard to believe he could be involved. He followed me around like a lost puppy most of the time." She shook her head. "People change, though, so anything is possible."

"A fact we know all too well. The quiet ones can be trouble." Jeremy handed her a menu. "Our research over the past few years has taught us that much. Do you want me to do a little background check on Jake Perry?"

"I never thought I would say this about my friends, but yes. And, while you are looking, check out Liam and Connor too." She could still sense him close by, and found herself looking around the restaurant at all the faces. At least he wasn't in there.

"I can do that." He looked over at Matt with a puzzled expression on his face.

"Sweetheart, I already had Jeremy checking Liam and Connor out. Now, I'll add Jake Perry."

"You always think of everything." She smiled at Matt. "I bet you thought I would be mad." She glanced at him, holding his gaze. He lowered his eyes.

"It had crossed my mind you might not like us checking out your friends."

"As you've told me in one of your many lectures, you have to rule them in or out. Connor told me they ran into someone else here from our hometown, someone besides Jake Perry, but I can't remember who he told me it was. I'll ask him the next time I see him. We might as well take them all on."

"You heard the lady, Jeremy; you're free to check away with no repercussions."

"I'll get right on it. Maybe we can flush this guy out, with a little help and a lot of luck." Jeremy smiled at her. "You know how I love this, and lately, you've been keeping me very happy chasing all these trails for you."

"I'm glad someone is enjoying themselves." Jessie

scrunched her face. "I, for one, would like a little respite from all of this. I don't like the idea that someone out there wants me dead. How many times does this make now?" She smiled, but it felt crooked. "Three or four, and I haven't been in Blue Cove even a year yet."

"I can see where you might not enjoy that part of it, but hey, you get to work with Matt and me a lot." He grinned. "So it could be worse."

"It could be a whole lot better, though. Oh, and"— Jessie frowned at Jeremy—"I'm not sure that Katie will be too happy about you checking out her brother."

"I'm aware of that, believe me, but it doesn't take away from the fact that I'm hooked."

"Jeremy, I think you should stop while you're ahead." Matt smiled. "You're digging a hole so deep it will be hard to climb out."

"Not to worry, Matt. Jeremy means well, even if he's too taken by the thrill of the chase. No one has pointed a gun at him yet. Anyway, I do like the intrigue and the investigative part of it myself, so I can't fault him." Jessie gave the door a quick look as it opened.

"Do you think he's still in the area?" Matt glanced around the room.

"I can sense him somewhere close by. He's not in here, though." She sipped her water. "He's near enough to see this restaurant." She gave the waiter her order when it was her turn and began to relax. She found herself answering Matt's questions about her days living in the city. After several minutes, she reached over and grabbed his hand. "Thank you."

"For what?" He smiled at her.

"For distracting me, I needed it." She studied

Matt's handsome face. "I think he's gone for now, but I'm wondering where to and for how long."

****

He had grown tired of standing there like some fool, his body pressed against an alley wall as he watched the restaurant across the street for any sign of her. The cold wind had a bite to it; he rubbed his hands together before he pushed them into his pockets. It felt like snow but what did it matter. A few minutes ago, the city had been pure magic, and he'd felt so alive. The devil moved out of his hiding place. What had happened? He had never been baffled like this before. He moved along the sidewalk, picking up his pace.

"Hey, pay attention, you idiot. Watch where you're going." The man's angry voice startled him.

What was he thinking? *Play it cool, don't let her get to you.* He lifted his head and watched the crowd around him, slowing to walk in pace with them. *Don't stand out, stupid.* He stopped in front of the police station. He started up the steps, but all of a sudden, uncertainty gripped him, and he walked back down them. All of his questions would have to wait for another day. She was messing with his head. How did she always seem to know when he was around? How could that be? She couldn't know who he was, he had been too clever in his disguise. But, she was aware when he was following her, and that both intrigued and now scared him. A shiver racked his body. Was she leading him into her web? He shook his head. He didn't like the place his thoughts were taking him. *How would it end?* Melancholy swirled around him like a gloomy mist. If he didn't get hold of himself, he'd be too depressed to leave his room. He was sinking, how he hated this feeling. His world was spinning out of control, and it couldn't! *He* was the one in charge; he couldn't let her have it. He would make her pay…yes, that's what he would do, he'd make her pay.

He packed his car, paid his bill, and left the city. It was time. The devil had to end the dance before she stopped him. He sensed that she could stop him, why was that?

Chapter 19

Jessie pulled her coat tighter around her as she stepped out the door. The temperature had definitely dropped.

Jeremy handed Matt a USB drive. "Here's what I have so far."

"Thanks, I'll check it out when I get back. Keep the info coming." Matt stuck it in his pocket.

Jeremy nodded. "You guys had better get started; it feels like you could run into some bad weather on the way home."

Jessie hugged Jeremy and started walking as fast as she could. The wind was blowing chills up and down her back, and she was more than happy for the warmth of the car. "Wow, I forgot how cold that wind could feel in the city. I can't say that I miss that part of living here. At least in Blue Cove, I can drive my car."

"Did you always walk?" Matt asked her.

"Not if it were far or too cold, then I would take a taxi or ride the subway. In a city with all these taxis, it's not always easy to get one when everyone else wants one at the same time." She felt herself thawing as the car got warmer.

"Do you ever miss it?" Matt glanced at her.

She shook her head. "I don't miss living here. I can come back for a visit or to go shopping when I miss the action and pace of it. Katie and I come in at least once a month. I'm cool with that. I'm always happy to leave, though."

"I know I couldn't live here." He checked his mirror and signaled a change of lanes. "I have a lot to process from our meeting this morning, but I think the police profiler had some great insight into how this guy's mind might work."

"I agree." She nodded. "I'm glad that we took the time to come. She confirmed some of the things you had already told me, and that I still find hard to believe."

"Like what?"

"I can't imagine how anyone could kill another person to begin with, but to have no remorse or empathy at all is beyond me. You told me something similar." She pulled a small notebook out of her purse. "I found her theory about how the boundaries between fantasy and reality become lost quite interesting. She made it easy to see how he might have created a new life to which he could escape. His fantasy becomes a part of his daily life because he can control it."

"I know. It makes sense. In your own world, where you're king, you can live detached from real truth and everything you do is right."

"Exactly." She nodded. "Dominance, control, sexual conquest, and violence are part of controlling your world. It's awful really, but the pain becomes of no consequence because he's all right in his world." She shook her head in disgust.

"You can see how the normal concepts of right and wrong can become skewed. He's been at this for a while, and no one has come close to capturing him. He must be emboldened by that. I got that feeling talking to the people at the church; he walked among them as if he was one of them. He was quite charming. They all liked him."

"I'm trying hard to think about people I know who might fit some of the reasons why a person becomes a serial killer." She frowned. "Nothing stands out yet, but maybe, when I have time to think, it will come to me. I know one thing for sure—it can't be Liam or Connor because they weren't in the city today."

"Do you know that for sure?" He glanced at her quickly.

Did she? A small chill walked her spine. "I...can't say that I do."

"There's one way to find out."

Jessie knew what he meant. She called Katie and put it on speaker. "Hi, we're on our way back. What are the guys up to?"

"Oh, they were in the city earlier. I thought maybe you'd run into them. Liam had to go to his office for something today. He called a few minutes ago to tell me they were back and wouldn't be here for dinner. It seems Connor challenged him to a game of pool at Patterson's. It has turned into the best of three, and you know what that means."

"I sure do, they'll be there for a while. I'll call you later." Jessie shook her head. "That blows that theory. We still can't rule them out after all."

"I think we'll be able to rule out at least one of them eventually." Matt made the turn off the main highway toward Blue Cove.

"I hope so."

"One thing that concerns me about this perp is that he might have started out organized and methodical, but now he's changing. Things seem to be happening more impulsively."

Jessie shivered. "That's the reason we have to catch him. He'll just keep it up until we stop him." She looked over her notes until she found the item she wanted. "The one thing that struck me is when she told us that a serial killer can become a visionary. They murder to appease something. I could see it in the dream I had of him. He was appeasing something or someone. He's getting worse."

"I feel the same way."

"What are we going to do about it?" Jessie turned in her seat to look at him.

"Right now, we aren't going to do anything. I'm going to study my case files until I know how this perp's mind works. I plan to talk to the other agencies and investigators involved until they're sick of hearing from me. Then, and only then, will we talk about what we might do about him." He looked over at her. "Look, I know, Jess, how hard it is to wait. We can't screw this up. We have to have all the evidence lined up so that when we get him, we can nail him."

"I know you're right." She shifted restlessly in her seat. "I feel so helpless. I know he'll do this again. I want to do everything I can to prevent him from hurting another young woman."

"We all want that, Jess. Believe me."

"I wonder how Audrey did at the store today. She should be closing up now." Jessie looked at her watch. "I'll wait a few minutes and give her a call."

"How's the store doing?"

"With all the bus tours coming to town, it's been doing well. I can only imagine how great it will be when the autumn bus tours begin, and we haven't even started the summer business rush yet."

"The concept you had of opening the doors between your store and Joe's was perfect. People who have a cup of coffee or tea love to read. It's a natural fit."

Jessie's phone started ringing. "Hey, this is Jessie." She stiffened at the hysterical flood from the phone. "What? Calm down, Audrey, I can't understand what you're trying to say. That's awful. Start driving toward the police station. I'll call Dylan and tell him you're on your way. We'll be in town in about ten minutes."

"What was that about?"

She held up her finger. "Dylan, this is Jessie. I'm sending Audrey, who works at my store, over to you. Someone threatened her and held a knife to her throat. We're about ten minutes out of Blue Cove. Watch for her, please." She put her phone away, feeling shaky. "Did you hear that?" She looked at Matt as he nodded.

"It would seem he preceded us back to town."

"Could he be the one who was casing the store? He didn't kill her. Thank God." She drew a shuddering breath. "If it was him, she is so *lucky*."

"Does Audrey fit the profile of one of his women?"

"Not really." Jessie frowned. "She's more mature than the others. Good thing." She laughed shakily.

"I think she'll probably have a message from our friend for us," he said grimly. "Which means he might be feeling a little desperate. I wonder why?"

"You and me both."

They went right to the police station when they reached Blue Cove. Jessie found Audrey in Dylan's office, bolted through the door to her, and wrapped her in a big hug. "I'm so sorry."

"It's not your fault." She patted Jessie's arm. "Look, my hands are still shaking. You never think something like this can happen to you."

"Why don't you sit down, and Audrey can tell us what happened." Matt handed Jessie a tissue.

"He grabbed me from behind and held a knife to my throat." She opened her collar a little to show the small cut where the knife had pressed against her. I was so scared. He kept yelling at me not to turn around, or he'd slit my throat." Audrey started to cry.

Matt handed her a tissue. "I'd like you to be checked out by a doctor and to talk to a victim's advocate. You have some bruising on your neck. You've had a traumatic experience, and I don't want this to continue to affect your life. We'll take you over there when we're done here."

"Okay…if you think I need to." She sniffled and blew her nose as she got herself under control again.

"I do." Matt pulled Dylan aside. "Is there anything else?"

"While the guy held the knife to her throat, he pressed a note into her hand and told her he was only letting her live because he needed her to give Jessie a message."

"And what was his message?" Matt leaned against the wall, his arms folded.

Dylan handed Jessie the piece of paper sealed in a plastic bag. "I've already taken precautions in case he left fingerprints.

You are cordially invited to be my dance partner for a memorable evening. The time and place will be of my own choosing. I promise you a night for me to remember.

"He sounds a little too sure of himself. I think he forgets I can sense when he's around." Absentmindedly, Jessie ran her finger over the plastic bag.

"Or maybe it's precisely the reason he's doing something out of the ordinary. He has never approached a woman beforehand to tell her what he's going to do. I think you may have him rattled. You're a challenge to him. This could work in our favor if it makes him overplay his hand.

"Oh, Jessie, I'm so scared for you. I don't think this guy is right upstairs if you get my meaning," Audrey gasped. "I think he could have killed me without a second thought."

"I'm sure you're right, Audrey. We'll do our best to protect Jessie." Matt walked over to her. "Let's get you to the ER to be looked at."

****

"I'm glad they're going to keep her overnight. I hope she'll be able to rest." Jessie leaned back against the car seat as they left the ER, feeling totally exhausted.

"The doctor said he would give her something to help her sleep." Matt pulled out of the hospital parking lot. "I'm hungry, how about you?"

They drove down Main Street. "It looks like Connor and Liam finished their game, along with a couple of others." She pointed to the small group exiting Patterson's.

"At least we know they didn't kill each other." He smiled as he glanced at her. "What sounds good to you?"

"I could use a little comfort food. You know, a hamburger with all the trimmings, and you know the best place in town."

"Sweetheart, now you're talking my language. I'm headed there already and damn happy you didn't say you wanted a salad."

"Although,"—she smiled at him as she said it—"now that you mention it, a salad sounds kind of good."

"Oh no, you don't. We're going with your first choice." He turned onto Blue Cove Drive. "Not to change the subject, but did you ever talk to Reba about your idea that he makes people see what he wants them to see?"

"No, I'm glad you reminded me. I forgot all about it, too many other things in my head. I'll call her first thing tomorrow." Jessie scribbled it down in her small notebook.

Matt parked the car, came around to her side, and opened the door for her. "I'm happy you suggested this place. I'll have to work out harder tomorrow because of it, though."

"You once told me Sally's Place was the best burger in town, and you were right."

Chapter 20

The next morning, Matt dropped her off at the store early. He had a meeting, and she had boxes to unpack. She dove into her work, grinning like a kid in a candy store as she looked over the titles. How would she ever choose what she wanted to read first? Books had to be one of her weaknesses. She placed several books on the counter and walked into the back room to get another stack. Business had been much better than she'd thought it would be. She had celebrated her early success by ordering books from a couple of new authors that her customers had requested.

Jessie was bending down to lift the final stack of books from the box when she heard the knock at the front door. As she walked out of the storeroom, she saw Reba standing outside, her hand raised to knock again. Reba's breath hung like fog in the cold morning air.

Jessie smiled, unlocking the door. "Brrr," A blast of cold air hit her face. "I hope you haven't been standing there too long." She locked the door again after Reba stepped inside. Jessie glanced at her watch—not quite time to open yet.

"I was only out there for a few minutes," Reba answered, taking off her gloves. "I think the weatherman got it right this time. It feels like snow is on the way. I wanted to stop by before I go to the market. If we get as much snow as they're predicting,

I'll be staying in for a few days, as will you." She unbuttoned her coat.

"I'm glad you did. I was going to call you this morning anyway. You always seem to know when I'm thinking about you and show up."

"That's because we need to talk, dear." Reba went to sit in one of the chairs and patted the seat next to her.

"Would you like a cup of hot tea?"

"Tea would be lovely." Reba slipped her coat off and placed her purse on the floor at her feet.

Jessie heated two cups of water in the microwave in the storeroom and made two cups of tea. "Do you take cream or sugar?" Jessie called out to her.

"No cream and one teaspoon of sugar, please, dear." She crossed her ankles.

Jessie handed the cup of hot tea to Reba and placed hers on the table. "If you need more sugar, let me know."

Reba smiled, her hands wrapped around the warm mug. "Oh my, this feels so good. There is nothing like holding a hot cup of tea with the steam rising up to greet you on a cold morning. I'm sure it will be perfect." Reba took a sip and set her mug on the table. "I heard through the grapevine that Emma's murderer was at our church. Is that true?" She looked over at Jessie.

"Yes, he was." Jessie nodded. "Matt questioned several people in the congregation." Jessie sipped her tea.

Reba shook her head. "People thought he was a charming man. You can imagine how shocked they were, and still are, when they heard that he might have murdered several women. It's hard to tell about folks sometimes. He looked normal enough, or so they all said."

"I can understand why they would be shaken. I find it hard to believe he would even want to be near a church considering the crimes he's committed." Jessie cradled the warm cup in her hands. "We were told by the profiler yesterday that serial killers don't process things the same way we do, and he probably feels no remorse at all." She shook her head. "Still, I find it hard to believe that, somewhere inside of him, he doesn't feel a little guilty."

"You have a good heart, girl, but don't be fooled by this man. He is no good, and he'll continue his rampage, given half a chance to do so. He's addicted. It's hard for me to say this because I try to find the good in everyone, but when I think of him, everything about him is dark and filled with cruelty."

"I know. I've seen what he's capable of in my dreams." Jessie glanced at Reba. "Did you know he was at the church the night Lawrence chased someone away from my store? I could feel him there."

"I know." She nodded. "I put that timeline together, but they're not the same man." Reba sipped and set the cup on the table again.

"I know they're not." Jessie's voice was soft.

Reba turned toward Jessie's chair. "Both of them are here to hurt you." Reba had a faraway look in her eyes. "They are both ruthless men who have killed before."

"I don't like hearing that, Reba." Jessie frowned and sat forward in her chair.

"You must, dear. One came with that purpose in mind. He's here to do harm to you and to Matt, I think.

But, you surprised the other man, and now he sees you as his next challenge."

"What am I supposed to do? I don't like being in the crosshairs." Jessie rubbed the back of her neck.

"Knowing is your first step to prevention. You have to know to plan a way to escape it. I'm not sure what the first man will do. He's a loner; he avoids publicity and hides in the shadows. He's watching you, calculating his moves. Our murderer loves the limelight. He's a true charmer, and he feeds on publicity. I wouldn't be surprised if he kept a scrapbook of every news article written about him."

"I wanted to ask you something." Jessie frowned, picked up her mug, and then set it back on the table. "Is it possible someone can control how people perceive them? The people at the church each described the man so differently when the police questioned them. The only thing they all said in common was that he was tall."

"Mind control, as you know from your last case, is a real possibility. All I know for sure, my dear, is that he has met his match in you. His end is in sight, but you must be careful." Reba picked up her mug and took another sip of her tea. She looked over the rim at Jessie. "I don't think Emma is resting peacefully. Have you seen her?"

"I've seen her outside of Matt's house, and I felt her in my room once. When she turned and looked at me, her face was so sad. I'll never forget that look." Jessie's eyes stung. "She was so young, with her whole life ahead of her. It's heartbreaking really." Jessie dabbed at her eyes with the napkin. "I think about her fiancé and family all the time."

"It's time that this awful man is taken off the streets. You'll remember something soon, and it will be the key to solving this crime, or it will come to you some other way. You are a part of the solution to catching him. I know that for sure."

"I believe that I know him, somehow, but I haven't been able to put it all together."

"You will, my dear, very soon." Reba stood up. "I must get to the market before the snow starts." She slipped on her coat. "Before I go, I need a book. Will you help me pick one? I may have to do some reading over the next few days. I don't drive in the snow anymore."

Jessie showed Reba some of the latest arrivals and Reba bought three. When Reba left, Jessie put the new books out on the shelves and thought about what Reba had told her. She wasn't happy to know there were two different situations to handle here; although, she had already known it in her heart. Hearing Reba say it aloud made it sound more valid. Matt would need to know too. At least, she found a small measure of hope in the idea that she would remember something soon that would help. She would hope it came true.

At this point, anything would be good. Please. She sighed and looked at her watch. It was time to open the store.

****

"I'll talk to you later, Frank." Matt hung up the phone. Frank had to delay his trip to Blue Cove due to the impending storm. If the predictions held, they'd be measuring the snow in feet and not inches. Damn, this was a major headache. Why did it have to snow now? Matt raked his hand through his hair. Buried under snow, the crime site would hold its secrets for a little while longer. With any luck, it might keep the suspect inside and keep him from murdering another woman.

Kenny popped his head in the door. "Matt, Tom Maxwell is on line one."

"Thanks." Matt picked up the phone. "Hey, Tom, what's up?"

"We tracked our missing guy to your area. We have a team of agents on the way. I'll be joining them tonight. We want them in place before the storm hits."

"How'd you track him? He flies solo and under the radar, doesn't he?"

"It was a lucky break. We're monitoring incoming calls to his sister. He always uses a disposable phone— one call—and then tosses it. He used a landline this time, and a track placed him in Blue Cove. He's definitely in your area."

"I'd be glad for the extra hands. I have mine full with this serial killer and the storm coming. We will be working around the clock trying to keep citizens safe, and we'll probably have some rescue situations. Hopefully, people will heed the warning and stay off the roads so emergency personnel can get through."

"Good luck with that." Tom snorted. "There's always the one person who likes to challenge the elements. They live for it."

"You've got that right." Matt made a face. He had done his share of rescues over the years.

"I'll stop by or give a call when I get into town. I'm going to stay at the Inn."

"That's a step up from the normal motels you stay in," Matt teased. "Did you come into some money?"

"Hey, it's a legitimate work expense. I have

another matter I'm looking into, and it's convenient for me to stay there. I'll give you the heads up on why when I see you. I want to get on the road."

"Okay, Tom. We'll talk after you get here." Matt turned his chair around to look out the window. He wondered what other matter Tom was looking into. The winter had been a mild one, and he wasn't looking forward to the snow. It complicated things. He reached for his phone.

"Idle Time Books, how may I help?" Her voice made him smile.

"Hi, sweetheart, I'm checking to see how my favorite girl is doing. Can you talk?"

"I can. As a matter of fact, I was about to call you. Reba stopped by before I opened this morning, and we talked. I asked her the question we were talking about."

"What did she think?"

"Anything is possible is what I got from her." He heard her take a deep breath. "She also told me two men were here. One had come here with the express purpose of hurting us, both of us." He heard her pause. "The other man, she said, was surprised when he saw me and thinks of me as his challenge. I'm thinking the guy in the green sedan may be watching you as well as me."

"She's right, and so are you. I've seen him tailing me a few times. I've also seen the car parked on a side street when I've left the station. I'm keeping my eye on him."

"Yet, you never managed to tell me about this. Why?" He could hear the tension in her voice.

"I figured you had enough to worry about without adding me to the list."

"I'll tell you when I've had enough. Believe it or not, I do care what happens to you, and besides, aren't you the one always telling me that we're partners?"

"That would be me." He paused and then chuckled. "It's nice to know you care about me."

"If you keep withholding information, I might have to rethink this whole caring thing."

He laughed. "Sweetheart, you can't help yourself, I'm just so damn charming."

"There's nothing like a humble man to sweet talk a girl off her feet." She giggled. "And you're nothing like humble."

"Come on, Jess, you know you like me...you may as well admit it."

"I think I'll just have to let you cool your heels for a while. You're too sure of yourself, and you're not keeping me in the loop. That's bad, Mr. Parker, very bad." He could hear the laughter in her voice.

"I'll have to do better. You want information, sweetheart. You'll be drowning in it until you beg me to stop. I'll be there soon. Don't leave the store until I get there."

"Like I can go anywhere! You're my ride. I'll be waiting for you, and you won't see me drowning. I don't even have a small wading pool of info yet." He could hear the smile in her voice. "See you soon. A customer is ready to check out."

Chapter 21

Jessie locked the door as the last customer left. It had been another good day in her store. If things were this good now, wow, what would the summer be like?

"Hi, Jessie." Molly stepped through the doors. "Do you have a minute?"

Jessie nodded. "I just locked up for the evening. What's up?"

"Business was good today. I guess people wanted to get out before the storm comes in." Molly hesitated, shifting her weight to the other leg. "I wanted to let you know I'm not pregnant." She made a pouty face.

"Are you happy or sad?" Jessie studied Molly's face.

"A little of each I think. I'm relieved because I would like to spend more time alone with Kenny, especially now, with him going to the police academy." Molly leaned against the wall. "I was sort of getting used to the idea of having a kid, so I'm feeling a little sad, too."

"I'm sure it will happen at the right time for both of you." Jessie walked over to the display table and picked up a book. "Here's a great book to read while Kenny is gone to class or working in the evenings."

"Sounds good. Ring it up, and I'll be over to get it after I close." Molly walked into Joe's to finish closing.

Jessie straightened books and tidied the store. She

had Molly's book ready for her when she came back. "I think you'll really like this one." Jessie handed Molly her change. "It's an extremely good read."

"I've read a couple by this author, and I like her style. I'll give this one a try."

"It's her latest." Jessie smiled at her. "You'll do a lot of reading if Kenny is working nights."

"I'm sure I'll be back for more. With Kenny gone almost every night of the week, I do get bored."

"I hear you." Jessie walked with Molly to the chairs to sit down.

"Kenny should be here any minute. He still won't let me leave alone at night. I'm kind of glad he looks after me." She leaned her head against the chair back, closing her eyes.

"I'm glad he does, too. I think that the guy is still around here." Jessie looked down at her folded hands and changed the subject. "What do you think? Are we going to get all the snow they are forecasting?"

"I hope not." Molly's eyes opened wide. "I've loved having these mild winter days. I'm not looking forward to snow piling up even a little, much less a foot or more."

"Well, let's hope they're wrong then. I'm putting in my vote for mild days with no snow. Do you think it'll work?"

"I doubt it, but it's worth a try. I'll stand with you." Molly turned to look out the window. "It looks like Kenny is here. I'll see you tomorrow, if we can make it without a sled. It looks like it's starting to snow." Molly stood up. "I'm glad you're my friend, Jessie, and you work close enough for me to stop in to talk to you."

"I'm happy that we're friends too." Jessie followed

her to the door and locked up after she left. Molly was right. It was snowing. Normally, she would love the possibility of a snow day, but not now. This storm was coming in at a bad time. It would slow their investigation down, and they didn't need that. Jessie wanted this murderer off the streets before he could kill another woman. If he had his way, that woman would be her.

Jessie picked up her phone and pushed speed dial. "Hey, Grams, it's me."

"Hi, honey. It's odd, but I was just going to call you. I've been thinking about you ever since I heard your weather for tonight. It sounds like a bad storm is coming in."

"It kind of does, and it has already started snowing. I was hoping these nice mild days would continue, but I guess it's not going to happen." Jessie made a face.

"It usually doesn't, but you didn't call to talk about the storm did you, dear?"

"No…" Jessie's voice trailed off.

"What's the matter? I know something is up." Jessie heard the concern in Sadie's voice.

"I guess," she hesitated. "I needed to hear your voice. I want reassurance that life somewhere is normal, and all is as it should be."

"What is normal, honey? Life is messy at best. It's often happy and sad all at the same time. It definitely is a mixed bag. As long as there are people in the equation, I suppose it will be this way. Don't confuse routine for normal. You're out of your routine, but who knows what normal looks like?"

"It certainly wouldn't be a serial killer. I know that much." Jessie sighed. "Why he's familiar to me, I have no idea."

"No, I doubt that *normal* would look like him. Is he still around your area? I was hoping he had moved on."

"He was at the church. People saw him, and he asked them questions about me. They were eager to give him information because they didn't know who he was. Even with a composite, I can't figure out how I know him." Jessie twirled a strand of hair around her finger.

"It will come to you. Don't beat yourself up about it."

"Pastor John thinks maybe he was wearing a disguise of some kind: a wig or colored contacts."

"Well, that makes sense, doesn't it? He's awful brash to walk into the church knowing someone would tell you."

"The strange thing is, I knew he was in the area that night. We were sitting out front of my store in Matt's car, and I knew he was nearby. I never thought of the church, though."

"It's hard to believe he'd go there of all places."

"He was in New York when we were there, too. Grams, I'm scared."

"I would be too. A little fear is healthy. It will keep you from getting lax and letting down your guard. You can always come home, sweetheart."

"Yes, I know, but he'd follow, and besides, Blue Cove is my home now. I see Matt's car out front. I'll call you soon. I love you, Grams."

"Love you, too, sweetheart."

Jessie gathered her belongings and stopped at the counter to get her purse. She listened to the messages on the answering machine, which were routine until she got to the last one.

"Hello, Jessie, don't worry your pretty little head about who I am. You'll know soon enough" She heard his sinister chuckle. "Our dance has only begun. I won't rush it. I've been waiting for this most of my life." She could hear Matt knocking at the door, but she was frozen in place.

Chapter 22

"Jess, are you in there?" His pounding got a little louder. Next, she heard him jiggle the handle. "Jess, are you okay? Come on, sweetheart, open up." He knocked again.

She finally started to move when her phone alerted her to a text.

—Jessie, you and Matt should come to the Inn for dinner—

She opened the door for Matt.

"What took you so long to open up?" He stared at her.

She held up her phone. "Katie wants us to eat dinner at the Inn tonight."

"Sure…" He followed her to the counter. "What's the matter, Jess? You seem a little off?"

She turned on the answering machine and let him listen. "I was listening to this when you drove up. Sorry, I didn't mean to worry you. I guess it took me time to process what I was hearing."

Matt listened to the message and then listened again. The hand at his side curled into a fist. "Damn, Jess, I hate it that I can't stop this from happening to you. Are you okay?"

"I will be. Did you hear the way he told me not to worry about his identity? Do you think he can hear me? I was talking to Grams about it earlier." She looked around her store. "There are a lot of places he could stash a listening device in here."

"Let's get you out of here. An evening with Katie is just what you need." He grabbed her hand.

She stopped abruptly and pointed her finger at his chest. "You do remember that Liam and Connor come along with it?"

"I figured as much, but right now, I'm concerned about you, not them." He took her hand again.

"Thank you." She smiled at him. "I'm ready to be out of here, too, just as soon as I erase the message." She pulled her hand free.

"You can't do that yet, sweetheart. You know the protocol. We have to enter this into evidence. We need to get the voicemail off your machine before you can erase it." He opened his hand for the keys.

"Okay." She dropped them into Matt's open hand and walked out the door he was holding open.

"Are you warm enough?" He slid into the car and closed the door.

"Yes. I can't believe how heavy the snow is already coming down. I was hoping it would skim past us." She rubbed the fog her breath had made from the window.

"It still might. It could push farther inland yet." He noticed her skeptical look.

"One can hope that nature is on our side. Several inches of snow could delay the investigation." She peered out at the snow that was now coming down in thick, white curtains. "We really need to get this guy, soon."

"We'll get him." He glanced over at her and then back on the road. "You don't think I'd let him threaten my girl and get away with it, do you? I'll tear this town apart to get at him, if I have to."

"There's my knight in shining armor." She chuckled. "You're not lost to me after all."

"You've got that right. I'm always hanging around. Call me crazy, but I think you need me." His lips curled up at her puzzled expression. "Whatever you do, don't ruin my illusion. Every man needs to think that the woman he loves needs him, and she'd be hard pressed to live without him."

"I thought only us girls thought that way. It's nice to know we're not alone in our daydream world."

"We men"—he flexed his muscles—"base our dreams on reality and not fantasy, my dear. I know you need me."

Jessie burst out laughing. "When did you come to that conclusion?"

"You know you do, sweetheart. You're always calling me when you're in trouble. Besides, I need you, too." This time, his smile was real—nothing teasing about it. "We make a damn good team, no fantasy about it."

"Okay, I'll give you that, and thank you."

"For what?" He grinned at her.

"Why for the best laugh I've had in a while." Jessie was still laughing when they pulled into the parking space behind the Inn.

"I think you're enjoying my discomfort a little too much." He closed the car door.

"Well, I think you did it on purpose to get my mind off that message. You're a genius. It worked for me." She was still smiling when they walked into the kitchen of the Inn.

Katie was pulling something out of the oven. "Hi." She glanced over at them. "What are you laughing about, Jessie?"

"Matt, but I won't repeat it because you had to be there." Jessie gave Matt a flirtatious smile. He was grinning at her.

Katie scrunched her face. "You mean it's personal and keep my nose out of it."

"I've trained you well, friend." Jessie peeked at Katie's creation. She could see melted cheese and pieces of chicken atop brown rice in some kind of creamy sauce. "Wow, does that smell good. What do you call it?"

"Dinner." Katie giggled.

"I, for one, am glad we're here." She sniffed the air again.

"I had another reason for asking you to come tonight."

"What's that?" Jessie lifted the lid on the pot cooking on the stove, and Katie slapped her hand. "Could you hurry? I'm starving?"

"You'll hear the news soon enough, so I'm going to tell you up front. Liam and Connor are doing a mini-reunion—or whatever they've coined it—here, a week from Saturday. Jake Perry will be coming in from New York. They are putting the invite out on social media to anyone from our high school who lives in the area and wants to come. Put it on your calendar because you'll have to be here. I'm not the only one who has to suffer through this." She spooned the broccoli into a serving bowl.

"I'll be here and so will my date because I need him." She looked over at Matt, fighting the smile that played at the corner of her mouth. "Ouch." She rubbed the spot where he had pinched her arm.

"I know something is up with you two. I'll be checking in later to get it out of you, Jessie."

"My lips are sealed. You may be good, but I'm even better. I can keep a secret. You never could." Jessie smiled at her.

Katie giggled. "It's true that I never could keep a secret. People told me things to their own detriment."

"You did keep things interesting. I always liked to talk things over with you, but I knew I could never tell you something that really had to remain a secret."

"Is that why you never tell me what's going on anymore?" Katie pursed her lips. "I did keep your secret about seeing Gina somewhat safe, if I remember." She handed Jessie the salad tongs.

"Yes, you did. I haven't told you much lately because I haven't seen you. I can't tell you anything that is case-sensitive. That's just the way it is. Besides, we're grown up, and we trust each other." Jessie tossed the salad.

"I would spill it all, I think." Katie laughed. "It's just as well you don't tell me too much. You could always keep secrets, but I couldn't keep even one. Flat out, I'm a social creature who loves to talk." Katie fluttered her eyelashes and grinned at them.

Jessie laughed. "You sure are. I can attest to that."

"What can you confirm about my sister?" Liam entered the kitchen. "This I have to hear. I've been trying forever to dig up dirt on her to use against her." He playfully pushed Katie.

"We were talking about her not being able to keep a secret." Jessie moved closer to Matt.

"You are so right, Jessie. I would tell her fabricated secrets, just to see if she would pass them on. She did every time."

Katie sucker punched him. "I can't believe you would do that to your own sister."

"It was easy after I told you about my feelings for a certain young lady, which you promised to keep secret. The next day, it was all over the school. I learned quick enough not to trust you."

"I remember that. What a mess it caused." Katie actually looked embarrassed—for a moment. "If I remember correctly, she didn't talk to you for a long time. She even went to the prom with that other boy. What was his name?"

"Bobby Angel. Yes, sis, you really mucked it up for me that time. From then on, it was fabricated secrets for you." He tousled her hair. "I still love you, though, only better now since you're not always butting into my life." Liam dodged the hand coming his way.

"Katie, you're my best friend, and you know I love you, but in high school, you were a real pain. Come to think of it, you've been busy interfering in my life, trying to hook me up since I moved here. Liam, I think it's time for us to work some magic and interfere in her life." Jessie gave Liam a high five.

"What is this, pick on Katie night? Matt, are you going to let them team up against me?" She put her arm through his.

He chuckled. "Katie, I think you've been asking for this for a while. I'm going to stay out of it."

"Why, Matt, are you a coward? I never thought I would see the day." She fluttered her eyelashes at him. "Since you're all being so mean to me, you can help me get dinner out to the guests."

****

Matt leaned back in his chair, watching as the tension melted from Jessie's face. He loved watching her interact with her friends. He looked around the table at each of them, and his grin broadened as she laughed. If he were a betting man, he'd bet neither Liam nor Connor were guilty of anything other than being flirts. They were a pain, yes, competition—more than he'd like to admit—but serial killer? He highly doubted it. He hadn't cleared them off his lists of suspects yet, but he was getting close to it. Matt turned his head when he heard the front door of the Inn open. Katie jumped up and returned in a few minutes, followed by Tom.

"Hey, all, this is Tom Maxwell. He's going to be staying here for a few days."

Tom nodded at them and sat down next to Matt. "Man, am I glad to be out of that car."

"Were the roads bad?" Matt looked over at him.

"Let's put it this way, I don't want to go back out there again tonight." He heard Jessie laugh and saw her poke Katie. "Jessie looks like she's having a nice time." Tom took a sip of the coffee Katie had placed in front of him.

"She grew up with all of them." His gaze went back to her.

Tom lowered his voice. "Between you and me, Matt, I'm here to keep my eye on the lawyer over there. Don't give me that look. I know he's Katie's brother. He's had some dealings with a couple of shady characters. The last one he defended was a particularly bad one, and the guy's not happy that they lost the case. Word on the street is Liam is on a short hit list. It could be his reason for leaving New York, or maybe it was all some kind of a setup. My job is to try and find out if he's involved, or if he's just a lawyer who took on a bad client."

"I knew he had defended some pretty tough characters. What we don't need here right now is another hitman. Blue Cove could become a little crowded with these guys."

"I hear you. You've sure had your share of big cases. At least the last one was in sunny Palm Springs. Are you making any headway with the serial killer?" Tom smiled as Katie set a filled plate in front of him.

"It has me perplexed. He's been doing some strange things, like hanging out at the church and asking questions about Jessie. He walked among folks as big as you please, not afraid he'd be caught."

"You must have a great description of him." Tom filled his mouth with a forkful of broccoli.

"That's the weird part. No two people saw the same man. We had so many descriptions that Jason almost went nuts trying to draw the composite. The only traits everyone agreed on were that he was tall and charming." Matt frowned. "I don't know where to begin to look for a tall and charming man." He chuckled.

"You're going to have to bait him with the one thing that will bring him directly to you: Jessie." Tom took another bite.

"Damn, I knew you'd say that. We're talking about it only as a last resort." Matt exhaled slowly.

"Matt, you know better than that. He's still here because of her. He won't leave until he tries for her. You know I'm right. It's better to set it up than to have it sprung on you with no plan." He took a sip of coffee.

"Look, we can plan it carefully and keep her safe. It's the best way to do it."

"I know…" Matt raked his hand through his hair. "I'll talk to her tonight, and we can sit down to a draw up a plan of action in the next couple of days. He might actually show up here next Saturday. They're having a small reunion for people from their high school who are visiting in the area. It seems like it's a perfect invitation for murder." Matt looked around the table. "How are we supposed to find a tall man among all these tall men? He has to be tall, remember."

"Yeah, but is he charming? That's the question." Tom elbowed Matt.

Matt chuckled and shook his head. He leaned over to Jessie. "Are you about ready to leave?" he murmured in her ear. "I have some reports to catch up on."

"Sure, let me help Katie clear the table, and I'll be ready in a few minutes." Jessie stood up, grabbed her dishes, and carried them to the kitchen. Matt followed her with his. They made short work of it and found themselves trudging through the heavy snow on the path to her place.

"Matt, I've been thinking." She gave him a sideways glance. "You're going to have to use me as bait to get this guy. It's simple, really, he wants me, and it's the reason he's staying on here. We can't pass up a chance to get him. You need to think about it, and we'll talk later."

Matt smiled inwardly. He could still bluster and put up a fuss to save his pride, but she was right. She had just handed him his way to approach her.

Chapter 23

The night seemed lighter and brighter than normal with all the white covering the ground. The freshly fallen snow crunched with each footstep.

"I love how quiet it is when it snows. The earth sounds insulated." Jessie opened her mouth to catch several snowflakes on her tongue. "I haven't done that in years." She smiled, turning in a circle. "So beautiful…"

"From where I'm standing, I would have to agree." Matt's voice sounded gruff.

They walked a little ways. At the door, Jessie stopped suddenly and grabbed Matt's arm. "This doesn't feel right. Someone has been in here."

"Didn't you tell me that Katie went in looking for you, and that Liam was with her?"

"Yes, but this is different. *He* was in here," she said breathlessly. "Be careful, Matt." She laid her hand on his back as he opened the door.

Matt pulled out his gun as he went in, followed closely by Jessie. He checked every room, and nothing seemed out of place. "Are you sure, Jess?"

"I'm sure he was in here. I can tell. I can feel him!" She shuddered and gripped his arm.

"Well, that answers one of my questions."

"What question?"

"Does he know where you live? He obviously

does, and he knows how to get in as well." Matt hung his coat up in the closet when she did.

Jessie went to the bedroom for her slippers. It felt good. Her feet were finally warm and snuggly. She grabbed her sweater off the chair when she passed Matt on her way to the kitchen. He followed her and reached for a glass in the cabinet. On impulse, Jessie took him into her arms and hugged him. "Thank you," she said quietly.

"What for, sweetheart?" He held her snug in his arms.

"You never make fun of me when I get all these weird feelings." She pulled away first, took the glass out of his hand, put ice in it, and filled it with water. She placed it on the table by his chair. "I feel strange enough without someone commenting on how odd I am." She smiled at him and then sat down at her computer. There was a note attached to the screen.

You found my little gift, hidden in plain view. You have a very cozy place here. It'll be easy to rent it out when you're gone.

"Matt, look at this." She pointed at the screen.

"Damn, Jess." His fingers curled into a fist at his side.

"I knew he had been in here. What do we do now?" She looked up at him, worried.

"One thing I know for sure, I'm not about to let you out of my sight. I guess Tom may be right." He paused.

"What is Tom right about?" she asked him pointedly. "While you're at it, you can tell me why Tom is here too."

He grabbed her hand and walked over to the sofa

164

with her. "He told me the same thing you said to me when we were outside. You have to be the bait because you're the reason the perp is still here." He sat on the couch pulling her into his lap.

"It'll be okay, really." She rested her head on his chest.

"We'll plan well and make it as safe as we possibly can. There are always risks, though. You know that I'm not telling you anything new." He frowned as he said it.

"I know, nothing is foolproof. We have to try, and I think Emma will help." She snuggled closer to him.

"I think he'll be here next Saturday night. If he's one of your friends from years ago, he'll be here, and if he's from New York, he'll crash it. I'm sure he'll show up. He's not afraid of people seeing him; he's sure of himself." He put his arm around her and held her tight.

"I might not know him when I see him. It's hard for me to believe any of my friends could be this maniac."

"Tom and I will be watching too." He patted her hand.

"This brings me back to my second question. Why is Tom here?" She lifted her head and studied him. He wasn't telling her something.

"Several agents are here because our hitman is here."

"Okay, I get that, but why is Tom here—and staying at the Inn?" Her eyes narrowed.

"This is where I have to say you must keep this a secret if I tell you." He looked at her seriously. "You said you're good at it, and I'm counting on you."

She nodded at him. "I can do it."

"The truth is, he's here to keep his eye on Liam."

His hand tensed around hers.

"Why?" She frowned.

"Liam has defended some shady clients. Word out on the streets is that he's on a hit list. Tom is here because the FBI wants to know if Liam is guilty of teaming with his clients, or if they're really out to get him. Tom thinks that might be the reason he left New York. He's hiding out here. He may be putting his sister in jeopardy without realizing it." His thumb rubbed against the palm of her hand.

"Then I'm glad Tom is here. He'll find out Liam is only guilty of defending questionable people."

"You're a loyal friend, sweetheart. A little naïve, but loyal." He smiled at her.

"You can say what you want, but Liam has a good heart. I would know if he didn't."

"Maybe or maybe not." He smiled gently. "As you said, it's hard to believe your friends could do wrong. As an investigative reporter, you know friends and family are usually the last to see it or believe it of a loved one."

"I know." Her voice was barely audible, "I'll let Tom do his job."

"That's my girl. I never doubted you for a minute. It might end up just like you said." He lifted her chin. "I want you to think about our serial killer, about how you might know him, and how we are going to trap him. Tom will get together with us, too."

"I can do that." She tried not to sound too eager. This waiting was driving her up the wall. She didn't like surprises; she would rather be the one giving them. "Matt, we'll get him. I know that we will. He picked the wrong town. I'm here, if for no other reason than to help you get this guy."

"I don't believe that for a minute." Matt leaned closer to her.

"What don't you believe?"

"We'll get him, I'm sure of it, but you're not here for him." He shook his head at her. "No, you're here for me."

"I am?" Her eyes widened.

He nodded. "I hadn't realized how bleak my life had become until you showed up and fought me every step of the way. I've never felt more alive than I do now. Emma was a stark reminder to me we can't take life for granted."

Her lower lip trembled and, for the second time in one night, she acted on impulse. She stood up, never taking her gaze from his, bent her head down, and kissed him with all the emotion she felt in her heart, leaving them both breathless. "That was the sweetest thing you've ever said to me, Mr. Parker. Thank you." She walked into her room, sat down on her bed, and gave way to the emotion that filled her.

****

He stared at the closed door. He could hear her crying, but he knew she needed to be alone and cry it out. He hadn't expected the kiss. What a kiss. He hadn't recovered yet. She constantly surprised him. It was one thing on a long list of things he liked about her.

Matt pulled out his case file and made a few notations. His first call was to Dylan.

"Hey, Matt, what's up?"

"I want you to take the lead working with the FBI agents on this hitman case. As I told you earlier, the bureau traced him here."

"I'll take care of it for you," Dylan replied.

"I don't need to remind you that our lives are on the line here."

"We'll do our best," Dylan assured Matt.

"I know you will. I'm working with Tom to come up with a plan to use Jessie as bait to lure in our other perp."

"Is Jessie okay with the possible risk?"

"She's been pestering me about doing it for several days. I'm against it, but Tom made me see it differently."

"How did he convince you to do it?" Dylan gave a short chuckle. "You're not easy to convince where she's concerned."

"He told me it's best to keep the element of surprise on our side." Matt sat forward in his chair. "I know he's right. This guy won't leave the area until he's tried to get her."

"Look, Matt, we'll get your stalker. You concentrate on Jessie. He's after her now. I imagine that Frank will be delayed by weather."

"Yes, he will." Matt exhaled. "Thanks, Dylan. We're going to do our best to get them both."

"With any luck, no one will get hurt in the process." He heard Dylan take a breath. "Are you going to Emma's service on Friday?"

"We'll be there. I'm sure our perp will be somewhere close by. I need to call Tom before it gets much later. We'll talk tomorrow."

"Okay, goodnight."

The call to Tom went right to voicemail. "Hey, Tom, you must be asleep," he said. "Jessie has agreed to what we were talking about earlier. We need to put our heads together and come up with a solid plan. I'll talk to you tomorrow." He disconnected then listened outside her door but heard nothing. She must have finally gone to sleep too. He was going to sleep on the sofa tonight. The killer had been in her house. Matt shook his head and scowled. Better have Gary sweep it for bugs. People could hear a lot with the new handheld listening devices. He grabbed a pillow and a blanket from the guest room and stretched out on the couch. He sure as hell didn't like the idea of using Jessie to get at this guy. Maybe Saturday would be the end of the line for him.

Chapter 24

The house was quiet, and she was wide-awake. Her bout of crying had left her drained but not sleepy. She pushed her hair from her face and tucked it behind her ears. Her eyes tracked around the room, straining to see the familiar in the dark. He had been roaming around in her space, which totally freaked her out. What had he touched? Had he gone through her drawers and handled her clothing? She shivered as she thought about it. Maybe he had lain on her bed or sat on her couch. She couldn't replace all her furniture, for heaven's sake. She didn't like to think of his hands that had killed so many women handling anything that belonged to her. But, he had touched her stuff. She knew it; she could feel him all around her. There would be no peace until they caught him. She would have an alarm system installed, but wiping the feeling of him from her room would take more work.

She stared into the darkness. Not everyone could hear and see what she did. Strange. Jess sat up in bed. She had never thought much about the supernatural. As a reporter, she had investigated a few psychics, and, for the most part, thought they were fakes. Yet, here she was doing something equally bizarre. She smiled. Who could have imagined her life headed in this direction? So much for her peace of mind. She shook her head. There wasn't any. Ghosts, girls talking in her head, and now, mind games. It was as if some far out story had snuck up on her when she wasn't looking for it. This sounded more like a novel than her real life. Darn, why couldn't she figure out who this creep was? Things would be much easier if she could put a name to him.

She couldn't manipulate this strange ability. If anything, it interfered with her life—coming and going when it wanted. She threw off her covers and stood. Sleep was never going to happen. She put on her slippers. Quietly, she opened the door and tiptoed past Matt on her way to the kitchen.

"Are you all right?" His deep voice startled her.

"I couldn't sleep. I know he handled my things and, to be truthful, I'm a little overwhelmed by how creepy it is. It makes my skin crawl just thinking about it."

"I'm sorry, sweetheart." He sat up and pulled her down beside him. "I wish I knew how to make it all go away."

"You can't, I know." She sighed.

"Jess, I think he'll be nearby during Emma's memorial service. He will want to gloat over it. I'm sure he will be at the Inn on Saturday night. You may or may not recognize him, but I think you'll know when he's around."

"Probably…but I may not know who to watch out for."

"We'll all help."

"I know." She stood up. "Do you want some water?"

"I'll get it and bring it to you. Try the guest room. I doubt he was in there for long once he realized which room was yours."

"Good idea." She went into the room and sat down on the bed. He was right. The room had a completely different feel to it.

He knocked and entered. "Better?"

"Much." She nodded.

"Goodnight. Call me if you need to." He bent down and kissed her.

She touched his face. "Thank you."

"See you in the morning." His voice sounded gruff. He shut off the light on his way out of the room.

She took a sip of water, stretched out on the bed, and was asleep in no time.

****

Another motel room. They all had started to look the same to him after a while. Jessie's nice little place made him almost long for a home. Maybe he would make this his last dance too and finally settle down. He let the silky fabric of her underwear slide through his fingers, rubbing it across his face, drinking in the scent of her. She would find it missing eventually. She already knew he had touched her things. That's what made this dance exciting. She just knew. Jessie didn't need a note to tell her. His body pulsated with excitement. He'd never run into anyone like her. He could lead most women like lambs to the slaughter, but she challenged him to use his brain. What a rush it gave him, and the tempo was building. All the snow made it more magical, crimson against the white. She could be his undoing. His breath came in ragged gasps. Feeling alive, he vibrated with his need to extinguish her. It might destroy him too. A sinister laughed filled the room, and he glanced at himself in the mirror. *But, what a way to go, eh?* He smoothed his hair back and reached for the remote. He had his invitation, and the reunion was only a little over a week away.

Chapter 25

Jessie awakened to less snow than they had predicted, but there was enough to make it slow going on the roads. Main Street was snow-packed, though the plows were making headway as they cleared a path for cars. The side streets were a little harder to maneuver on, but Matt was able to get her to work in time to open the store. She heard on the news that about twenty minutes west of Blue Cove, the snow was still falling at the rate of an inch per hour. Blue Cove had gotten a foot before the snow let up. The storm had hit harder inland.

She was supposed to work at the church today if Audrey made it in okay. She was just happy Audrey still wanted to work at the store after her scare at knifepoint. Matt had promised Audrey she wouldn't have to walk to her car alone in the evening and that they would follow her home when she worked. Jessie wouldn't blame her if she never wanted to come back to the store.

Would the store be busy or slow today? She had no idea what to expect. She walked to the front window. This was Blue Cove's first snowstorm since she had opened. It could go either way, she supposed. Although, New Englanders were a hardy bunch. If they stayed in when it was cold, they would never get out during some winters.

She lingered at the window. The church looked so pretty this morning against its snowy backdrop. The sun was peeking out from behind the clouds, shining down on the snow, making it shimmer. Pastor Kevin was out with the snowblower, clearing a path to the door. Pastor John was making his slow way in from the parking lot, which one of the church members must have plowed earlier. Life went on, as odd as it seemed sometimes. Emma's service was in two days, another sad event for a congregation that had seen more than their fair share lately. She rubbed her temple. He would be somewhere nearby. Emma would be, too. Jessie was sure of that. She turned away from the window.

She busied herself straightening the books on the table, which were still nearly perfect from when she had straightened them the night before. Idle hands or an idle mind, what did Grams always say? She got her duster out and went over a couple shelves of books, then went into the back room to get the cash bag out of the safe. The bell over the door rang.

"Jessie, are you here? It's me, Audrey."

"I'll be right out. Did you have any trouble on your drive in?" Jessie walked toward her.

"It's a little slick in places, but my four-wheel drive makes it easy if I don't go too fast. Who cleaned your walks?"

"Matt did when he brought me in this morning. My car is not good in the snow." She put the cash in the register as she talked. "It's perfect for warm summer days, though."

"We haven't had much snow this winter, so this moisture is needed, I suppose." Audrey grimaced. "I shouldn't complain about the weather, but I probably will. These warm days have been glorious." Audrey put her gloves in her purse and unwound the scarf from around her neck. She hung her coat up in the back room.

"I know what you mean. I was about to run over to Joe's and get a coffee. Would you like one?" Jessie asked her.

"I'll go for you. You can get ready to go to the church." Audrey nodded when Jessie told her what she wanted and gave her the money. She walked into Joe's to get their coffee.

Audrey would work out great. They had hit if off from the first time they'd met. She was good with the customers and a hard worker. Audrey was back in a moment with the coffee and two bags.

"I'm a great fan of their scones too. Today's is one of my favorites: mixed berries with a creamy whipped icing. You'll love it." Audrey placed the small tray on the table.

"I thought we were kindred spirits, but now I know it." She smiled as she took the bag. "I'm sure I'll like it. I'm addicted to these things. I have to work out all the harder because of this sweet little addiction. I don't let myself have one every day anymore. Once a week is all I allow. Unless, of course, someone else buys me one." She winked. "In that case, I'll never turn it down." She smiled at Audrey. "You have my number, I'm right across the street, and I'll be back at lunch to relieve you." She grabbed her purse from the counter.

"I won't need you unless it's a business question, I'm sure. Enjoy your morning."

"I hate what he did to you, Audrey." She paused at the door. "It still makes me mad to think about it."

"I still have a few nightmares about it." Audrey shrugged and then shivered briefly. "There was something scary about him, even though I couldn't see him. You're the one I'm worried about. He let me live, but I'm not sure he'll let you."

"No, I don't believe he means to." Jessie slipped her coat on and wrapped her scarf around her neck. "I'll see you in a little while." She opened the door and stepped out into the cold air. She made her way across the street, pulling her coat tightly around her. Her shivers were from more than just the cold air. She waved at Pastor Kevin, still working to remove the snow on the grounds, as she made her way to the front entrance of the church.

"Hey, Blondie. Boy, I'm glad to see you." Melinda headed her way as Jessie walked through the doors.

"Hi, Red." Jessie stopped and looked around. She felt something different in the church—familiar, yet different.

"I was watching for you. It's been dull around here without you. Although, I think our ghost is back." Melinda started for the office, and Jessie followed her.

"What makes you think that?"

"You know the regular weird stuff. I swear I heard Gina singing the other night. Do you think she's here to help because of…you know…Emma?"

"I never thought about it. It's conceivable, I guess. I mean none of this stuff ever happened to me until I started working here, so I'm not sure how it works." Jessie shrugged. "Anything is possible."

"And now you're back, and it's happening again." She scrunched her face, looking over the top of her glasses. "Mighty perplexing I would say, wouldn't you?" Her red curls bounced up and down as she nodded.

"It sort of is at that." Jessie pulled off her coat and hung it up on the hook.

"Matt told us the fella that was here asking questions about you was most likely Emma's killer. Maybe Gina's going to help you get him. I think that would be pretty cool, don't you?" Melinda pushed her glasses back up on her nose.

"I guess it would be." An icy cold chill ran down her spine.

"Maybe Gina and Emma will team up to save you this time." Melinda slapped her leg. "A ghost tag team. It would have to be something pretty important to bring Gina back here, don't you think, Blondie?"

"I guess it would have to be, if she's back." And she plainly was. Jessie had known it was true the minute she'd walked into her office.

"Oh, she's back, there's no doubt about it. And, you're the reason they're both here. Even Reba feels it. She told me the other day." Melinda plopped down in the chair in front of the desk. "Don't go getting all weird, Blondie, this is a good thing. Just think about it, the three of you working together to trap a serial killer."

By the time Melinda left her office, Jessie's mind was in overdrive. Gina was here; she could tell. Maybe it was true that she was here to help find Emma's killer. She didn't know what to think about it. She smiled. If she didn't know better, she'd think she was losing it. Ghost tag team! That was crazy, or was it? Jessie took out a pencil and wrote down a few things Melinda had said.

"Gina, I know you're here, and I'd appreciate any

help you can give me," Jessie whispered. She walked to Pastor John's office. "I wanted to let you know that I'm here."

"It's good to see you back, Jessie. How's the store doing?"

"Better than I anticipated." She smiled. "We've had several bus tours stop, and they like to shop. They visit Joe's and migrate into my store. Sales have been good." She sat down in the chair in front of his desk.

"Do you mind leaving it to work here in the mornings?" Pastor John gave her a pointed look.

She gave him a reassuring smile. "Not at all, Audrey is great, and she'll do fine."

"I don't mind telling you that we were all shocked to learn that the serial killer walked through our church as big as you please, asking questions about you. Everyone thought he was a potential new church member. He seemed like such a nice man." John frowned.

"How could you know?" Her fingers were tapping quietly on the arm of the chair, and she stilled them. Yes, creepy that he was here. Almost as creepy as him in her house. She crinkled her nose.

"I feel so bad for Emma's family every time I meet with them. Her fiancé is brokenhearted and yet irate enough that he'd love to get his hands on the man who did this."

"I'm sure the same could be said of the other victims' husbands and fathers." She started to stand. "Let me know if you want me to do anything."

"Jessie, I'm sure Melinda will tell you, but some odd things have been happening around here again." John sounded troubled. "They're telling me it's a lot like when people saw Gina before. Some are saying she's back again, and they've actually seen her. I don't know if I believe that, but there are some unusual things going on. I thought that you should know."

"Melinda caught me on my way into the church." Jessie smiled at him.

"Oh, she already got to you, huh? I guess my warning is a little late. I won't attempt to explain what I'm not at all sure of, but I've heard and seen some things, and so has Pastor Kevin."

"I know. Everyone is a little on edge with Emma's murder, and then her killer was in the church. Who could blame people for seeing strange things? It's an unusual situation for sure."

"You're right about that. Say, let me know if you see her. You did last time, and I'm curious to see if you can figure out what's going on."

"I will." She nodded thoughtfully. "One thing I know for sure, Pastor Gina was a loving person, and if she could, she would watch out for this congregation." Jessie walked back to her desk as the phone rang. "First Community Church, this is Jessie speaking."

"Hello, Jessie dear, have you seen her yet?" Reba's cheerful voice came over the line.

"No, but I know she's here. I could feel her around this morning."

"We are all taken aback. I didn't see this coming. I was so sure she was free from this place once her murderer was dead."

"It could be like Melinda said: she is watching over this congregation. Maybe she's here to help find Emma's killer, and maybe she doesn't like the fact he was in her church. I'm speculating, of course, and feeling a little silly about it." Jessie smiled and waved at Pastor Kevin as he walked through the door.

"No need to feel silly, dear. We can't explain all of life with simple black and white answers. There are many unknowns, for sure. Why, I'm surprised all the time."

Jessie chuckled. "I am, too; at least, I have been since I moved here anyway."

"I think you could use a little help to keep you safe. It's possible that Gina and Emma are both around for that purpose."

"A ghost tag team of sorts, as Melinda told me this morning." She smiled; although, the thought was actually comforting.

Jessie heard Reba laughing. "Oh, that girl is too funny. You never know what she's going to say next. Although, I have to admit, a tag team is not a bad way to describe it."

"I'll let you know if I see anything."

"You do that, my girl, and in the meantime, I'll keep my eyes open. We'll all work together to keep you alive and to get Emma's murderer."

"Thank you, I need all the help I can get." Jessie nodded as she looked around the room. She could feel Gina watching her. Reba hung up, and Jessie got to work. Before she knew it, her morning was over. She dialed the store.

"Idle Time Books. This is Audrey."

"I was thinking of bringing you some lunch. How does a chicken salad sandwich from Joe's sound?"

"Great. The store has been busier than I thought it would be," she said cheerfully. "Lunch sounds good."

"Okay, I'll be there in a few." Jessie put in a call to

Joe's to order the sandwiches, straightened the office, and said goodbye to the pastors. Watching for icy spots, she made her way across the street. Matt was supposed to talk to Tom today; maybe they would come up with a plan. She wondered what they would think if she told them Gina was back.

She felt someone was watching her cross the street and did a quick scan of the area before she went into Joe's, but she didn't see anything out of the ordinary.

Chapter 26

Matt watched her walk across the street and grinned. She wasn't even aware he was around. He was monitoring the car that had been tailing him the past several days. The church parking lot was the perfect vantage point from which he could observe the green sedan. Jessie looked preoccupied as she headed for Joe's door. She was as pretty as a picture. He couldn't help but notice how her hair shone in the sunlight. Watching her was his favorite pastime.

Keeping her safe was becoming his full-time occupation. He could think of many worse things than staying close to her.

"This is Matt," he answered his phone. "What's up, Dylan?"

"Our guy hasn't moved, which has me wondering what he's up to."

"Is there any other way out of his room, other than the door?" Matt asked.

"No, the window in the back is too small; we've already checked. For a guy that prides himself on being elusive, he's done some things that make little sense to me."

"What are you thinking?" Matt took a sip of his coffee.

"Why is his car parked where it can be seen? He's staying at a motel on Main Street, for heaven's sake."

Matt heard Dylan take a breath. "He tried to break into Jessie's store, which got him noticed. None of this makes any sense. The agent with me said they watched him for months and never saw him come or go. He was stealth itself. This guy could be a decoy, hired to keep you from noticing the real hitman in the shadows."

"I hate to admit it, but that sounds about right. It can't be this easy, nothing ever is."

"He's what we've got for now. The best we can hope for is that he inadvertently leads us to the man we're searching for. What should we do?" Dylan asked.

"Stick to him like glue and hope he makes a mistake." Matt looked over at Jessie's store as the door opened.

"That would be my call too."

"I'll get back to you. I have another call coming in." Matt took the incoming call.

"Matt, this is Gary. We had a call from the police chief at Pine Junction. They found another woman's body this morning. I thought you would want to know, so you can call and compare notes. This may or may not be the work of the serial killer." Matt jotted down the number and called to talk to Mack McCoy.

Yes, it seemed that their man had struck again. Matt hung up the phone feeling grim. "The woman had been out walking her dog when he attacked her. The dog's incessant howling alerted a neighbor to call the police. She wasn't the usual age of his victims, but all the other criteria were there. Mack described the scene as brutal and almost surreal with all the blood against the white snow. Hell, he hated this. The perp was working himself into a frenzy getting ready for Jessie. He left them with no choice. Jessie had to be the bait whether he liked it or not. He was coming after her, and they all had to be ready.

****

"Thanks, Jessie, lunch was great." Audrey crumpled up her sandwich wrappings.

"My pleasure, I'm happy that you still want to work here."

"I enjoy it. It's good for me to get out, and the people who come in here are so nice." Audrey smiled. "Besides, my friend, what's not to like about working around all these lovely books? Reading is one of my favorite forms of entertainment. If I owned this store, I would cut into my profit margin with all the books I'd buy for myself."

"So far I've done well. I've had to learn to pace myself over the years, or I couldn't afford my habit."

"I know the feeling. I was going to ask you if you knew of a feel-good type book. Something lighthearted? I'm not ready for a murder mystery."

"I have just the book for you." Jessie got up and picked it off the shelf. "This will leave you feeling happy. She's a wonderful author, and her books always have happy endings of the best kinds."

"Sounds perfect." Audrey turned the book over and read the blurb on the back.

"If you like it, this is the first book in the series, so there are several more for you to enjoy."

"Why don't you give me the second book now?" She carried it to the cash register. "It's snowy and cold: perfect weather for a warm blanket, a book, and hot tea."

"You described a perfect day to me. Enjoy!" Jessie slipped both books into a bag.

"I'll see you in the morning, and I'll be here Friday, so you can go to Emma's service."

"Thank you, Audrey, I appreciate it." Jessie walked her to the door and saw Matt walking across the street toward her.

Jessie watched him take Audrey's arm and walk her to her car. She busied herself straightening the chairs around the table. She smiled at him when he finally walked into the store.

"Hi, sweetheart, how was your first day back at the church?" He gave a quick kiss on the cheek.

"I think you need to sit down for this one." She led him to the two comfortable, wingback chairs and sat down next to him. "Guess who was at the church today?"

"Reba." He shifted in his chair.

"No." She shook her head at him.

"I have no clue. Tell me who was there."

"She's back…Gina is back."

"Are you sure?" His eyebrows rose.

"I'm sure. Is that crazy or what?" Jessie studied his face. She couldn't imagine what he was thinking.

"I don't know what to say."

"I'm not the only one aware of it. Reba, Melinda, and even Pastor John are aware of the rumors and the strange things happening at the church. He won't go so far as to say what he thinks it is. Reba thinks she's there to team up with Emma to help catch her killer. I don't know what to think."

"I guess we'll take all the help we can get, even if it is of the strange variety." He grabbed her hand. "You come with a strange group of characters."

"I didn't bring them with me, for heaven's sake."

She let her breath out in mocking exasperation. "They found me when I moved here. It has to be this town."

"Either way, sweetheart, you're in the middle of it all. It seems to center around you."

"I know, and I would like to know why that is. So far no one has given me an answer to *that* question." She frowned at him. "I went to work at a church where there was a murder, and the victim's ghost picked me to find her murderer. That story is too preposterous to believe, even for me, and yet it happened to me." She watched him shrug his shoulders. "Still nothing to say? Has the cat got your tongue?"

Matt started laughing and laughed harder when she punched him. "You have to admit it *is* kind of funny. In all my years of police work I've never heard anything like it."

She fought back her smile. "I'm the one it's happening to, and I say it's not funny." Her giggle ruined it.

"I hope they're here to help, Jess, because we're going to need it." Matt was serious again. "He's killed again. A woman in Pine Junction was murdered. They found her body this morning."

"Oh, Matt, that's awful. You're right; we do need everyone's help to get him." Jessie's eyes stung with tears.

"I think we'll need a lucky break and a great plan. We will get this guy off the streets one way or the other." He handed her a tissue from the counter.

"We can work on the plan." She took out a notebook.

He stood up and paced. "I have no idea where to begin."

"We can start with the fact that Gina's here. It must be getting near the time for us to get him or there'd be no need for her to be here." She started jotting down ideas. "He was in the church, and maybe she's looking after the congregation. I feel ridiculous speculating about this, but it's a part of my reality right now."

"Or," he stopped pacing to face her, "it could be as Reba said, and she's here to help you."

"It could be." She shrugged. "She could point us in the right direction, and Emma could confront him. That would be justice."

"Now you're thinking. He'll be around on Friday and next Saturday, I'm convinced of that. Watch for any sign she gives you." The front door opened, and a customer walked in. "I'll be back to get you at closing time."

She walked him to the door. "Okay, see you then." She waved at him as he stepped through the door.

He turned back, briefly. "Keep thinking about it, Jess, something will come to you. Think about how she helped you the last time. I'm sure it will come to you why she's here. When it does, let me know."

"I will." She closed the door and walked over to her customer to see if she could be of help.

Chapter 27

Jessie had time before Matt arrived to jot down a few notes. Gina had come back for a reason. Gina would be watching over the church, and she would be watching for any sign from Gina. She smiled crookedly. This was life for now. She saw ghosts, she heard people in her head, and she saw things other people didn't always see. Live with it! If it saved someone's life, then it was worth it.

Katie had told her that twenty-five people were coming to the get-together. They either lived in the area or would be here on the Saturday of the party. Their perp could very well be one of them. She would trust her instincts, and with a little luck, she would figure out who he was before it was too late. Matt, Tom, and the others would be watching out for her too.

She was out the door as soon as Matt pulled up. "Hi." She slipped into the passenger seat.

"I would have come to the door to get you." He glanced her way as she put on her seatbelt.

"I know, but I was ready to be done. It's almost six, and the store closes at five. I get a little stir crazy. I'll be happy when I can drive again and don't have to put you out anymore."

"I'm sorry I was late, but Tom and I were going over ideas. Besides, I don't mind picking you up; it gives me a chance to see you." He pulled out of the parking space onto Main Street.

"I appreciate that, but I like the freedom to come and go as I want. I'm sure you do too." She smiled over at him to take any sting out of her words.

"Freedom is highly overrated. I like being with you. I like everything about you, even the quirky things."

"Now aren't you just too sweet." She laughed at her attempt at a Southern drawl. "I have decided not to let Gina's arrival rattle me. I think she's here to help us, and I'll let it go at that."

"You know, Jess, you amaze me. Most women, and men for that matter, would be flipping out over this. You just take a ghost all in stride."

"I don't know about that, but I am learning to live with my weirdness for now. Could we get something to eat? I'm so hungry." She folded her hands in her lap.

"Once again, I'm sorry." He looked over at her. "What sounds good to you?"

"Patterson's is fine, and we don't have too far to go to get there."

****

Matt had enjoyed being with Jessie tonight. She had beaten him soundly at both pool and darts. Of course, he was too busy enjoying the view to keep his mind on the game. He grinned. She had even pulled Dylan and Kip into the game. Her appetite and energy were over the top tonight. Maybe it was her way of dealing with nerves. They needed to talk, but she went directly to her room when they got to her place, and she still hadn't come out.

"Jess, are you okay?" He glared at the closed door, waiting for her answer.

"Yes, I'll be right there." She came out wearing a pair of sweats and fuzzy slippers. "I think I overdid it at dinner. I may be a wee bit nervous about next weekend."

"I wanted to talk to you about that. We need to bounce ideas off each other."

She placed her trusty notebook and pen on the table beside her. "Where do we begin?"

"Let's start with Emma's service. He'll be around, maybe in disguise, somewhere in the area to watch and gloat."

"He can't show up looking the way he did before, or everyone he talked to would recognize him." She leaned her forehead into her palm.

"True, but he will be there. I don't think he'll try anything because I'm never going to leave your side. You're not going to leave mine either." He leaned back with his hands behind his head and made steady eye contact with her. "For all practical purposes, we are glued together. I'll stand outside the bathroom door if you have to go. I may even check it before you go in."

"I get it." She covered her eyes with one hand. "I'll watch for any sign of Gina or Emma, for that matter. No one else has seen him up close and personal the way Emma did."

"To tell you the truth, Jess, I'm more concerned about next weekend." His eyes narrowed. "I've been working out a plan with Tom and the others. I'm not going to let you know about any of it because I don't want you watching them. I don't want you to be concerned with anything they do. Just pay attention to those in the room."

"Okay, I guess." She pressed her lips tight together.

"It's not what you think." He crossed his arms as he recognized the signs here.

"Exactly what do I think it is?" She pointed her pen at him, her face flushing.

Yep. He was right. He sighed. "I'm not trying to withhold information from you, if that's what you're thinking. You'll have enough to do. You're going to be the bait trying to lure our suspect in. I think that's enough to ask of anyone. I want you to concentrate on that, knowing we are watching out for you." He frowned. "We have another issue, which is the hitman. Your hands are full enough, and we will do our best to deal with the rest."

"If he's the guy in the old beat-up green sedan, why can't you arrest him?"

"No. We're pretty sure he's only a decoy, not the one we have to be concerned with now. We're hoping he'll lead us to our suspect. That's why the FBI agents are here. They've been tracking him for a long time." Matt raked his hand through his hair. "You'll need your gun, and you can't be afraid to use it on him." Oh, God, he hated to have to talk like this, hated to see her take this risk. "Understand?"

"I understand." She lowered her eyes and looked away from him.

"Look, Jess, we're both a little tense about this. It's no different from any other case we've worked. I trust you to follow your instincts. You're good at it, sweetheart." He turned her face toward him.

"I'll do my best." She blushed.

"With a lot of help, we're going to get through this." He stroked her cheek. "We're going to get him. Oh, I almost forgot. Frank and Radar will be arriving on

Friday, which should give us one more weapon. If you have any questions or concerns, be sure to let me know."

"I will. I should say the same thing to you."

Matt grabbed the remote. "Do you mind?"

"Be my guest." She walked over to her computer, turned it on, and scrolled through her emails. "Matt, Jeremy wants you to call him when you get a chance. He said he tried to call you and left you a message."

"Tell him I'll call. I want to catch the scores first."

"Men and their sports," she muttered under her breath. "I think I'm going to bed." She turned her computer off and stood. She walked over to him instead, and stood in front of him, chin up, with her hands on her hips. "I have one question for you."

"I figured you might. I was waiting for it." He grinned. "Go ahead and ask away."

"Since when do partners withhold information from each other? And while you're at it, you may as well tell me why you asked for information from my friend behind my back."

He put his glasses on. "Earlier, Katie gave me the list of guests who were coming, and I asked Jeremy to check them out. I didn't want his findings to influence you. Your instinct will kick in, and you'll know who bothers you without reading this list, but I'll let you read it if you want." He reached for the paper and held it toward her. "As for going behind your back, I didn't. I sent him the info as soon as I got it. That's all there is to it." His eyes narrowed. "There was no grand conspiracy to keep you out of the loop. I do lots of things during the day at work, and I don't tell you all of them any more than you have to tell me every last thing you do."

She could feel the heat on her neck and blinked back tears. "You don't have to show me the list. I understand."

"Jess, I'm trying to make this as easy for you as I can. If you want more information, ask me. I will give you whatever I can."

"Thank you." She shook her head. "I don't understand what's wrong with me."

"I do. I feel wound as tight as a top. Jess, the stress you've been under for days would make anyone edgy, including me." He patted the open space beside him. "I'm getting a cramp in my neck looking up at you."

She sat down beside him. He turned on the TV, and they watched it together. She relaxed into his side and leaned her head on his shoulder. It would be okay.

Chapter 28

Jessie awakened Friday morning to an overwhelming sense of sadness. The sun was shining over the cove, but she could feel the grief hanging over the small community, ripping at its very soul. Her pillow was wet from the tears she had shed throughout the night.

If she felt this way, what did Emma's family feel? Maybe she was experiencing what they felt. She turned the water on in the shower and stepped in beneath its steady flow. The tension eased in her body. If only she could rid her mind of thoughts so easily. "Emma, everyone is so sad. He might have killed you, but he couldn't extinguish the light you were to those who love you. Matt Parker will do everything that he can to bring your family justice." She spoke the words aloud, sending them into the air, hoping Emma could hear her.

Her heart was a little lighter when she walked out of the room an hour later to the smell of coffee and bacon. Matt was busy cooking. She could live with the idea of a man who would cook for her. She smiled. He was so handsome standing at the stove. Yes, she could live with him standing in the kitchen every morning.

"Good morning, sunshine." He glanced at her and then back at the skillet on the stove. "How was your night?"

"It was a sad one. I guess what the Wilsons and

Emma's fiancé are going through finally hit me last night."

"I know, today won't be easy for the family. The Wilsons have been a part of this community a long time. They have so many friends whose kids went to school with their son, Brett. He married Lisa, a girl from Rocky Pointe, and they moved to Providence many years ago. Emma and her sister Kendra spent most of their summers here in Blue Cove with their grandparents before Kendra got married." He flipped the bacon over.

"People in a small community tend to know each other, and their lives intersect. Dick and Amanda have longtime friends here who will support them through the hard days ahead, and they will need them." Jessie sighed.

Matt nodded. "By the way, they loved the story you wrote about Emma. Amanda made me promise to tell you."

"I'm glad. It was nice of her to think of me." She looked out the kitchen window at the bright sunshine. "At least it's not another gray day."

"I agree with you there. The sunshine is better than a gloomy day." He whipped the eggs in the bowl, poured in the cream, and added several different spices.

She leaned her hip against the counter, content to watch him. "I wonder what surprises this day holds for us?" She looked up, tilting her head. Would he be there? She glanced again at Matt. "Mmm, that smells so good." She closed her eyes. "What can I do?"

He handed her the bread. "Toast this."

She put the bread in the toaster. "What made you decide to cook this morning?" She buttered the slices as they popped up.

"It's how I deal with stress. Breakfast sounded good, and I'm hungry. Coffee is ready, grab a cup and sit down while I finish." Matt handed her a mug, and she added the coffee and little cream.

She stood where she was and watched him. "Do you think he'll show today?"

He glanced at her and reached to turn off the burner. "There's no doubt in my mind that he'll be there or at least nearby, so he can gloat." He handed her a plate and then scooped some eggs onto his. "Let's eat while it's hot."

She put a slice of toast, a piece of bacon, and a spoonful of eggs onto her plate and noticed him watching her, shaking his head. "I don't usually eat much for breakfast."

"Jess, you have to eat more than that. You'll make the cook feel bad." He grinned at her and placed another slice of bacon and a large scoop of eggs on her plate. "Now you have breakfast."

"I can hardly think of eating this much when I know he'll be there today." She set her plate on the table and sat down.

"I won't let anything happen to you." He sat in the chair across from her.

"I know you won't, but that's not what bothers me." She leaned her chin against her hand and looked down at the table. "It's the idea that he will be somewhere in the shadows gloating while Emma's family is suffering. Life seems so unjust." Her first bite of eggs hit her taste buds with a burst of flavors.

"It does at that." He lifted her chin. "Sweetheart, you can't think about the injustice, or you will never do any living. My only thought is to get justice for the family." He ate a piece of bacon.

"I know you're right." She frowned and took a bite of her eggs. "Oh my, these are good." She took another bite. "What's in them?"

"My secret recipe. If I told you, I'd have to kill you." He watched her eat another bite. "It looks as if you might eat breakfast after all."

"I've never tasted eggs like this before." She wiped her mouth with her napkin. "As good as these eggs are, and the cook, too, I admit I'm still worried about today."

"Look, if it's any consolation, I have several officers who'll be watching for him in the vicinity of the church. A team was there all night to make sure he didn't get in and hide. They'll go over the building from one end to the other and double-check. The problem is that we don't know who we're looking for. He might have changed his appearance. I'm sort of counting on you and your head, sweetheart, to tell me if he's close by."

"What if it doesn't work this time, and I don't know?" She frowned. It could happen.

"Not to worry. We'll just do it the old-fashioned way with manpower and observation. Don't put any unneeded pressure on yourself, Jess. Things have a way of working out." He took her hand in his. "If you have any premonitions, see any ghosts, or get feelings, please let me know." He locked eyes with her.

"I'll tell you." She looked away from his intense gaze and took a sip of coffee. "I can't promise anything, though."

"I'm not asking you to. Just stay close to me. Don't

leave my side for any reason without letting me know. That way, I can keep my eyes on you. And it makes my job easier. I like looking at you and having you close by." He gently turned her face toward him again.

"You don't have to worry. I won't be going anywhere without you today," she told him.

"Good to know. Now, eat and stop worrying, please." He finished everything on his plate. Jessie noticed.

****

Matt took her hand as they walked into the church. She reached for the bulletin the usher was handing out.

"Is this one of your creations?" Matt asked her quietly.

She shook her head. "These were done by the funeral home." They got in line, and both of them signed the guestbook. They walked toward the sanctuary, and that's when she saw the floral dress. Gina and Emma were standing in the hall. Jessie felt drawn to them as she observed their actions. They were staring at her. She shivered. Interesting!

"Did you say something?" Matt tugged on her hand to get her to move.

"They're here." She kept turning her head to watch them until she couldn't see them anymore.

"Who's here?" He let her slip into the row first and then followed her.

"Gina and Emma are standing in the hallway. I saw them." She slipped off her coat and arranged it on the pew beside her.

"I can't believe how nonchalant you are about seeing two dead people standing out in the hall. I can still remember the first time you saw Gina. You were as

199

pale as she must have been."

"I may appear calm, but my insides are in turmoil. They're here for a reason." She smiled at Reba, who made a beeline for them.

"Hello, Matthew," she said as she scooted by him when he stood. "Are your parents going to be here today? If I remember correctly, they knew the Wilsons." Reba sat beside Jessie.

"Yes, they are friends with Brett and Lisa, but they won't make it. They wanted to be at the service, but they've been on a cruise in the Mediterranean, and there was no way they could get back in time." He smiled at Reba.

"That's too bad. I was hoping to see them. They'll have to meet this lovely young woman at some point, won't they?" She glanced at Matt. He smiled and nodded.

Reba leaned over and whispered in Jessie's ear. "Have you seen them yet? You know who I mean."

"Yes, they're here." Jessie reached for a tissue when Pastor John walked in followed by the family and Pastor Kevin.

"I'm surprised that Gina is here. Once they are free, they don't usually return unless...it's as you said, she's watching over the church," Reba said softly. "Or maybe it's more about justice."

The music started to play, and a video of Emma's life began. "Emma is here too." Jessie dabbed at her eyes with the tissue. Reba patted her hand, and that's when Jessie felt him. Panicking, she forced herself to take a deep breath. She looked around the church, but no one stood out to her. Gina was agitated, moving up and down the aisle. She knew he was there, too. Emma was at the front of the sanctuary, her eyes fixed on her family.

Jessie bent her head to whisper in Matt's ear. "He's somewhere close. I can sense him close by and so does Gina."

"In the building?" he asked.

"He could be...I don't know." Jessie turned her head again to look at the back of the church.

"I'll text Dylan to keep his eyes open." He took his phone from his pocket.

****

Jessie watched the family file out at the close of the service. She closed her eyes for a moment. A flash of the murder scene went through her mind. He was taking a sick delight in what he had done. She shivered. Jessie felt Reba lean toward her, and she opened her eyes.

"Funerals are never easy, but when it is for someone so young, it's harder still." Reba touched a tissue to her cheek.

"I know." Jessie grabbed Reba's hand and held it for a moment. The atmosphere in the church felt different. He had been here all right, but where was he now? She glanced around the sanctuary. Could he be hiding? The sick, nauseating feeling slowly was replaced with outrage.

"Is he still here?" Matt stood up as people started to leave the sanctuary.

"I don't think so...I don't know." She stood up beside Matt and waited for Reba to gather her things. Jessie grabbed her purse and coat.

"We should have left when you felt it." He frowned at her.

"You told Dylan. What more could we have done?

I don't know if he was even in the building." She glared right back at him. "You would have disturbed the service, not to mention the family."

"I hope we didn't miss our chance."

"We didn't." She grabbed his arm. "This isn't the time or place. We don't even know who we're looking for. You'll get him."

"I hope your faith in me isn't misplaced," he whispered in her ear.

"Never," she mouthed at him and saw him smile.

"We should go and talk to the family." He moved into the aisle so Reba and Jessie could get out. Matt took her hand and led her toward the kitchen area.

Jessie stood beside Matt while he talked to Brett, Emma's dad. She let her eyes travel around the room. People shouldn't wait for moments like this to talk. She needed to call her parents and invite them to come for a visit. They would love her store. At least, her mom would. Her dad would have to pout first.

"Hey, Blondie…" Melinda touched her arm. "Did you see her?"

"I did." Jessie turned around to visit with her.

"I kind of like having her around."

"Why's that?"

"I don't know. Maybe it makes me feel a little safer to know that someone cares about what goes on in this crazy life we live."

"Most people would be scared, but not you, Red."

"Scared of Gina? Never!" She gave a short laugh. "But there're plenty of living folks I'm afraid of. Earlier, I saw this old man walking down the hall. He scared me."

"Why?" It was him! Jessie knew it.

"There was something creepy about him. He was tall, but all hunched over and wrinkled. Something was off about this guy. His eyes didn't look right, maybe too young for the rest of him. I went out of my way to avoid him." Melinda twisted the ring on her finger. "I can talk to anybody, you know me. When I said hello and shook his hand, I wanted to get as far away from him as I could." Melinda grimaced.

"I'm glad you did. I've learned that if someone makes you feel uncomfortable, there's usually a darn good reason for it. Go with your instinct every time." Jessie waved at someone who called her name. "Have you ever seen him before?"

"Not that I know of, but there was something about his eyes that seemed familiar." Melinda shuddered, her red curls bouncing on her shoulders. "I guess I had better bring some of the other desserts out from the kitchen. It looks like we're running a little low." She started to turn around and then came back to Jessie. "Oh, I almost forgot. He said to give this to the church secretary…maybe it's a contribution for the family. She handed Jessie an envelope, Jessie ripped it open and read the note inside.

"He was here in disguise," she said to Matt the minute Brett walked away.

"What makes you think that?" He studied her face.

"Something that Melinda just told me." She related Melinda's words to him. "And this." She handed him the note.

Jessie, my blue-eyed angel, are you ready? It's almost time for our dance.

"Damn, he was here, and we missed him." Matt took the envelope and note from her hand. "Evidence," he mumbled. "Melinda told you something important you need to remember."

"What?"

"You'll know him by his eyes. You said the same thing when you looked at the composite. There was something familiar about his eyes. No matter how he changes his appearance, you'll be able to tell him by his eyes."

"You're right." Jessie felt herself getting excited. She had something to go on now. Maybe looking at pictures from high school could trigger something. After they'd talked to Dick and Amanda, they left.

"I hope you don't mind leaving early." He opened the church door for her.

"I don't mind. The fresh air feels good; it was getting stuffy in there." She took a deep breath. "I need to get to the store."

****

When they reached the parking lot, Matt motioned for her to wait and made a call. "Hey, Dylan, did you see anyone strange this morning?" Matt glanced in Jessie's direction. She waited by his car, her head turned away from him.

"Not until right before the service. I stopped and talked to an old man who was wandering the halls. He said he was looking for the family. When I took him to the area, he didn't go in but said he needed to use the men's room. I saw him standing there later when the family came out, and he got in line behind them, but I never did see him again with the family. I thought that was a little strange."

"What does your gut tell you about him?" Matt took a deep breath as he waited for Dylan's answer.

"He was nice enough, I guess. Something seemed off about him though. The family didn't acknowledge him when he got in line, and I don't remember seeing him go into the church with them. Just before the family went into the sanctuary for the service, he slipped out of line and went to the men's room again."

"You said he was an older gentleman?" Matt clenched his fist.

"He was, and I remember thinking he must have bladder trouble." Dylan paused. "Why, what's on your mind?"

"Melinda described a man to Jessie that she had seen at the church. Something about him bothered her." He relayed the details Jessie had given him. "Does that sound like the same guy you saw?"

"That's him, but like I said, he told us he was a part of the family. I didn't think to question him any further."

"I understand. We think that he may have been our perp in disguise. Did you notice anything else about him?"

"If it was him, it was a hell of a disguise." Dylan's eyebrows rose. "He looked like an old man except for maybe…his eyes. Their shade of brown surprised me, along with how young they looked. They weren't brown exactly but more like an amber color, which is very unusual and easy to remember."

"The color was probably from tinted contacts. Earlier, witnesses at the church described the color as emerald green, so who knows what his true eye color is. The one constant is that he's tall. Let me know if you remember anything else. We'll talk later." Matt hung up and glanced over to find Jessie watching him. "Dylan noticed our guy."

"I figured that out listening to your side of the conversation. What happened?" She walked over to where he stood.

"The man told him he was a part of the family. Hell, how sick is that? Dylan noticed his eyes, too. Amber in color, he says, which tells me he's wearing contacts. His eyes are the standout, so you need to concentrate on that."

"I will." She took a deep breath and closed her eyes.

Matt could almost see the wheels turning in her head. "Think hard, Jess, you have to know who those eyes belong to."

"I've done nothing *but* think about them. They have a dreamlike quality to them. Dreamy eyes, who do I know who has dreamy eyes?" She scrunched her face in thought.

"I can't help you there. I never thought of any guy as having dreamy eyes."

"No, but plenty of girls have. I'm trying to think of someone that the girls at school used to say had dreamy eyes."

"I think of him more as a chameleon with all of his disguises. That's our code name for him." He took her hand. "I'll walk you to your store." They crossed the street. "I'll be back to get you after work. What's on your agenda for the day?"

"I'm going to look in my yearbook to see if I can find the boy that belongs to those eyes." She went in and stood at the window watching him until he was in his car driving away.

Chapter 29

He waited until the last moment. Grabbing a few cookies from the kitchen, he left the church to traipse through the woods behind the building. He smirked as he remembered their grief-stricken faces. Looking over his shoulder more than once, he followed the path, dodging behind trees at the slightest sound, to the place where he was staying. The old fleabag motel suited his purpose. Off the beaten path and away from prying eyes, it was a dream spot for him. He wanted to stay longer, but something had felt different about the church this morning. He shivered. He had felt someone watching him, but he never saw the person. A cold chill ran down his spine.

"Ah, home sweet home," he muttered as he stuck the key in the lock.

He looked around the room. What a dump. From the orange shag carpet to the brown bedspread with big orange and blue flowers, it was an eyesore. He opened the small refrigerator and grabbed a soda.

Pulling the tab, he walked over to the old beat-up dresser on the other side of the room and stood in front of the mirror. The wig came off first. He took a swig of the soda. How good it felt to get that damn thing off his head. It made him all sweaty. He ran his hands through his black hair, tousling it. Placing his hands on both sides of his face, he carefully rolled the disguise from it.

He grinned. He had removed years from his face in a moment. He chuckled as he pulled off the old man's sweater and tossed it aside. His fake gut followed quickly, and he scratched his stomach as he released the itchy material from his middle. He looked down and admired his six-pack abs that he had worked hard to maintain. Jessie would be impressed. The contacts were the last item he took off. He placed them carefully in their box. Brown eyes were nice, but he liked his own better.

He stretched out on the bed with his arms stacked behind his head. What a morning! He had walked into the church as a grieving relative. Only she knew he was there. She always knew. They were simpatico. It was getting exciting. His body throbbed with anticipation. He had waited a lifetime for this dance. She was almost his equal but not quite. His note was a nice touch, and by now, she knew he definitely had been there.

He would have liked to have stayed and played the game with her, but the cop never left her side. Besides, he hadn't liked what he felt. The fear had taken him by surprise. He couldn't stay around Blue Cove much longer. He might have stayed too long, but he couldn't get rid of the obsession he felt.

She was in his dreams, always at the edges of his thoughts, and in all his fantasies. He needed to leave, but he had to stay. He jumped up, turned the shower on, and stared as the water swirled down the drain. He would stay…he had to. He had a few more surprises up his sleeve. A diabolical laugh slipped from his lips. The devil was in the mood to play; yes, he was. It would be over too soon.

Chapter 30

During a lull in business, she looked up her yearbook online and went through it page by page, scrutinizing one photo after another. No one stood out. He could be older or younger. She glanced away from the computer when the bell on the door rang. She'd check a few years ahead of and behind her class later on.

"It's just me," Molly called out to her. "I've come to get a couple more books in that series I'm reading."

"You liked it. I thought you would." Jessie walked toward Molly. "She's such a fun author to read."

"I could hardly put them down. Now, I need my fix. With Kenny taking classes at night, I have to keep myself busy."

"I've always found a good book is the perfect way to be entertained when you're alone."

"As fast as I read those, maybe I should buy four this time." Molly lifted the next four books in the series from the shelf. "At this rate, I'll single-handedly keep you in business."

"I'm happy to oblige you." Jessie carried the small stack back to the counter. "Now, you can go home and read."

"Not yet. I'm on my way to the market. If I don't get there today, we won't be eating tonight. I had to stop here first, though. Some things are more important than food." Molly paused to laugh. "I'm sure Kenny wouldn't agree, but he doesn't need to know." She grabbed the bag Jessie handed to her and turned to leave. "Oh, look, Reba's here. You two have a cozy chat, and I'll catch up with you later." Molly held the door open for Reba on her way out.

"Thank you, Molly. I see you've been shopping. That's what I've come to do myself." Reba walked toward Jessie, a smile on her face. "Do you have this book? I read a review on it this morning and thought I would give it a try." She handed a piece of paper to Jessie.

"This book came in the delivery that I just opened." Jessie walked to the counter where she had placed the books she had unboxed earlier. "It's on the bestseller list already." She picked up a copy and handed it to Reba.

"I'll take it." She took her wallet out of her purse. "That was a sad service this morning, but a beautiful one. It's odd how that works."

"I know what you mean." Jessie gave Reba her change, placed a bookmark in the book, and slipped it into a bag. "Here you go." She handed Reba the bag.

"We'll, I'm off, but I did want to mention to you that a third person will cross your path, and you'll have to deal with him. He's not here for you, but your paths will intersect. That's all I know about him. You have a lovely evening, Jessie dear, and don't worry. It's all going to be all right. I know you might find that hard to believe right now, but it's true nevertheless." She waved and hurried out of the store.

Darn her. Jessie stared at her as she left smiling. How could she drop a bombshell like that and just leave? Another person here in Blue Cove? What was up with that? She looked at the clock on the wall. Thirty minutes until closing time. Grabbing the stack of books, she carried them to the front of the store and arranged them on her special display table. One more piece of information to add more weight to Matt's overtaxed mind.

****

Matt had talked to several agencies in the various towns where the perp had left his murderous trail. Each agreed to send one officer to help on Saturday night at the Inn. He could cover more ground with the extra officers and stood a better chance of catching the guy. With the FBI agents keeping an eye out for the hitman and more than a little luck, they might be able to come out of the evening unscathed.

Matt answered his phone. "Hey, Frank, what's up?"

"I will definitely come on Friday to be there to help out on Saturday. If you have the clothes your victim was wearing at the time of her murder, your suspect's scent will be on them. If he's still in the area, we'll find him."

"Great, Frank, your help is appreciated. He's after Jessie." Matt filled him in on the man's appearance at the funeral service.

"We'll get him," Frank answered. "I'll see you on Friday."

"I think you're right. We'll talk when you get here. Of course, you're staying at my place."

Things were starting to come together. Matt didn't know for sure that their man would show up on Saturday. He had a hunch, though, and he was working it as if it were a fact. His plan was coming together. In one more week, the monster would either be dead or put away.

"Matt, you have a call on line one." Joe's voice came over the intercom.

"Thanks, Gary." Matt picked up the receiver and pushed line one. "This is Matt."

"Matt, I've been going over the info you gave me. I think I might have some possible suspects for you to look at. I thought I might drive to Blue Cove next week and bring the photos with me. I just emailed you what I have."

"Thanks, Jeremy; we can use all the help we can get. I'll look at what you have and get back to you later." He drummed his fingers on his desk.

"Sounds good. See you."

Matt looked at his watch. Time to pick up Jessie. Matt straightened his desk and stood up to leave. He picked up his file, put on his jacket, and closed his office door behind him.

"Hey, Matt, wait up." Dylan caught up to him when he stopped. "Can I meet with you first thing Monday? I need to fill you in on what's happening in my case."

"We need to get everyone together. I've been on the phone all day with the other jurisdictions involved, and a plan has started to come together. We should coordinate with everyone involved. I'll let Maxwell know, and you can tell the other agents working with you."

"What time works for you?"

"First thing Monday. Let's say nine." Matt started to walk away and then turned back. "If you think I need to know anything before that, give me a call. I think these cases are starting to intersect. The man you're watching has to know about our serial killer. He's calculating his next move, I'm sure. I need to pick up Jessie, so why don't I call you after dinner?"

"That's fine with me." He walked with Matt to the door and told him a few of his concerns on the way.

The minute he pulled up to her store, she was out the door and locking it. "Reba came by the store today, and I bet you can't guess what she had to say."

He grinned at her. "I probably couldn't, so why don't you just tell me and make it easy for me, sweetheart?"

"Well, you know how Reba said there were two men here for the purpose of getting us? Not anymore." She shook her head. "Instead of two, it's up to three."

Chapter 31

If Matt had been driving instead of parked, he would have slammed on his brakes. Instead, he lifted his hand quickly, hitting the review mirror and knocking it cockeyed. "What the hell do you mean there are three?"

"My thought exactly. She simply dumped it on me and left the store before I could ask her any more questions. She did say that he wasn't here for me, but our paths would cross. Whatever that means! To tell you the truth, Matt, I'm a little tired of these men even getting near my path."

"I don't know what to tell you." Matt shook his head, feeling gut-punched. "Why is it that every criminal in the area has decided lately that Blue Cove is his or her destination of choice? Do you think Reba has an answer for that question?" Matt adjusted the review mirror and glanced at her. He'd love to brush this off, but Reba's predictions were about as accurate as Jess's.

Jessie was frowning as she latched her seat belt. "It reminded me, though, that I have to take this threat seriously."

"Damn, right you do," he snapped back. She'd better take it very seriously. "This isn't over by any means. As of matter of fact, a few new developments have surfaced that we need to talk about. Let's go to dinner, and I'll fill you in." He pulled onto Main Street, heading back toward Blue Cove Drive.

"Where are we going?"

"There's a great little café in the Seaside Resort. It's nice and quiet there this time of year. We can talk. Plus, they serve a great blue plate special."

****

She loved the quaintness of the place. From its intimate table arrangements to its Parisian café feel, it was perfect. The panoramic view of the cove must be great in the summer months when the doors were open, and people sat outside at one of the patio tables. She could imagine the place packed with tourists. It was too dark to see much other than the reflection of the lights dancing across the water. She chose a grilled chicken breast on a bed of greens, and Matt ordered the fish and chips.

"This is what I love about this town." She gestured toward the windows. "The view of the cove is amazing from so many places. I never tire of looking at it."

"I've lived here so long that I guess I just don't notice it much anymore."

"How is that possible? It's so beautiful. Go live in New York for a while where all you see is one building after another. You'll come back here and notice quick enough."

"I suppose you're right. Don't get me wrong, I love the days when I can take the time to enjoy it, but some days when I'm working it's the last thing on my mind."

"What came up today that we need to talk about?" She placed her hand over his, stilling his drumming fingers.

"I talked to Jeremy and Frank. Jeremy has been looking into some possible suspects on the list of folks coming on Saturday. He's also headed our way for a few days next week. Frank is coming in on Friday. He wanted to make sure to be here on Saturday."

"I know you can use the extra hands. With Tom and the extra agents that are already here, you should be in good shape." She studied his face.

"I also talked to the other jurisdictions involved." He stifled a yawn. He hadn't felt this beat in a long time. "Each one has agreed to send an officer to help secure the perimeter on Saturday."

"Won't it tip him off when all these cops descend on the town?"

"That's where our plans started to centralize. He uses a disguise, and so can we. They'll be coming in as ordinary citizens, with no patrol cars. I'll have them stationed in various spots around the Inn and through the woods. We can't forget that we also have a hired gun in the area and, now, this third man. If he exists." He stopped talking as the waiter approached the table with their meals.

"I'm pretty sure he's for real. Reba hasn't been wrong yet." She sounded so calm. "Only time will tell how he plays into it. You may as well accept the fact there is a third man here that will impact Saturday in some way." She took her first bite of salad. "This is so good." She closed her eyes, and a smile lit up her face.

"I love your expression when you enjoy what you're eating," Matt grinned at her; although, he felt like pounding on the table. How could she be so calm when this whole thing seemed poised to spin out of control? He poured a little vinegar on his fish and chips. "We are meeting on Monday to finalize our plans. I'll have more details for you then. But, as you know, the best-laid plans can fail. We now have a third guy, and it may come down to you taking one of them out."

"I understand that. I think I can do it." She glanced at him. "Although, it might be harder for me if I recognize him."

Oh, crap, that's right. He could be an old high school friend. "Hell, I didn't need to hear that," he said heavily. "You won't be able to second guess yourself, or you might end up dead. You'd better work this out in your head now." Too late, he realized how harsh his tone sounded and winced as she flushed.

"I have a few days so quit crabbing at me. I'll work it through." She stabbed her fork into the salad. "Right now, I want to eat my meal in peace. No wonder you're so crabby. You can't have good digestion when you always growling and thinking about worst case scenarios."

He blinked. She had stunned him. But she smiled back when he gave her a weak grin. He reached over and tousled her hair. "You're something, you know it? I do get a little crabby when I'm in the middle of a case."

"A little?" She rolled her eyes. "A lot would be more accurate." Her smile widened. "Do you treat everyone this way, or am I the only one that gets the brunt of your charm? I use that last word loosely."

"I never acted this way until you came along." He put on an expression of mock despair. "I think you're a bad influence, or you've cast a spell over me. I'm really a likable guy."

"That's debatable. I'll cast a spell over you." She gave him a playful slap on the arm.

"Seriously, I find myself worried about you often." He dropped the banter. "And it does make me a little crazy."

"That's sweet of you; you don't need to be. I'll work with you to keep me safe." Her lips curved into a smile. "I kind of like living. Besides, this odd relationship thing we have going has me intrigued. I'm curious to see how it's going to turn out."

"You and me both, sweetheart..." He reached across the table and traced his fingertip from her cheek to her chin, pausing at her lips. "I'm extremely interested. My future happiness is invested in it."

"There you go. We are both committed to keeping me alive, and we both have good reasons to do so. I'll put up with a little growling if you put up with my doubts. Just remember, my strong caveman guy, you trained me, and I can take care of myself."

They shook hands on it playfully and then ordered a hot fudge sundae to share for dessert.

****

The weekend flew by, and Monday was a cold, crisp morning. Some of the snow had melted and the week was supposed to be a warmer one. Matt hoped the weather predictions were right. The less snow they had to contend with, the better.

"Are you about ready? I need to get to work," Matt called out to her as he poured her coffee.

She opened her bedroom door, walked into the kitchen, and saluted him. "Aye, aye, captain..." She reached for the cup he held in his hand.

"Be careful, it's hot."

"I have an early delivery this morning." She sipped her coffee.

He watched her open the freezer and drop a piece of ice into her coffee. "I told you it was hot. You just defeated the whole idea of a cup of hot coffee."

"I don't mind hot, but a burnt tongue is not what I'm looking for." She took another sip. "Now that's better." She sighed.

Matt shook his head. "This is the week, so stay alert. He may not be predictable."

"What do you mean?"

"He might show up before Saturday and test the waters. Truthfully, I don't know what to expect. I'm throwing out random warnings. I know you might not like hearing them, but it makes me feel better." Matt unplugged the coffee maker and rinsed out his cup. "Do you want something to eat?"

"No." She shook her head. "I need to get to work too."

"Are you sure?"

"I'm sure." She kissed his cheek. "You can hand out your warnings as you see fit. I'll take it in stride. I don't want you worrying about me. You have enough on your plate."

"Worrying about you might be a full-time job, the way your past keeps showing up in Blue Cove." He gave her a swat on her backside with a towel. "Let's get going. I've got a big meeting, and I need to meet with Dylan first."

She put on her jacket and grabbed her purse. "You do know that I can drive myself, and I can stay at my place too."

"Like I'm ever going let that happen while this maniac is in our area. You're going to have to put up with me hanging around and like it."

She grinned back at him. "Okay, since it's your choice, not mine, you'll have to be patient as you wait."

She walked out the door.

He turned in time to see the snowball come flying at him. She was in for it now. He chased her down in a few seconds and tossed a handful of snow in the air over her head. Her laughter made him laugh too, and it actually made him feel better. "What was that for?" He tried to catch his breath, but he couldn't stop laughing.

"You're too serious, Mr. Parker. Sometimes you need a good laugh. It helps. Believe me, I know."

They walked to the car hand in hand, and he couldn't stop grinning at her. He loved the way she looked in the morning…any time of the day for that matter. She made him laugh and want to pull his hair out, but mostly she made him dream about a life with her by his side.

****

The Devil had watched the little scene play out between them. He didn't like it. Jessie was his. The vein in his neck pulsed, his jaw clenched, and his hand curled into a fist. He cursed and slammed his fist against the trunk of the huge pine tree repeatedly. A warm sticky sensation penetrated through his rage and pulled him back to reality. His eyes opened wide, and he slapped his bloody hand to his forehead. Feeling faint at the sight of his own blood, whimpering, he curled into a fetal position and slept.

Chapter 32

"I'll be back to pick you up at five or maybe a little later, but don't go anywhere." He parked the car in front of the store to let her off.

"As if I could." She sighed. "I don't have a car, remember?" She unhooked her seatbelt and reached for the door handle.

"You know what I mean. Hang tight, I'll be here. Call me if anything comes up?"

"I will. I work at the church tomorrow for a few hours, and Audrey will be here." She opened the door.

"Jess," he called after her. "Have a good day, sweetheart."

"You too," she said and waved as she shut the car door. She unlocked the store and went in, locking the door again once inside. She noticed the mail on the floor beneath the mail slot and bent down to pick it up. She carried it with her to the counter to sort through it. The computer on the counter came on. It was time to catch up on her accounts and pay some bills.

Her stomach grumbled as she called Molly's cell number. "Are you working today?" she asked when Molly answered.

"I am. What can I get you, as if I need to ask?"

"You don't." She smiled. "I'll meet you at the doors in ten minutes with my money in hand plus a tip."

"All right, ten minutes it is."

Jessie paid Molly, locked the doors, and went back to do her work. She took a bite of the scone. Mmm, this was one of her favorites. With mixed berries, a light glaze, and just a hint of lemon, it made her taste buds sing. She looked at her watch when she finished her accounts and found she still had forty minutes before opening time. The stack of mail on the counter was next. The letter opener slid through envelope after envelope until she came to the last one. There were a few bills, a letter from Mom, and…what was this? She eyed the blank envelope with no stamp as she slit it open and took out the folded piece of paper. "Here we go again!" she mumbled.

It simply said,

On your mark, get ready, now run for your life.

She turned it over several times. Possibly the same writing…she took a closer look, but she wasn't sure. It didn't sound like him, though, or feel like him for that matter. She had known when he had handled something before, and this didn't feel the same.

She turned it over again. It had to be him, didn't it? Could someone else have sent it? But who and why? Whoever it was would have to take a number and get in line. She knew Matt was busy this morning, but she tried him anyway. No go. He was still in meetings, so she left a message with Gary to have Matt call her when he had a break. She opened her store and didn't look at the clock again until lunchtime. Joe's was busy and so was her store. She hoped the trend would continue. She had a five-year plan for making a profit, and as of today, she was ahead of schedule, which was a good turn of events. Retail was fickle. She heard the bell ring and looked up to see Katie waving at Liam and Connor, who had just dropped her off.

"Honestly, those two don't let me out of their sight. I'm tripping over them every time I turn around." Katie removed her coat and sat down in the nearest chair. "I'm here to see my best friend and catch up on the news. The boys are shopping for Saturday and made me promise not to take one step outside your store until they come to get me."

"I'm glad that Liam is taking this threat seriously. He's your big brother, and he should be looking out for you." Jessie sat in the chair across from Katie and kept a watchful eye on the customers in the store. "How many are coming?"

"So far, we have twenty-five confirmed and two maybes."

"That's quite a few; it should be an interesting night." Jessie stood up when a customer walked to the counter to check out.

"Did you find what you were looking for?" she asked him.

"I did. You have a nice little store here." He looked around the room. "It was a smart move on your part to open up your store next to the coffee shop. I'm sure it has been good for both of your businesses. You see the combination in a lot of large chain bookstores in major cities but not so much in small towns." He handed Jessie his credit card. He looked around the store several times and over at Katie. "You have some business savvy."

"Thank you, I think it's worked out well for both of us." She swiped the card and handed it back to him, then watched him sign his name. "Have a nice day." She placed a bookmark in his bag. *That was weird.*

Jessie watched him leave. *What a strange little man.* His signature matched the one on his card: Ian Brewster. She had never seen it before.

Before she caught up with Katie again, she checked out three more customers. "Do you remember when we read Corrine's books together?"

"Of course. We had so much fun reading them. I hate waiting for the next one, but I'm sure she can't write them as fast as we can read them." Katie picked up a book from the table and read the blurb on the cover. "Do you have any recommendations for my next read?"

"As a matter of fact, I do." She handed three books to Katie. "This is a new author I discovered, and she's really good. She has quite a few books out, so you can read hers while you wait."

Katie nodded. "Sounds good. I like reading in bed at night. It helps me settle down."

"I know what you mean; although, lately I've had too much on my mind to enjoy it."

"I'm going to run over to Joe's." Katie pointed at the connecting doors. "If Liam comes back, you can show him where I am. I want an iced tea. Do you want one?"

"Sounds perfect." Jessie straightened things while she waited. There were no customers at the moment, so she had time to talk.

Katie sat down in one of the leather chairs and placed the two glasses of tea on the table. "I'm afraid, Jessie."

"Why? I mean other than the fact we have some guy running around town who kills women, what's there to be afraid of?"

"You're being sarcastic." She raised an eyebrow. "You always get like that when you're nervous."

"No one knows me better than you do. You've seen all my flaws and are still my best friend." Jessie twisted a strand of hair around her finger. "I'm totally sarcastic when I get nervous. Truthfully, I'm afraid too. He could be there Saturday night, and what if, this time, I don't know it?"

"I suppose anything is possible. I don't know how you do know it, so I guess I wouldn't be surprised if you didn't know it. Does that make sense? It sounded a little odd to me."

Jessie giggled. "It's weird, but it made perfect sense to me."

"I hope Matt is taking this seriously. I can't handle the thought that this man is here to get you. We could know him. Have you thought about that?" Katie tapped her hand.

"I've thought about it often enough. Lately, I've been trying to figure out why Gina has shown up again."

Katie's eyes narrowed. "What do you mean Gina's back?" Katie's head tilted, and she crinkled her nose.

"She was at Emma's funeral and so was Emma."

"You are beyond peculiar; you see these crazy things and talk as if it's a normal occurrence."

"It's sort of becoming that to me." Jessie rubbed the nape of her neck. "I don't know what to do about it. I can't get distressed every time I see or hear something. It's happening too often right now."

"What else aren't you telling me?" Katie pointed at her. "I know you well enough to know something's bothering you, and you haven't told me about it yet."

Jessie handed her the note. "This arrived today. I haven't had a chance to show it to Matt yet. He's been in meetings all day." Jessie stood up and paced. "The other day Reba told me there is a third person we need to be concerned with. Add a ghost into the equation, and you can understand that I have a lot on my mind."

"Oh, Jessie, I don't understand how you deal with this. It would be too much for me."

"That's probably why I'm so sarcastic. You have to keep this to yourself. I don't want to mess up Matt's case. This is one time you have to keep a secret; someone's life may depend on it."

"I'm not a kid anymore. I get it that this is serious stuff." Katie's smile evaporated. "You can count on me. How do you keep all of this junk inside you?"

"I'm obviously not doing a good job at it because I needed to talk about it to somebody. You walked in at the right time—or the wrong time, depending on how you look at it."

"All I know, friend, is that I'm not going to let anything happen to you, so I'll be keeping my eyes open too. Liam and Connor are here. Are you ready for this?"

"Sure, but Matt will probably show up now and not be happy."

"I think Matt needs a little competition. He moves far too slowly for a man in love."

"No, he doesn't. I'm the one dragging my feet." She felt her face getting hot. "I'm into him and no one else. But, I'm not ready to turn control of my life over to a man, any man, just yet. There are times when I've gotten close, though. Matt is so different from anyone I know. He gets me."

"Don't leave him dangling too long. There are plenty of women who would love to be in your place."

"He's not dangling. We're just taking it slow."

"Yeah, whatever." She rolled her eyes. "Matt's not the kind to hang around you like some of the others you've dated. You'd better remember that."

"What should she remember, sis?" Liam threw his arm around Katie as she stood up.

"None of your business, brother dear."

"Don't let my sis boss you around, Jessie. Put her in her place." He grabbed Jessie and pulled her into his side.

"If I were you, brother, I'd take my hands off Matt's girl. He's not going to like it much, and he just pulled up."

Jessie saw his reaction the minute he walked through the door. He walked over to her and kissed her cheek. "Hi." She looked into his eyes and smiled.

"Sorry, I didn't call you. I got the message as I was leaving, and I figured I would see you in a few, so I'd talk to you in person."

"We'll see you guys later." Katie started dragging Liam toward the door. "These two lugs don't know it yet, but they're taking me to dinner."

"Why don't you both join us?" Liam was trying to free himself from Katie's clutches, but she held tight.

Jessie eyed Matt, and he nodded. "Where are you headed? We'll catch up in a few minutes."

"Patterson's," Liam shouted out. "If we're paying, then we're choosing."

"See you when you get there." Katie waved at them. "Bye, and don't do anything I wouldn't do, which gives you plenty of wiggle room." Katie giggled and pulled Liam out the door.

"We don't have to go with them if you don't want to. I can still call and tell them we aren't coming." Jessie turned to look at Matt.

"It's fine. You relax when you're with your friends. I don't mind Liam once in a while."

"I need to show you something." She grabbed Matt's hand, led him to the counter, and handed him the note. "This was in with my mail. It must have been pushed through the mail slot."

He looked at it and then at her. "Damn, Jess, it never stops with you. At least, I know who this one is."

"Do you mind filling me in? I would like to know what I'm up against." That ticked her off—that he knew. And she didn't!

"This is the hitman who was in Palm Springs watching us. I guess he decided to get in the game. He always notifies his victims of the hunt before he starts." Matt frowned.

"That's awfully sweet of him." She lifted her chin, her eyes narrowed.

Matt rubbed his temple. "I admit I'm a little surprised. These guys like to get in and out with a clean hit. He has to know that our suspect is also watching you. I don't know what to think. I need to let Dylan know, and I'll turn this over to the agents."

"You can call Dylan while I close up the store." She closed the doors leading to Joe's and locked them. She put the money from the register into the safe, shut off the back room lights, and joined him with her coat and purse in hand.

"Are you ready, sweetheart?" He reached for her coat, holding it for her to put on.

"All ready." She smiled at him. "I was thinking that there are so many bad guys vying to get me that maybe they'll trip over each other and hurt themselves." She laughed at his expression. "What, you don't you think it's possible? All I'm saying is it could happen."

"Not likely."

"Aren't you the one always telling me that they're just men and not invincible? I agree with you, they're merely men. They made a big mistake picking on this girl this time. I'm tired of bullies." She shut off the lights in the main part of the store.

"The way it's been going, these two are going to have to stand in a long line of folks wanting to get at you. In the end, they are going to have to fight their way through me." He took the keys from her and locked the door.

"You're sweet. I love it when you get all tough and protective. You are my knight all over again." She slipped into the car when he held the door open for her.

"The reason we have this hitman now, if I remember correctly, is because you got all tough and protective and shot another hired gun to save me. Doesn't that make you my knight?" He grinned at her.

"I don't know." Her brows rose. "Do they knight women? I'm not sure of the tradition. If they do, I guess that makes me your knight. Either way, women are more than capable. "

"You're telling me, sweetheart. I think you could do almost anything you set your mind to."

"I'm glad to hear you say that because it might take everything I have to stay alive through all of this. I wonder…" A brief sadness swept over her.

"What."

"I wonder if I'll ever be able to enjoy the quiet life I envisioned when I first moved here."

"You haven't been bored, that's for sure."

"That's true."

"You've had some good times and met some nice folks." His fingers drummed on the steering wheel.

"True again." She laughed, that fleeting shadow gone as quickly as it had fallen over her. "So what's your point?"

"Outside of a ghost or two, being shot at, and nearly blown up, it's been good so far, don't you think? I mean, haven't you always dreamed of a life like this?" He chuckled. "Let's meet our friends and eat. I might even be generous tonight and not knock Liam out if he puts his arm around you again."

"How magnanimous of you, Mr. Parker." She laughed, liking this man so much. "I'm sure Liam will appreciate your restraint on his behalf. Not to mention his face will be happy."

"You're in a good mood considering the note I just read."

"To tell you the truth, I'm trying to figure out how Gina fits into all this. I haven't given much thought to the note yet. I'm sure that will come later on. Speaking of being in a good mood, why aren't *you* blowing a gasket over this?'"

"I've spent all day in meetings. I've planned as much as anyone can for the situation that we now find ourselves in, and I'm optimistic." He grinned at her. "I think you're rubbing off on me in a good way." He grabbed her hand. "I have a good feeling about all this. Besides, the good guys win; all the movies tell you that."

She hadn't seen him so playful in a while, and it was a good thing. He'd been too tense. "Well, there you go," she said gaily. "We're the good guys, and they are definitely the bad guys. I guess they may as well pack it in. Their days are numbered." She rubbed her hands together and gave him a teasing look. "I suppose somebody ought to tell them about it."

"Why, Jess, that's exactly what we're going to do, sweetheart. We're about to serve their eviction notices and give them a new permanent address in a location far away from here, where they'll never bother us again." He opened her door. "Let's eat. I'm hungry." He took her hand. "After dinner, it's you and me, sweetheart, and some darts." He turned her face toward him. "The game is on."

Chapter 33

Audrey was at the shop, and Jessie sat at her desk at the church. Last night had been fun. Matt had beaten Liam and Connor at pool, darts, and wits. She smiled just thinking about it. Liam, at one point, had told her that Matt was a real stand-up guy, but it didn't mean he was giving up. They weren't married yet. She felt her smile broaden. Liam would figure out soon enough that she wasn't interested. He'd always been a bit thick headed.

Melinda came bouncing into her office, sat down in the chair in front of her desk, and slid a piece of paper toward her. "When Pastor John gets here, he needs to call this lady." She slapped her hand to her forehead in a dramatic fashion. "I've done my duty, but I don't know why. You should have seen her this morning. She came in earlier, wanting to talk to a pastor. She was indescribable." Melinda shuddered and made a strange face.

"What makes you say that?" Jessie looked at the name, Bertha Worth, written on the paper.

"Well, let me tell you." Melinda's eyes opened wide. "She looked like a Russian woman weightlifter or something. She was freaking big and lumpy. I could see her tossing cabers at a Scottish festival and holding her own. Her hands were twice the size of mine..." Melinda held up her hand and turned it over. "And her glasses…" Melinda's voice grew louder with each word. "They were so thick that they made her eyes look all distorted."

"Was she an older woman?" Jessie saw movement out of the corner of her eye and caught a glimpse of Gina's floral dress as she moved quickly past the open doorway.

"I sure hope so; her face had enough wrinkles on it. She walked all hunched over with a walker, but she could really move that thing. After I told her the pastor wasn't here and got her phone number, she booked it out of here." Melinda was shaking her head. "She was here, and then she was gone. I don't mean to be unkind, but she was one ugly woman." She pulled her glasses off. "I was wearing these, too. My eyes may never be the same."

Chill spider-feet tracked down her arms. "Did she say what she wanted to talk to the pastor about?" Jessie had her eyes on Melinda but was aware that Gina was now watching them.

"She said she needed to set her house in order—like maybe she was dying or something."

"That's sad…the poor dear." The chilly spiders were galloping now. There was more to this story than met the eye. Way more. "I'll make sure he gets the message."

"Tell him to talk to her on the phone or be sure to have tons of backup around in case of an emergency."

"She couldn't have been that bad." Jessie bit her lip as she tried hard not to laugh.

"You didn't see her. I'm telling you, she was scary. She had a wart on the end of her nose."

Jessie laughed. "Oh, Red, you are something. I

think you may be embellishing her looks a wee bit."

Melinda shook her head. "Just be sure to tell Pastor John what I said. I've never seen a woman who looked like that before."

"Tell who what?" Pastor John startled them both.

Melinda proceeded to tell him. "I mean it; don't let her come in here unless you have at least five or six men with you. In case she gets upset."

"Melinda, I think you might be exaggerating a little." John smiled at her. "I'll remember your recommendation, though. In fact, I may never forget it." He chuckled.

Melinda jumped up out of the chair. "Okay, I've taken care of it. I'll get to work." She waited until the pastor walked down the hall toward his office, then bent close to Jessie. "All I know is that Gina didn't like her," she said softly. "She was all stirred up, and I don't want to see her again either." Melinda walked out of the office.

Jessie shook her head. It wasn't possible, was it? No, she shook her head again. It couldn't be, or could it? She felt that chilly shiver down her arms again. Maybe…The lighted line indicated that Pastor John was on the phone. To Melinda's mystery woman that upset Gina? She got to work and kept busy with several phone calls of her own.

"Hi, sunshine." Gary walked into the office followed by Matt.

"What are you two doing here?" She tilted her head to look up at them.

"We got a call from Pastor John, saying we needed to talk," Gary answered her.

"I'll let him know you're here." She picked up the

phone. "Pastor, Matt Parker and Gary are here to see you." She nodded. "He'll be right out." She smiled at them.

Pastor John walked into the reception area and shook their hands. "Jessie, I think you need to join us on this one. We can let the phone go to the answering machine, or Pastor Kevin will answer it when he gets here."

Jessie followed them into the office and sat down in one of the chairs. Her heart was racing. She had a feeling that her earlier guess had been right. "Are you sure you want me in here, sir?"

"Yes, this concerns you, I think. Melinda told me a story about a woman who came to the church this morning." He looked from one man to the other. "I thought she might have been embellishing her descriptions a little, but now I'm not so sure." He proceeded to tell them what Melinda had told them earlier. "I talked to her for a while, and the conversation still has me puzzled."

"What did she tell you?" Gary asked sharply.

"Her name is Bertha Worth, but I'm not even sure about that, anymore. Anyway, she told me she called because she needed to set her house in order, and she wanted me to absolve her of her sins. I told her I wasn't a priest, but I could pray with her for forgiveness if she wanted." John frowned, closing his eyes for a moment. "She said she needed forgiveness because she had cheated on her ultimate dance partner. She said she'd been saving a dance for a special person, but she blew it and danced with an unworthy partner and that nothing would be the same now." John looked at Matt. "Does any of this make sense to you? It doesn't to me either, but there was something about her tone…." He broke off and frowned. "I thought I maybe needed to bring you in on this. Considering what has been going on here."

"The chameleon has changed his colors again." Matt looked at Jessie, then back to the pastor. "I think you were probably talking to our suspect. He was telling you he killed someone other than Jessie. Dance to him is murder. He was saving himself, trying not to kill anyone else until his ultimate dance with Jessie, but he cheated on her by killing someone else—perhaps our recent murder victim."

John shook his head. "That's sick," he said unsteadily. "I prayed for the man or woman for forgiveness."

"You couldn't know, Pastor. You were doing your job."

"Melinda told me before she left my office that Gina didn't like the woman and was stirred up."

"Are you telling me people actually see Gina? I've heard the rumors." Pastor John raked his hand through his hair.

Jessie nodded. "Something is up. That's for sure."

"I'm sure it was probably a disposable phone, but let's try to call big Bertha." Matt tried the number, but sure enough, there was no answer. "Gary, see if you can trace it. I'm doubtful, but they're never as smart as they think they are."

"What should I do? This isn't the first time he's come into this church." Pastor John's voice rose. "How do I keep the women safe here?"

Matt frowned. "I think we need to put someone in the building to keep an eye on things, if that's okay with you."

"I'd be happy to have one of your men here. It bothers me that Melinda met this person when she was alone in the building. I think Jessie shouldn't work here until he's caught."

"I agree with that." Matt glanced at her, clearly worried. "If Jessie had been in here alone, it wouldn't have been good."

"I hate to let him think he's won by scaring me away from work. Maybe I could work in the afternoon when you're all here."

"No." Matt shook his head. "Pastor John is right. Your presence will keep him coming into the building and putting others at risk. I doubt that you'll miss more than a week of work. It seems to be coming to a head." Matt looked at John. "I'll get someone in the building to watch over the church. Do you have an extra key?"

"I do." He handed the set of keys to Matt.

"You may need to let Melinda know, or I can talk to her before I leave if you want." John nodded. "She needs to understand she has the right to ask to see a badge if someone is in the building. If this guy knows we have someone in here, he might try to impersonate an officer."

"I never thought of that." John frowned.

"Melinda has met him three times now, twice when she was alone in the building. I think it might be good if she doesn't come in until you are all here." Matt glanced at the John.

"That's a good idea. I don't want anything to happen to her." John wrote a reminder on his notepad. "I hope you get this guy soon."

"We do, too, Pastor." Matt stood to leave. "Thanks

for the call. Let us know if you see anyone who looks suspicious to you. You can't be too careful at this point."

"I agree." John stood to walk Matt out.

She felt the anger start to rise. Her lips pursed. No, she shook her head, not this time. This was no ordinary situation. She was glad to have a man take charge. She didn't want anyone else to be hurt.

****

Matt's voice startled her.

"Jess, I don't want you to think I was high-handed in there. I know you can take care of yourself, but I need to look out for the other women in the church too. Our chameleon is getting out of control. Don't be mad, sweetheart."

"I'm not, really." She looked up through her lashes at him, her head tilted. "Okay, well maybe, at first. Old habits die hard," she sighed. "But you're right, I realized it pretty quickly. I don't want to be the reason Melinda gets hurt or anyone else."

He lifted her chin to look her in the eyes. "I have every confidence in you. You know that, Jess, don't you? If your not working here for a while makes him think he has won, it might work to our advantage. He might relax and make a mistake. We need every advantage we can find."

"I thought of that, actually." She smiled. "I know you're right, and I'm okay with it."

"Thanks for understanding, Jess." He looked so relieved. "We have a chance to stop this guy, that's what is important now. You're going to be bait, as it is. You don't want to attract him at the wrong time and place." He started to leave but turned back around. "Do you know what I think? If you're honest with yourself, you need to admit you're scared. He's getting to you. "

"How'd you jump to that dumb conclusion?" She felt her face get hot and heard the edge of sarcasm in her voice.

"You feel you can't control what he does, and it bothers you." Matt's eyes were on her face. "He's invaded your world and your friends. You know I'm right. You're feeling out of control."

"Even if you're right, what can I do about it?" She felt her shoulders slump.

"You're the one who taught me you can't always be in control when others are involved. You have to go with your gut." Matt's tone was gentle. "You'll do what's right, and I'll be standing by you to help."

"I like everything to work the way it should, and when it doesn't, I need a plan to get it back under control. You're right." She clenched both fists. "I can't control him or his movement. He doesn't fit into some neat little package, and the closer I come to facing him…" she shivered. "Matt, I don't know if I can do it."

Matt placed his hand on her shoulder. "I hope you never have to and that we get him before he gets that close to you."

"You know there's no way around it." She looked up to meet his eyes, found them full of compassion. "We're going to have to meet. That's what this is all about."

"Yes, but can I say that he's never met the likes of you before." Matt smiled. "He's going to lose this one."

"Thank you, Matt. I needed to hear that." She leaned into him briefly as he kissed her cheek.

"I need to go. Gary is talking to Melinda." He walked out of the office door. "We'll get him, don't worry," he called back over his shoulder.

Chapter 34

He knew what Jessie was feeling because he felt that fear every time he thought of her near the perp. Matt sat at his desk, staring at the faded calendar on the wall without seeing it. The best plans could always go wrong. He'd seen it happen more than once. If something went wrong, he could very well lose her. He let his breath out in a rush. Even the thought of it made him sick. Every case, he felt the same way. At some point, he had to believe she was capable, or he would worry day and night.

"Matt, can we talk a moment?" Dylan knocked on Matt's open door and stepped in.

"Sure, what's up?" Matt leaned his elbow on the desk. "Sit down."

"We've been following the man in the green sedan hoping he'd lead us to our hitman. No such luck so far. We know he's around the area, but have no idea where. We did notice something, though, on one of our stakeouts."

"What was that?"

"When you were out the other night with all of Jessie's friends, we noticed a new tail. When you all left the restaurant, this guy followed Liam and Connor."

"You actually saw him?"

"Yeah." Dylan nodded. "We decided to follow him. He followed Liam's car to Blue Iris Lane where he pulled over when they turned. He sat there in the car. About twenty minutes later, he drove back to the Inn, turned around, and came back to the highway. We followed him until he drove out of town."

"Tom thinks Liam might be in the crosshairs. That's why he's here. He thinks that could be the reason for him suddenly showing up in Blue Cove."

"Liam's putting Katie and Jessie in danger, doesn't he realize that?" Dylan asked.

"I doubt he's even aware that they know where he is. He probably feels safe." Matt glanced at his open file. "If I hadn't gotten wind of the hitman stalking us in Palm Springs, I never would have thought about it. We've put people in prison before with no hired gun and no problems."

"The last time was different, though, we all knew retaliation was a possibility. Our Jessie shot a hitman. Booker wasn't too happy about his takedown by a rookie—and a woman to boot. He probably hired the guy from prison." Dylan chuckled and grinned.

"True, my girl seems to be at the center of almost everything going on in this town that is of a criminal nature." Matt's smile faded.

"She attracts her fair share of them, that's for sure." Dylan stood. "So what do we do about the guy watching Liam if he shows up again?"

"I'll let Tom know what you saw. He's the one handling Liam's case." Matt made himself a note to call Tom. "Did you hear about what happened at the church today?" Matt told him about his conversation with Pastor John.

"It makes you wonder how he'll look when he shows up for Jessie." Dylan shook his head.

"One can only guess. I think his pride will make him want to come as himself. Whether he will or not remains to be seen. Remember, he is trying to impress her. This chameleon has taken the meaning of the word to a completely new level. I'm not sure what to expect, and neither is Jessie." Matt frowned. "It has me genuinely worried."

"She'll know, don't you think?" Dylan leaned his hip against the wall.

"I sure as hell hope so."

****

She liked being in her store. Matt was right, she needed to stay away from the church for a while. The thought of him being alone in the building with Melinda was more than Jessie could handle. Melinda was quirky, unconventional, and unique. She made even the mundane seem interesting.

The afternoon was quiet with only a few customers in the store. Joe's was quiet too. Jessie picked up a book on the table with the idea of reading it. Instead, she found herself lost in thought until the bell on the door pulled her back to her immediate surroundings. A man came in. She noticed as she stood and set the book back on the table that a tour bus had parked across the street. People were starting to exit the bus. No time to read now. The man's back was still to her.

"May I help you?" She started to move but stopped when he turned toward her.

"Yes, I think you might be able to." He smiled, and her stomach turned queasy.

Jessie gripped the back of the chair. Don't you dare faint now! She noticed his eyes, but the rest of him didn't make any sense. His hair color didn't seem right.

Another color change. Mesmerizing eyes, almost hypnotic. There was no doubt it was him. She found her voice. "What do you want? I have other customers coming."

"Yes, I know. I had to risk seeing you for a moment. You're just as sweet as I remember. I have to leave now, but I'll see you again real soon."

"Do I know you?" She saw him nod.

"Of course, you do. Did I mean so little to you that you have no memory of me? I think about you day and night, sweet Jessie. Soon enough, you'll know who I am." He started to move toward her.

Her legs felt heavy and unable to move. "You could just tell me your name."

"No." His chuckle was menacing. "We'll reminisce together soon. Remember to save the last dance for me." The bell above the door rang. He smirked, waved, and slipped through the doors into the coffee shop.

She followed as soon as she could get herself to move, but he was already gone. He wasn't anywhere on the street. How had he moved so fast? She fumbled her phone out of her pocket. "Matt, this is Jessie. He was here with me. In my store." The words tumbled out.

"Calm down. I can hardly understand you. He was there?"

"Yes, he was here."

"Are you okay?" Matt's voice was hoarse. "I'll be right there."

"I'm fine; he's gone. He left when a bus tour arrived. He was here…" her voice trailed off.

"Jess, I'm coming."

"I knew him, don't you see, I'm telling you that I knew him."

"You know his name?"

"No, no, I knew it was him. He won't be able to take me by surprise." Jessie smiled at the folks coming in the door. "His eyes are a dead giveaway. They're almost hypnotic. The minute he smiled, I thought I would be sick. Just a minute, Matt." She showed a woman where a book was. "I'm back, but I need to go. I have customers."

"I'll be there in a few minutes."

"You don't need to. I'm okay."

"I'm coming." He hung up the phone

Secretly, she was happy he was coming. She was still a little shook.

****

He slipped out the back door, peeling off a few layers as he went. No time to pick up what he dropped. Keep moving. He crossed the street and headed to the wooded area behind the church, walking through the graveyard. What a day this had been. Smiling, he could hardly contain himself. A chuckle rumbled through his chest and made it to his lips. He looked at the church building as he passed by it. The devil had gone to church this morning, yes he had. A smile spread across his face. The building was still standing and didn't look any the worse for wear. He'd even had a conversation with the pastor, which had started his day off with a bang. The roof hadn't collapsed either. Duly counseled, prayed for, and forgiven, he was ready to get on his way. A devil, a happy devil.

He had seen her. The excitement coursed through him. Risky, yes, but worth it. His body vibrated with his craving. A few more days…she would recognize him in a few more days.

What was that? He saw the movement out of the corner of his eye. He rubbed them, not trusting what he saw. It couldn't be. His heart raced. She was coming closer. He ran. Impossible! He pushed through the brush, the limbs of the trees slapping at him, tearing his skin. She was right behind him. He felt her icy breath on his neck. *Keep running, you fool. Don't look back.* He jerked his head around. The burning stitch in his side left him breathless, gasping for air. The heart pounding in his chest felt like it was going to explode. He had to get to the car. Scrambling, he slid down the hill, rolling part of the way to the pavement below. He flung the car door open and fumbled the key into the ignition. His eyes wide with terror, he drove the back road out of Blue Cove.

Be rational, he kept chanting, it was only a hallucination. He would return in a day or two. He had to, she was there, and he was addicted. Only for Jessie would he go back, only for her. His body shivered and twitched. It had been a powerful hallucination; he could still feel the effects of it.

Chapter 35

Matt walked into the store and waited for Jessie to finish with a customer. The minute she was free, he was by her side. "Are you okay?" He paced in front of the counter.

"Yes, please sit down, Matt. Your pacing will scare away my customers." She sat beside him and told him what she could remember of the conversation. "His last words to me were, 'remember to save the last dance for me.' I followed him once I unfroze, but I couldn't see him in Joe's or out on the street. He moved fast."

"What do you think? Do you know him?" Matt leaned forward in the chair.

"He definitely knows me and seemed a little upset that I couldn't recall who he was. All I know are the eyes and the sick feeling I get. He had another disguise of some sort on because the rest of him didn't make sense. His face was too thin for his body size." Jessie described what she could remember to Matt.

"Do you want protection while you work here?"

"I don't think it's necessary. I don't think he'll be back. He took a risk today with all the people around." She patted his hand. "I'll be safe."

"That's not a sure thing, Jess. This is serious." His face looked almost gaunt with worry. "This guy is brazen and getting bolder all the time, I'm going to be sending someone in to keep an eye on things." He saw her shake her head. "Yes. He won't be here all the time, but he will come. This is not open for discussion."

Her shoulders slumped. "You do what you think is best."

"That's exactly what I plan to do. We still have a few days until Saturday."

"What if he doesn't show on Saturday?" She reached for his hand.

"We'll be on guard until he does show. He's going to try for you at some point. On that, I think we can both agree." Matt stood up and looked around. "Your store is getting busy. I'll be back in a little while to get you." He kissed her lightly, turned, and walked through the connecting doors into the coffee shop.

"Hi, Matt, what can I get you?" Molly looked up from drying a frothing pitcher.

"Nothing, I need to ask you a few questions." He leaned against the counter.

"Fire away." She cleaned the counter with the rag in her hand.

"Did you see a man come through here? Jessie described him as a large man, thick around the middle, light hair, with a large nose." Matt waited impatiently for her response.

"I did. He asked for the bathroom and never came back this way. I figured he might have gone out the back door. I hope that helps."

"Thanks, Molly, you've been very helpful." Matt went out the back door. He bent down and, using a napkin, picked up a strange looking object on the ground. It looked like a fake nose. Interesting, He called his team in. They found several items tossed carelessly into the trash. All were a part of the disguise he'd worn.

They got DNA, yes, but the Chameleon wasn't in the system.

Matt noticed there was some kind of padding in the sweater they found, which would make him look bigger. He remembered Jessie saying his face looked too thin for his body. Matt noticed a dark hair and a lighter one on the sweater. He took a pair of tweezers, carefully lifted the hairs, and slipped them into the plastic bag. With any luck, one of these might be his real hair color.

The man must have walked out the door, removing each of the items as he went. What did he change into after this? Matt looked again at the nosepiece. He pulled out his phone. "Jared, this is Matt. I'm curious about something." He explained to Jared about the nosepiece. "Do you think you can reconstruct what his actual nose might look like from this?"

"It's possible. I can change the nose shape on the composite once I see it. I'll swing by to pick it up, and have it ready for you sometime tomorrow."

"Thanks, Jared, that would be great. I also found a light hair and dark, almost black hair on his sweater. Try him with black hair too. You never know what facial feature or hair color might trigger Jessie's memory of this guy."

As soon as Jared arrived, Matt wrapped it up and went to the store to get Jessie. It had been a long day, and dinner at Mindy's Grill was his peace offering for making her wait.

****

She was too quiet. He could only see her profile. She had turned her face from him, lost in her own thoughts, staring out the window. "Sweetheart, Jess."

He patted her hand. "What are you thinking about?"

"He was in my shop today. I should have shot him. I wasn't ready. I didn't have my badge or gun. I should have. I could've stopped him."

"Jess, cut yourself some slack, you didn't know he would come today, and you've had very little training to do this work. I've asked too much of you." His thumb stroked the back of her hand.

"I'm tired of him killing at will. I can only hope he will face his accusers because I didn't seem capable of doing anything at all today." She dabbed at her eyes.

"You were faced with a scary situation, and you did all right. If there is any justice at all, he will pay for his crimes. We have to hold on to that for the families' sake."

"I was scared, but more than anything, I'm mad at myself for not being ready. I knew a confrontation was possible, and I got caught not looking. His calm, arrogant manner makes me angry every time I think of him standing there."

"I get that, but what's this all about really, Jess?"

"If he comes into my store again, do I have to wait until he attacks me to shoot him?" She frowned, drumming her fingers against his hand. "If I just shot him on sight, would you arrest me?" He didn't answer but let her talk. "I wanted to wipe that sick smirk off his face." She rubbed her forehead. "I'm ashamed to say it's contrary to who I am. It bothers me that I felt such an intense hatred for him. I wanted to cause him the pain he's caused others, but instead, I just stood there and did nothing."

"There is a protocol, and you know it. You'd have to try to follow it."

"I knew that's what you'd say, and I know you're right. It's the only way I wouldn't lose my humanity, but I've never felt that kind of anger before." She shook her head.

"Now you know what I battle." He let his breath out in a slow sigh. "That's why I remodel things and need someone like you to help keep me in check. Hell, I don't know anyone who wouldn't want to blast that guy off the face of the earth."

"So what's your advice to me?" She gazed into his eyes.

"Write about it, sweetheart. Don't give him the power to make you hate. Tell your readers about him and his crimes. Carry your gun. Wear your badge. You can attempt an arrest if he comes in the store again. If he comes after you or tries to flee, you can shoot him as long as it doesn't put anyone else in jeopardy. It is a store after all." He smiled at her. "Are you better now, or do you want to leave?"

"I can eat now. It's just that…well, I was so angry with myself for doing nothing. I just stood there, frozen in place, and let him leave. He could kill again, and I could have done something to stop him. I don't want to feel this unprepared or angry again." She opened the menu.

"Jess, you constantly amaze me." He was dumbfounded. "Here I was worried that you were traumatized by seeing the guy, and you were angry for not stopping him." He touched her cheek and gazed into her eyes. "It's no wonder that I love you."

"The feeling is mutual you know." Her smile reached her eyes this time. "Thanks for listening."

Chapter 36

Matt walked into her store with the new composite drawings to show her. She was standing in the open doorway to Joe's talking to Molly. They were laughing about something. Her whole face lit up, and he felt the familiar catch in his heart. What had he done to deserve her? Whatever it was, he was grateful. He placed the folder on the table and walked up behind her, wrapping his arms around her and resting his chin on the top of her head.

"Hello, Mr. Chief of Police." Molly smiled at him.

"How's it going?" He nodded at Molly.

"Good." She smiled, her eyes dancing with mischief. "Why, Matt Parker, are you sweet on my friend?"

"You could say that." He grinned at Molly.

"It's about time that you two figured it out." Molly shook her head.

"Is that right?" Matt grinned.

"We all got it even if you two couldn't see it. It's been a waiting game with bets on the outcome placed all over town." She laughed. "Kenny will have to pay up now. I can see a new couch in my future."

"I think we're catching on, what do you think, sweetheart?"

"I think Molly needs to get to work. There's getting to be a line at the counter." She pointed, and

Molly's eyes followed. "I also think you must be here for a reason. It's the middle of the day. But to answer your question, officer, I would say that unless they placed their bets on us getting together, they're going to lose money."

"See you two lovebirds later; as you said, I need to get back to work. Remember, guys, the doors are open," Molly called over her shoulder as she walked away.

Matt led Jessie over to the table and pulled out a chair. He sat down across from her. "Jared worked up a new composite based on some of our new evidence. I wanted you to look at them." He pushed the first of two pictures toward her.

"So that's what his nose looks like. I'm not sure." She frowned, her eyes on it. "Something is still off."

He pushed the second sketch over to her. "Take your time."

Her eyes moved back and forth between the sketches but rested on the second one. "This one reminds me of someone I've seen before. Now if I can only figure out who he is and how I know him, we'll have it made." She pushed the sketch of the man with dark hair back to him. "His hair is definitely dark. The other must be a wig. It didn't look right on him."

"Good, Jess, we're one step closer than we were. The rest will come to you." He handed her the drawing back. "You can keep it, we made copies."

She opened her jacket and showed him her badge. "I took your advice. The gun is in my drawer at the counter. I didn't want to scare my customers. I doubt that he'll come back, but I'm ready if he does."

"Frank will be coming in tomorrow. He seems to

think that if we take the dog to the scene of the crime, Radar can track all the places in town where our suspect may have gone, including where he might be staying."

"That's good. It would be great if we could get him before he does anything more. Don't forget we have dinner tomorrow night at the Inn. We have to help Katie get everything ready for Saturday."

"I told Frank we would be at the Inn tomorrow night." He stood up. "I need to get back to the station." He smiled, wishing that he could simply take her hand and go spend this day with her. "It's a warm day out, and I almost hate to go back to work."

"That reminds me." She smiled up at him. "I wanted to ask you if we could run outside tonight. It's so nice. I feel like I've been cooped up inside forever."

"Sure, I'll run with you. I know you don't like the gym as much as you like running outside."

"Thanks." She walked with him to the door. They got there just in time for him to hold the door open for Reba, who was coming in. "See you later."

****

"I had to stop by to see if you have any more books by the same author. I really enjoyed reading the last one. I find I'm in a reading mood now." Reba followed Jessie over to the shelf that held the author's books.

"I thought you would enjoy her books. As you can see, she has quite a few."

"I think I'll pick up several. They're easy reading and enjoyable." Reba spent a few minutes reading the book descriptions and picked out three.

"How have you been?" Jessie rang up her purchase.

"No small talk for us, we're beyond that, girl." The

bell above the door rang, and she lowered her voice. "There's an extremely unsettled aura over Blue Cove. I'm at a loss to explain it. Gina is here, no doubt about it, and so is Emma. We've seen them, but I think there is something more going on here. It's been crazy active, everywhere I go." Reba watched the woman walk into the coffee shop. "I'm not trying to scare you, but something big is about to happen."

Jessie leaned toward Reba and spoke quietly. "They're here to help us catch their murderer. I can't believe I'm even saying this. My, have times changed."

"My thoughts exactly. It could get real interesting around here." Reba patted Jessie's hand.

"I'm not afraid. I was, but I'm not now. Blue Cove is where it will all end for him. I can't tell everybody this stuff, but I know you'll understand."

"My dear girl, he'll be sorry he ever came to our town." Reba walked toward the chairs. "Do you mind if I sit down? I would like to chat with you when you're free and read when you're busy."

"That sounds like a perfect afternoon to me. Would you like a cup of tea?"

"I'll just pop next door and get each of us one. I'll be right back." She returned a few minutes later with two cups of tea and peach scones.

Jessie helped a couple of customers and then sat down by Reba. "Thank you for the tea." She took a sip.

Reba placed the bookmark in her book. "I think this should all be over soon. It's so active I don't even know where to start." She made eye contact with Jessie. "This man is from your past and not recently either. He's been around the edges of your life for a long while. He doesn't look like he once did." Reba paused to look at her. "The minute you see him as he is, you'll remember him. He's a problem, but he'll never be able to hurt you. That's what Gina and Emma are here for." She took a bite of her scone.

"I thought the same thing, but I needed to hear it from someone else, I guess." Jessie slumped forward in the chair with her face in her hands. "What about the man you saw outside the store? When you sent Lawrence to the rescue that night?"

"That's a little tricky to figure out. He's in plain sight, but there is someone behind the scenes. I'm a little concerned about him. I haven't been able to figure out what he's going to do. He's been observing until recently, but I think he's in the game now." Reba wiped the crumbs from the scone off her lap.

"He must be the hitman. He sent us a note telling us to run for our lives a few days ago."

"That must have been when he made his decision." Reba appeared thoughtful.

"Who is the third man you told me about the other day?"

"Ah, yes, the third man—I can't figure him out at all. He's here, and he's in it, but not after you. That's all I know. He may be the most dangerous of all because—well—I just don't know." Reba's brow furrowed. "I wish I understood all of this, but you only see what you see. I know you understand."

"It's okay. It's amazing what you do know. Somehow, we'll get through this, and then I'm done with all of it. I've had enough of all this crazy stuff. I moved here to have a nice quiet life, and this has been anything but that." Jessie sat up straight, a determined look on her face.

"Just let me say, my dear, it doesn't work like that. You can't make it happen, and you can't make it go away." Reba picked up her book and opened it. "A customer just came in the door."

Jessie stood up. "I'll find a way."

"I've been trying to find it for years, dear, and here I am. Now smile and go take care of your customer. I'll sit here and read a while."

****

Matt hung up from one of several conference calls with the various agencies that would send officers in for the weekend. They were, in theory, ready for the weekend. He watched the activity in the park from his window. Plenty of folks were out enjoying the nice warm day. The snowstorm last week was a fast fading memory. An even warmer day was on tap for tomorrow, which boded well for Frank's dog having a successful track. The only snow left would be in the areas that didn't get much sunlight. The murder site was one of those spots, but they had the clothes they'd gathered at the scene with her scent and his on them. Frank thought that would be enough.

"Matt, do you have a minute?" Tom walked into his office.

"Sure, what's up?' Matt turned his chair around.

"I'm pretty sure we have a potential problem. Ian Brewster is in the area. We caught him on camera. Ian has an extensive record and close ties to the Murray family. Liam was defending one of the sons in his last case. The case he lost." Tom pushed a photo of Brewster toward Matt.

"You mentioned you were here to make sure Liam wasn't somehow involved." Matt looked at the photo.

"He's not. His nose is clean, but his client isn't happy. I'm sure Brewster is here to settle the score." Tom frowned, his fingers tapping on the arm of the chair. "I'm concerned for Katie, and anyone at the Inn for that matter. He's not going to leave the area without doing what he came to do."

"I wonder if Jessie knows him. Probably not, that would make it too easy." Matt shrugged. "It looks as if the Inn will be attracting a lot of attention for the next several days. We need to get more eyes in the area, starting this evening. I can spare a couple of officers."

"I'll put a couple of my agents on it too."

Matt nodded. "By Saturday, I'll have several more officers from different agencies who will stack the odds in our favor. Until then, we'll have to make do with what we have. What are we looking at, Tom?"

"It can only be one of two things, as far as I'm concerned. He's here either to rough him up and scare the hell out of him or kill him."

"Sounds like a nice fella. Our town is getting too crowded with them."

"Yeah, what's up with that?" Tom's eyebrows rose.

"Ever since Jessie moved to town, we've been inundated." Matt looked at Tom. "Don't ask me why, I don't have a clue."

"You can't pin any of this on her."

"I'm not, but for some reason, she has become the main attraction." Matt shook his head.

"I'm telling you, hide her, it might help." Tom laughed. "Good luck with getting her to stay hidden."

Dylan knocked and then walked into the office with a grim look on his face. "I needed to let you know that we got a tip on the suspect. Bushman and Hansen were following him from a small town west of here back this way when he gave them the slip. We lost sight of him. He could be anywhere in the area. You and Jessie need to keep your eyes open."

"Damn, the good news keeps rolling in." Matt rubbed his temples.

"We're looking for him, but man, this guy is slippery." Dylan leaned against the wall, his arms folded across his chest.

"I suggest keeping your eyes on the Inn. Everyone seems to be headed there," Matt told him.

"It couldn't hurt." Dylan pushed away from the wall.

"Speaking of the Inn, I need to make my way back there. I don't want to be late for dinner." Tom stood up. "I'll get my guys in place."

"So will I," Matt responded.

Chapter 37

Their running shoes pounded the pathway in tandem. They were making the final push up the hill toward the Inn when Matt suddenly shoved Jessie to the ground and landed on top of her. The bullets had narrowly missed hitting them. What had made him do it? Instinct? Something hadn't felt right, and he'd gone with his gut. It had saved them.

"Ouch, why did you do that?" Jessie tried to sit up.

"Stay down." He pushed her head back down.

"Are you crazy?" She heard the rapid *pop, pop* and laid her head back down fast. One bullet scuffed the dirt not far from them. "Is that what I think it is?

"Yes, keep your head down and stay low to the ground." One bullet ricocheted off the tree trunk to the right of them, spraying bark into the air. "Stay down; we're going to crawl under the cover of the trees so we're not such an easy mark." Matt phoned the station. "Tell them to come with lights and sirens. We're pinned down here on the path from the marina, and we're going to make our way to some trees for cover. We're out in the open now. Call Tom, too!" Two more quick pops sounded.

"Where is he?" She huddled into his side.

"I don't know. If he had intended to kill us, we would already be dead. This is part of the thrill of the hunt for him."

"Only a part of it? Uh, is he nuts?" He could feel her anger.

"Shh, listen." He put his finger to his lips.

"What am I supposed to listening for?" She whispered.

"Any sounds. Is he coming toward us? It's too quiet. We may have to run."

"I can hear the sirens in the distance."

"It's not them that I'm worried about." Matt put his arm around her straining to hear the sounds around him. Where was he? A twig snapped. "Let's run." Keeping low, they zigzagged through the trees. Another bullet scraped the limb above their heads sending pine needles raining down upon them.

Jessie covered her ears with her hands. "I'm tired of being shot at," she said quietly.

"I know, sweetheart." Matt had his Glock out of the holster. "Give me your hat." When she handed it to him, he put the hat on a stick and lifted it above the bush. "Be ready to move." *Pop, pop*. "Run." They ran as Matt fired off a couple of rounds. The woods came alive with the sound of gunfire, and then it was quiet for what seemed like a long time.

"Matt, are you and Jessie okay?" Tom's voice called out to him.

"Did you get him?" Matt stood up and walked toward Tom.

"Not yet, they're still looking."

"You won't find him. He was toying with us. You know his MO. If he had wanted to kill us, he could have. He had us dead to rights coming up the hill. This is the chase before the kill."

"Judging from the look on Jessie's face, I don't

think she was happy with that piece of information." Tom looked over at Jessie, who was sitting on the ground.

"I'm sure she isn't. She's at her limit." Matt turned to look at her. Her nose was crinkled, and she was squinting at the hat she held in her hand. "What's the matter?" He watched her turning the hat over and frowning at it.

"He shot a hole clean through my favorite hat. I wear this when I run. First, it was my car and now my hat. What's next?" She frowned

"As long as it's not you, the rest can be replaced."

"Well, duh, he was shooting at me, wasn't he? If my head had been in this hat, it would be a different story, wouldn't it?" He could see the tears gathering in her eyes.

"I know this isn't easy, but you did shoot Booker, remember? There are a few repercussions for doing that, as you can see." He sat down next to her.

"Matt, are you trying to make me mad?" She glared at him.

"Yes." He smiled at her. "You have to stay in the game and not get defeated. He's not done yet. He'll be back, and if he can get a kill, he'll do it."

"Okay then, I'm good and mad, and you don't have to worry about me." Her eyes sparked. "I'll have to get him before he gets me. I'm not going to be anyone's punching bag anymore. Do you hear me?"

"Yes, I did. They could hear you all the way to the Inn." He winced when she sucker punched him.

"Ha, ha." Jessie frowned at Tom, who was laughing. "What are *you* laughing at?"

"The two of you and I can't help but wonder how

you ever got together." Tom started back up the hill, still laughing.

"Shall we go?" Matt stood up and reached his hand down to help her up.

"Sure, why not." When her hand touched him, he pulled her up. "Thanks." They walked the rest of the way to the cottage. Tom was standing by her back door when they got there.

"It was as you called it. He vanished. We do have some spent shell casings and hopefully a print or least a partial. A Remington 700."

"What does that mean?" Jessie crossed her arms.

"It's a high-powered sniper weapon of choice. Through a scope, our suspect can hit something from a thousand yards." Tom saw Matt shake his head at him too late.

"That's just great. Now, I can be shot and killed from long distance as well as up close and personal." She dropped the key from her pocket into Matt's open hand. "Is that all you men do? Sit around and think up better ways to hurt and kill each other?" She pushed past Matt when he held the door open, mumbling under her breath.

"Sorry, man, sounds like you're going to have a rough night." Tom tried to hide his smile.

"She's right, you know. It's dumb that people keep inventing more high tech ways to take someone's life."

"I know, but we can't stop them. It is what it is."

"It would be nice if we could. I know, I know." He didn't even have to look at Tom's expression. "I'm idealistic."

"I think we've all wished for it at some time. That's why people move from the cities into small towns, but crime has a way of finding them there too."

"I admit that it might be nice to go back to the quiet days of policing Blue Cove when giving a speeding ticket or investigating a barking dog was the highlight of the day."

"Keep your ears open. We'll have extra eyes watching this place tonight." Tom turned to walk away and then turned back with a grin on his face. "You'd better get inside and see if she's okay. To tell you the truth, I feel sorry for the man coming after you. I think he might have met his match in her.

"You may be right. Thanks, Tom." Matt walked inside and closed the door. "Are you okay?"

"Sure, I'm getting used to bullets flying in my direction on a regular basis." She frowned, glancing at him. "I've made a decision."

Matt held his breath for a moment. "Yeah, what's that?" He wasn't about to let her leave town. Unless he could move with her.

"Since I can't seem to stop this stuff from happening to me no matter what I do, I have to become better equipped to handle it. What I need is a little fine tuning, if you know what I mean." Her fingers began tapping on the arm of the chair.

"I'm not sure I understand," He exhaled his breath. God, what would he do if she decided to move away?

"Maybe I need to go to the academy, like Kenny. All I know is that I had better learn to defend and protect. Writing has become a very dangerous job for me." The tapping increased.

He watched her, fascinated by this side of her. "I'll think about it, but I'm not sure it's necessary unless you want to be a cop on the force. You have your store to look after and your writing. I like you on my team, and we work well together. So far, we've handled everything thrown at us together, haven't we?"

"Of course, you're right, I wouldn't want to work at the station or give out tickets." She made a face. "I do love my store and all of my customers. Besides, my self-proclaimed dance partner is about to come face-to-face with a few of his partners from earlier dances." Her chin lifted, and a look Matt hadn't seen before crossed her face.

"What do you mean?" This sounded like Reba talk.

"I mean, I know Gina and Emma are in town, but there is something bigger going on. Reba didn't know what it was exactly. She called it an unsettled aura. I personally think he's in for a dance he didn't bargain for." Her lips turned up at the corners.

"You almost sound like you're looking forward to it." Matt couldn't believe he was saying it.

"I guess I am. He's messed up so many lives. I think that the women he killed should have the last say. Emma gets to end the dance the way *she* wants it to end."

A chilly finger brushed down the back of his neck. She sounded so…sure of this. "Sometimes you completely take me by surprise." He scratched his head. "I thought I was coming in here to be yelled at, and you are thinking of ghostly justice against the Chameleon."

"Now, why would I want to yell at you? You haven't done anything wrong." She looked genuinely puzzled. "He was shooting at you, too!"

Matt shook his head. "Well, for one thing, you weren't too favorable toward men and their quest to find ways to kill each other a moment ago."

"Oh, that." There was a hint of a smile on her lips. "I had just been shot at, cut me some slack. I was speaking of men in general and not you."

"Oh, I see. Or at least, I think I do." He sat down in the chair. Her line of reasoning could make his head spin at times.

"Nothing against you personally, it seems such a waste of life for grown men to spend time figuring out the best ways to cause death when it should be all about living. That's all I'm saying."

"I can agree with you there, but until that happens we have to keep ourselves up with the latest, don't we?"

"I guess, but where does it end?" She pursed her lips. "It's all such a waste. I would prefer to think about other things myself."

He stood up and walked over to her, leaned down to put his hands on the arm of the chair, covering hers. He bent down enough to see eye to eye with her. What would you rather think about, sweetheart?"

"You know friends, travel, and other happy things. Anything would be better than thinking about the next way to take someone's life." She took a deep breath and swallowed.

"I would add *us* to that list." He gazed at her, watching each expression as it crossed her face. "I'm making you nervous again, huh?" He saw her nod, bent closer until her lips were right in front of him, and leaned slowly to whisper in her ear. "I think I'll make us something to eat." He pushed up, grinning, and walked in the kitchen. He didn't turn to look, but he knew and grabbed the pillow before it hit him in the back of the head. She wasn't so lucky.

Chapter 38

Matt had dropped her off at the store, making her promise to call if she needed anything. She smiled. He had emphasized the word *anything* several times and then grinned. She loved that crooked grin of his. True, he could make her nervous with those smoldering eyes of his, but he was fun to be with, too. When he looked at her the way he had last night, it was hard to breathe. She could almost feel her resolve to remain single for a while longer slipping from her grasp. He knew what he was doing to her. He'd said he would wear her down with his charm. She didn't mind making him work for it. What a ride. She fanned her face and walked to the front of the store.

She straightened the display table and answered her ringing phone. "Hey, Jessie, did you remember you're coming to the Inn for dinner tonight?"

"I did, and what good thing are you going to be feeding us?" Jessie glanced out the window. Pastor John and Kevin walked toward the church. Jessie rubbed her eyes. Who was following them?

"My secret, but I will tell you this much, I am serving that wonderful chocolate mousse we had in Palm Springs."

"Yum, I'll be there for sure. Knowing what you went through to get the recipe from the chef is the icing on the cake." Jessie shielded her eyes from the sun's glare with her hand trying to get a better look. What were they doing? They were mingling outside instead of following the pastors into the building. Gina. Emma. There were others moving in and out of her view. She squinted, trying to see if they were in the cemetery. Numerous spirits had gathered at the church.

"Are you listening to me?"

"Of course, why?"

"I told you something, and you didn't say a word." Jessie could almost hear Katie's tapping foot.

"I'm sorry. I must have gotten distracted. I was watching someone walk into the church."

"Would you please pay attention?"

"Sure, repeat what you said." Jessie made herself pay attention. She could see the fluttering of Gina's dress and barely make out someone besides her at the door of the church.

"I said you can help me put together the welcome baskets for everyone, if you don't mind." Katie was clearly irritated.

"Sure! I would love to help you. It sounds fun to me. Of course, you know me. You'll have to show me each step. I can be such a klutz when it comes to making things."

"I have one done, so all you have to do is arrange it the same way. I'll put the bows and everything else on."

"I'm in." Oh my gosh! Jessie's eyes opened wide. They were everywhere. Their suspect was in for a big surprise. Jessie couldn't believe what she was seeing. "I'll see you tonight, Katie. I have to get my store ready to open." Finally, Pastor John and Kevin walked into the church, unknowingly followed by a large group of unseen guests. Jessie almost wished she were at the church.

****

Matt walked with Frank to Emma's murder site with a search warrant in his pocket. He touched it. He had petitioned Judge Sanders to issue one just in case they got lucky. He hoped Radar could get a hit and find the suspect or, at the very least, some of the places where he might have been. Matt handed Frank the bag with Emma's clothes, which also held the man's scent. "This is where we found Emma." Matt pointed to the spot. "Jessie had been jogging in this same area a little earlier when he chased after her. She was able to escape, but Emma wasn't so lucky. Because she saw the murder in a dream, we were able to find Emma's body before the animals got to it."

Frank bent down beside Radar and held the clothes up to him. "Find the man, fella." The dog started the process now familiar to Matt. Radar sniffed the ground around the area and went to the path and back up the hill. He sniffed around Jessie's cottage several times.

"I think he must have been here at some point." Frank looked at Matt.

Matt nodded. "He was, which is scary. It's cool how he can retrace the suspect's steps by his scent."

Frank gave Radar his lead. "He's good at what he does when he gets down to business."

The dog went near the Inn and out to the street, slowly making his way into town. He stopped at the door to Jessie's store. "Do you think he was here?"

"He was here." Matt opened the door, and the dog went through the open doors through Joe's to the back door. Matt smiled at Jessie and waved as he went through. "I know he was back here, too." Radar sniffed

269

around the area and the trash where they had found the sweater the suspect had tossed.

The dog continued down the alley to the side of the first detached building on the street, crossed it, and headed back toward the church. "Do you think he's still on track?" Frank asked. The dog was pulling on his line, and Frank's arm was getting a workout.

"Yes, the suspect has been at the church several times." Radar then went to the cemetery, sniffing his way through it and along the back, through the wooded area. After walking a short distance, they came out in the parking lot of a rundown motel. Matt had almost forgotten this place was here. It was off the beaten path and not a place where a lot of folks would want to stay. Radar sat down in front of room number six. "I'll be right back."

"Can I help you?" The man in the office glared at Matt, scratching the stubble on his face.

"Is anyone staying in room six?" Matt flashed his badge.

"I don't want any trouble, Mister," the manager whined, rubbing his chin. "I run a good establishment here."

"Just answer my question. Is there anyone staying in room six? I need the key." Matt held out his hand when the man nodded.

"I'd have to see a search warrant before I can give you a key. You know how it works, officer." He held the key, his hand tight around it.

Matt pulled the warrant out of his pocket and handed it to him. "The key, now!"

"A real nice gentleman is staying there. Paid me in advance, he did. I haven't seen him in a couple of days, but the room is paid up until Sunday, so it's no skin off my nose where he's at." He pushed the room key toward Matt. "Is he in some kind of trouble?"

"He could be." Matt took the key and walked out of the office.

"What did you find out?" Frank asked him.

"He's paid up until Sunday but hasn't been seen around in the area for the past couple of days. He must be planning to come back." Matt unlocked the door and opened it to reveal a dark, sparsely furnished room. "You can't accuse him of living a lavish lifestyle. This place is a dump." Matt flipped on the light and roaches scurried for cover. The suspect had left behind some personal belongings and a few of his disguises. "I'm sure he would have taken this stuff with him if he knew we were going to visit. This is a goldmine of evidence." Matt made a call to get his team there.

"Looks like your guy left in a bit of a hurry." Frank looked around the room.

"It sure does. He's been so clever about never leaving evidence behind. It has me wondering why." Matt took gloves out of his pocket and put them on. He picked up a case and opened it to find all kinds of make-up, nose changes, colored contacts, and several hairpieces.

"It looks like he could create a new look at will." Frank looked in the case. "Maybe even a woman if that wig is an indicator."

"He went to the church as a woman." Matt could hardly believe what he was looking at. The man had taken the art of disguise and murder very seriously. "At least now it makes sense to me why each agency I talked to had a different description of this guy." Matt saw a thick scrapbook under a stack of newspapers. He opened it. "Look at this."

"What is it?" Frank walked over to join him.

"A book with news articles about him." Matt showed him a page.

"Wow, a horrific record of a sick man's life, if you ask me."

"It appears he has been labeled a devil more than once. I think he likes that name. See how he underlined it repeatedly in the headlines." Matt pointed it out, and Frank nodded.

"I'm sure the women he murdered felt that way about him." Frank scanned the pages as Matt turned them.

"His actions make a little more sense to me now. He sees this as some kind of legacy of greatness, just like the profiler told us. It's sick to us, but he doesn't see it that way." Matt closed the book and handed it to Marcy when she came up behind him.

The rest of the team got right to work, tagging and bagging each item into evidence.

Matt needed air. He walked outside, scanning the area around the motel. Where was the sick monster right now?

****

He watched, hidden, from his vantage point in the wooded area across from the motel. Damn, he should have taken all his stuff with him the other day, but whatever he had seen in the cemetery had freaked him out, and he hadn't been thinking clearly. He still couldn't rationalize or explain it, but whatever it was hadn't hurt him. His book was in there. He clenched his teeth. The record of his greatness would be what he missed most of all. Everything else was inconsequential. They couldn't take the triumphs from his mind, though. He bared his teeth in a grin. He would start a new book soon. The only way the other stuff would incriminate him was if they had him in custody, which they didn't. He sat back with a smirk to enjoy the show. The police entered and exited his room with bags. The cop came out and looked right at his hiding place. He stood up, his body tense, not taking his sight off the cop. A bloodhound came out of the room and started sniffing the air. Damn, the dog knew. He was pulling the man with the leash straight toward him. *Move!* Running back to his car, he drove quickly out of town on the back roads.

****

"What's up, Frank? Why is he acting like that?" Matt watched Radar pulling and pacing back and forth.

"He must have caught the guy's scent in the area." He let Radar have his lead and followed him up the hill. "If he was here, he's gone now." Frank looked around the area.

"He was here all right. Look, these footprints are fresh." Matt pointed them out. "He must have been watching the motel from here."

"We're getting close, and he knows it. Do you think he'll skip now?" Frank bent to look at the tracks and Radar leaned into his hand. "Good boy, Radar." Frank patted the dog's head.

"I don't think so. He's arrogant, and he wants Jessie. I think he'll be more careful, but he's coming after her. I know it."

"Then I guess we had better be ready for him when he comes." Frank patted Radar's head again. "Radar knew his scent right away. He started sniffing the air the minute we came out the door. He will be helpful."

"You've got that right. We'll all be ready; we have to be."

Chapter 39

The bell over the door rang. Jessie watched Frank walk in with Matt. She smiled, waved at them, and hurried over to where they were standing.

"I'm glad you get to see my shop, Frank. I'm really proud of how it turned out."

He looked around. "It's great; you have a nice place here. I think I'll take a look around."

"When you're done, be sure to sit down and make yourself comfortable. It's almost closing time, but I still have a few customers to take care of. I'll be ready to go in about twenty minutes. Katie is expecting us all at the Inn for dinner." Jessie went to the register.

"Did you find everything you were looking for?" she asked the woman as she placed several books on the counter.

"I did, thank you. You have a nice shop here. I know I'll be back." She swiped her credit card.

"I think you'll enjoy this author." Jessie put the books in a bag.

"I read her first book in the series and loved it, so I'm sure that I will like these, too." She took the bag from Jessie's hand.

"I hope to see you again."

"You will." She smiled and waved as she walked out the door.

Jessie rang up the last customer, locked the doors

opening into Joe's, the front door, and turned the sign around to *Closed*. She took the money from the register, placed it in the cash bag, and locked it in the safe. When she was done, she walked over and stood behind Matt, who was sitting by Frank. "Did you boys have an interesting day?"

Matt looked over at Frank. "Interesting might be a good way to describe it. What do you think, Frank?"

"That would be one way to define it." He paused, his eyes crinkling at the corners. "I would call it remarkable at the least and right up there with exciting."

"Will one of you just tell me what went on today?" She flicked Matt's head.

"Oh, you wanted to *know* about it? Sorry, my bad." He clenched his lips to keep a straight face. "Why didn't you just ask?" He proceeded to tell her about Radar, the old motel, and the evidence they found when they got inside the room. "It looks like he has had many disguises over the years."

"Radar is amazing, Frank." She touched his shoulder. "You must feel very proud of him on days like today."

"He did great." Frank beamed. "It makes me happy when he does."

"Speaking of Radar, where is he?"

"We took him over to Matt's, and the last time I looked, he was sleeping." Frank smiled. "Something he does better than anything else."

"He deserves it; he had a hard workout today." Jessie sat down in the chair across from them.

"Trust me, Radar lies around whether he's worked hard or not. He's a hound." He grinned. "That's what he does best."

"I could handle a little more of it myself." Matt stood up. "I think it's called down time, and it sure sounds good to me."

"I hear you." Frank exaggerated a wince. "That dog practically yanks my arms off every time we do this."

"Come along, you two old men. It's time for us to go eat now." Jessie giggled as she pulled Frank out of the chair. "Do you want me to drive?"

"Be nice, sweetheart. We walked a long way today." Matt gave her a playful push.

****

It looked as if every light in the Inn was on, inviting them in. The wonderful smells that hit her senses when she first walked through the door made her tummy grumble in response. Katie had once again outdone herself. It was possible tomorrow would be great fun after all. Maybe Radar had scared him off, and he was gone. Forever.

"Hi." Katie smiled at them as they came in. "Jeremy arrived about ten minutes ago, and Liam already has him doing something."

"Something sure smells good in here." Frank found the first comfortable chair and sat down. "You've been busy baking cookies and bread, I think."

"Very good, you got it right. I'm putting the cookies in the welcome baskets, and you get to eat the bread tonight." Katie smiled at him.

"I hope I get to sample the cookies, too."

"Of course." Katie started to leave and then turned back around. "I almost forgot, Matt. Jeremy wanted to talk to you the minute you got here."

"Point me in the right direction, and I'll go find him." Matt headed in the general direction of Katie's pointing finger, and they nearly collided.

Jessie couldn't hear what they were saying. She tried. She did everything but walk behind them and had to settle for watching them walk into the library and close the door. "I wonder what that's all about." She sat down next to Frank.

"I'm sure you'll find out eventually." Frank gave her a lazy smile. "When Matt wants you to know."

"I suppose so, but darn, this curiosity of mine finds it hard to let it go. I hate being left out." She glared at the closed door. "Will you be okay here?" She looked at Frank and saw him nod. "I think I'll go see if I can help Katie. If I happen to walk by the library and overhear something, there's nothing wrong with that, is there?" She moved before he could answer and lingered outside the closed doors. She heard nothing but the mumble of voices beyond and Frank's chuckles behind her.

Next, she went in search of Katie and found her in the kitchen. "Do you have something for me to do?"

Katie had her put the fresh chopped veggies into the lettuce for the salad. "You can take the salad out to the buffet table. I have it marked where I want it to go."

Jessie picked up the huge bowl of salad and carried it into the dining room. She placed the salad right where it was supposed to be and noticed on her way back to the kitchen that the door to the library was still closed. Darn, she would love to be a fly on the wall. "What's next?"

"Go tell Matt and the others that it's time to eat."

Jessie went to the closed door and knocked. Matt

opened it up. "Dinner is ready. What are you two doing in here?" She tried her best to look innocent.

"It's killing you not to know, isn't it?" Matt chucked her chin. "I'll tell you later, don't worry."

She heard Jeremy laugh in the background.

"I'm glad you're enjoying yourself at my expense." She stuck her head in the door to glare at him. When he laughed harder, she frowned at him. Then she turned around and walked back to the kitchen to help Katie.

****

Jessie enjoyed dinner with all her friends. She looked around the table and watched each of them for a moment. Nostalgia mixed with a strange undercurrent she couldn't name ran through her. Tom, Jeremy, and a few agents she didn't know sat across from her. Liam and Connor were being their normal entertaining selves. Frank and Matt were in a deep discussion to the right of her. Katie was at the height of her glory, enjoying the compliments the men were throwing her way after her wonderful meal. Jessie had to admit she had cooked the roast to perfection. Katie's face couldn't hide how pleased she was. Jessie loved these folks, Dylan, Kip, and Gary included. Would she be here for another meal? The reality was setting in, and nerves were rearing their ugly heads. Matt stood first, followed by Jeremy, and along with a few of the others, they headed for the library and another closed-door meeting.

"Abandoned again to clean up their mess," Katie said as she started clearing the table. "They like to eat it, but move fast when it's time to clean up."

"You've always had to do this, even when you were young."

"True." Katie made a face.

When they finished, Jessie sat at the table to help Katie with the welcome baskets. "Your guests will love them." She picked up a finished basket.

"What do you think they're up to in there?" Katie pointed to the closed library door. "They've been in there for a while."

"It's shoptalk." Jessie placed a book in the basket that she was working on. She had donated one for each of the baskets. She figured that trading the books with others to get the one you wanted to read would be a great icebreaker.

"Well then, why aren't you in there? Doesn't it concern you, too?" Katie handed her a bow.

"I'm sure they'll come for me when they have something that concerns me. Until they do, hand me another basket. I'm here to help you." Jessie put the first few items in the basket. "These are really nice. I want one." She stuck a package of Katie's homemade cookies into it.

"They are turning out nice, even the ones you did," Katie smirked. "I knew you could do it."

"A kindergartener could do it with the instruction sheet you gave me." Jessie waved the paper at her.

"I think people will like them." Katie held a finished basket up to examine it closely and then set it back on the table.

"What's up with you and Jeremy?" Jessie glanced up at Katie.

"Nothing." She frowned at the next basket. "He seems to be dragging his feet. It looked for a while as if it might be a great relationship. I don't know. We have nothing to talk about because we're too different. He's a brain, and I'm a social butterfly. I can't get into all that computer stuff." Katie stared off into space.

"I was hoping you'd be a couple." Jessie started on the next basket feeling sad for Katie. Well, she had defined the two of them correctly.

"Me too, but honestly, Tom and I can talk for hours." Her face brightened. "So I'm not sure who I like right now. I'm thinking of giving up men permanently. Don't you dare laugh. I'm serious." Katie glared at her.

Jessie bit her lip. "You have to admit that would be a first. I mean, I'm a little skeptical that you could pull it off." Jessie couldn't stop the laugh from coming out, and Katie pinched her arm. "Ouch! Give it up, Katie, you'll never be able to do it."

"You can just wipe that smile off your face right now and keep your comments to yourself. I'm considering it, that's all." Katie smiled when Jessie lost it and laughed outright.

"Ladies, it sounds as if you're having a good time. I hate to break up the party, but I need to talk to Jessie." Matt waited for her to stand up.

"I'll be back to finish this, leave it for me." Jessie pointed at the basket she had been working on.

Tom and Dylan were in the library waiting when they got there. Matt closed the door. "We need to go over the plan for tomorrow night." He smiled when he said the word plan. "Jess, you'll stay here at the Inn the entire time until you leave with me. We don't want you leaving to go anywhere with anyone besides one of us. If I have to leave for any reason, there will always be someone to keep an eye on you right here. Does that work for you?"

He was learning. He had *asked* her. That was pretty

cool. "That's fine." She rewarded him with a smile. "If I can make your lives easier by staying where I'm supposed to, I'm down with it." She opened the door to leave; she didn't want to think about it anymore.

"Wait up a minute, Jess, we aren't done here yet." He caught the door. "Jeremy has some photos he wants you to look at. All of these are men who will be here for the weekend." He slipped in a picture of Ian Brewster. "Are any of these men familiar to you?"

She studied each one. "I know some of them, of course. Jake Perry and I went together for a while." She pointed at the picture of Brewster. "He was in my store the other day."

"When? You didn't tell me." Matt sounded perturbed.

"I didn't know who he was." She frowned at Matt. "He bought something and paid with a credit card. I thought he was a little peculiar but harmless."

"What about the rest of the photos?" Tom asked her.

"I can't tell you much more. A few of them I can vaguely remember." She leafed through the pictures again. "And some of them not at all. I guess I'm going to have to get up close and personal with our guy. It might be the only way that I'll know him." She glanced at each one of them again. "He may not even show up."

"I think he'll show up. He may be an invited guest or an unexpected visitor. We might need to devise a signal so you can let us know he's near, and I'll tell the others to watch for it too." Matt smiled when she whispered in his ear what she thought it should be. "That's not a signal, it's a distraction."

"I could swing my purse with the gun in it at his

head," she suggested.

"Not very subtle." Tom laughed. "I want to know the other one that she whispered in your ear."

Jessie gave Matt a look that said he'd better not. "She can't use it. I wouldn't let her. Enough said."

"The truth is you'll know if I sense him because it will be written on my face." She felt her smile slip away. "I can't hide my emotions when he gets near me."

"We'll go with that." Matt glanced at her.

"What do you know about the man after Liam?" She looked around the room.

"You don't need to worry about him, sweetheart, we have eyes on him." Matt was using his persuasive voice. "You concentrate on *here*. You just need to do your part and show us some emotion."

"Got it. Now, can I go finish what I was doing?" She looked around the room.

"One more thing," Tom spoke up. "Neither of you go anywhere alone." He looked at them both. "You'll be too easy to pick off, and we've lost our visual on the guy. Not only does she need to stay put, but you do too, Matt."

Katie came through the partially opened door. "No more talking, we need to get things finished up here." She grabbed Jessie's hand and pulled her toward the door.

"Yes, ma'am." Tom stood up. "You heard the lady. She needs our help."

Jessie enjoyed watching Katie boss the guys around. She was in her element and doing a great job at keeping them hopping. Matt swung by where she was working on baskets. "Is she always like this?"

"If she has an event, she is. She's good at what she does and wants it to be perfect. Maybe she's a tad like you in that respect." Jessie patted his hand.

He looked totally affronted. "I'm not like this, no way."

"Do you mean overbearing, something of a tyrant, and always telling folks what you want them to do?" He nodded and she laughed. "Oh yes, you are." She rubbed her arm where he'd pinched it. "Ouch. You don't have to be mean about it."

He came striding toward her. "I'll show you a tyrant." He picked her up out of the chair, tossed her over his shoulders, carried her, laughing like crazy, into the sitting area, and tossed her on the chair. "Stay where you're put." He grinned.

She was still laughing so hard she could barely catch her breath. She stood up with her hands on her hips. "You just proved my point," she sputtered out.

He had a dangerous gleam in his eye. "Umm, I think I like playing the caveman type. I picked you up without any problem. Remember *that* the next time you think you can walk away from me." Both of them turned at the sound of Frank's hearty laughter.

"I don't know when I've enjoyed myself more. You two are something. You might actually survive this weekend if you don't kill each other first."

Chapter 40

Jessie worked in her store Saturday until closing time at two o'clock. She loved the small town winter hours. She wondered if he would even be there tonight. They were all speculating at best, but she knew in her heart that he'd be there, and they would come face to face. Her phone rang, and she checked the caller ID.

"Hi, Katie, how's it going so far?"

"Quite a few are already here. Most of them I know, which is kind of fun." Katie sounded out of breath.

"Are you okay?"

"Sure, I've been running around showing people to their rooms. The Inn is a big hit and so are all the welcome baskets."

"I bet! Wait until they get a taste of the spread that you have planned for them tonight and tomorrow morning. You'll get some repeat customers for sure."

"One can hope. Oh, and they love the icebreaker with the books. I admit you had a great idea there."

"I'm happy to hear it. I hope they are prepared to have their socks knocked off. You're the best."

"Stop it, you're too kind, and I'm not used to it." She giggled. "You usually pick on me."

"Katie, you're so bad at lying. That's not true, and you know it." Jessie heard her laugh again.

"How are you, Jessie? I mean, you have to be a

Iona Morrison

little nervous. Have you thought about what you're going to wear?"

"Katie, you know what this night might become. I've hardly thought about clothes, truthfully." Jessie frowned. What was she bringing upon her friends if this guy showed up? Katie couldn't even begin to understand, but she did. She had seen what he was capable of. He was a monster.

"Well, do, that's all I'm saying."

"I'll be there and dressed. That will have to do for tonight."

"While you're off catching the bad guys, I fully intend to have a good time. There will be plenty of single men around tonight."

"Have you made up your mind yet?" Jessie found herself smiling in spite of her nerves. Katie was nervous too. Jessie knew all the signs.

"I'd settle for Jeremy, but he's not to be found. I kind of like the hunky FBI man, but he's not here either. I'll settle for an old school mate. At this point, anyone would be nice."

"Don't sell yourself short, no pun intended. When you make up your mind, they might, too."

"I find it hard, with all these great men, to focus in on just one."

"Maybe you're not as ready for marriage as you think." Jessie laughed as she imagined Katie's face.

"You may be right. At least not tonight anyway. I plan on having fun and flirting with any single male who is here." Jessie heard Katie's heavy sigh.

"Katie, don't forget that I've known you for years. You're chattering about stuff that doesn't matter to cover up your nerves. They'll do all they can to keep us safe."

"I know, but I don't want to lose you or any of my friends. I'm scared, Jessie, really scared. It helps me to pretend things are normal, but I'm terrified."

"I am, too! I'll be there soon, and somehow we'll get through this."

"Promise me you won't get killed, please. I want you in my wedding and there for my kids."

"I'll do my best. See you later."

****

"Are you ready yet? We're going to be late," She heard Matt call.

"I'll be out in a few minutes. We aren't late, and you know it." She glanced one more time in the mirror and slipped her lip-gloss into her purse. She didn't think anyone would notice the slight bulge from her badge in the pocket of her dress or the gun in its holster strapped to her thigh. The dress was loose enough to hide it. She slipped her feet into a pair of ballet flats just in case she needed to run. She could run fast if she had to.

"Finally," he said, as the door opened. He stared at her, grabbed her hand, and pulled her toward the door, pausing to pick up her coat and hold it for her while she put it on.

"I didn't know what to wear. Is this okay? I've never dressed to trap a murderer before," she muttered. She held out her arm for the sleeve of the coat.

"It'll work, believe me. You can wear anything and look good, sweetheart. I can't afford to lose my focus right now. Why do you think I'm in such a hurry to cover you up?"

"That's sweet, I guess." She buttoned the first button. "You give such strange, mixed messages."

"Nothing sweet or mixed about it." He leaned in and kissed her. "It's all about focus and preservation right now. If we get through this night alive, then I'll show you my real feelings. Let's get going. Frank and Radar are there already."

"I'm sorry. I didn't mean to hold you up. I guess I'm a little nervous."

"I'm just as tense, and we're not late. It's all good." He held the door open for her. He was silent for the time it took to get to the Inn. Jessie eyed his stark profile, his slight frown. He was going over every detail they had talked about in his mind, she knew. Her stomach was tense. How would this night turn out? Would they both be okay at the end? She looked away, tightening her lips. They'd both come through fine. She had to believe that. He turned on Blue Iris Lane heading back toward the brightly lit Inn.

"Look at all the cars. Katie must be frantic trying to take care of everyone." She glanced at Matt's stoic expression. "It'll be all right." She reached across to touch his hand. They both had to believe it.

"Sure…remember, you stay here, sweetheart. I'll open the door for you." He got out of the car and walked around to open her door. He leaned in close as she got out. "You look beautiful; I should have told you earlier. Better late than never, I guess."

"I understand, Matt." She squeezed his hand. "Don't worry. I'll stay put." The minute she stepped out of the car, the hair on her neck stood up. The night seemed to scream with strange sounds. Was she the only one who heard it? She glanced at Matt out of the corner of her eye. He must not hear or feel it.

They walked side by side to the big wrap-around

porch and up the stairs, his hand resting on the small of her back. Through the window, Jessie could see the people milling about and heard laughter as it spilled through the closed door. Strange. It all looked normal, but she knew it wasn't. Matt placed his hand on the door to open it. "Are you ready for this, Jess?" He waited for her nod and opened the door into the crowded Inn.

Katie rushed over, looping her arm into Jessie's. "I'm going to steal her," she said to Matt. "People have been asking about her all evening."

"I'll leave her in your capable hands." He mouthed the words *watch her for me* so Katie could see, and she nodded. "I have some things to take care of, so I'll see you soon, sweetheart."

Jessie freed herself from Katie's hold. "Please, take care of yourself out there. I have a strange feeling about this night."

"I will. Don't worry." He kissed her cheek. "I'll watch over you."

"Thank you." She gazed up through her lashes at him and let Katie pull her away into the crowd.

****

Matt went outside and made his way to the command site near Jessie's cottage. Strange feeling, she'd said. Hell, that couldn't be good. Her premonitions were always right on, even if he didn't understand them.

"How's it going?" Matt looked at Gary, who was handling the incoming radio calls.

"Everyone is in place. Some are walking the perimeter with Frank and his dog. We still don't have visual contact with any of the suspects, but the grounds are secure."

"Matt, what are you doing here? You aren't supposed to be out in the open. You'll make our job harder for us." Tom frowned at him. "You should be up at the Inn with your lovely gal. Now, I'm going to have to walk you back up there."

"It's tough to stay away from the action. I doubt you could do it either."

"Probably not, but who's to say? All the action might be up at the Inn tonight." He gave Matt a small radio. "We'll keep you updated, but you need to be away from here. It's my job to keep you safe."

"I know, and I would be saying the same thing to you if I were in your shoes." He shook his head, wanting to stay outside to keep all of Jessie's friends safe. "I just can't stand waiting around. I want to do something."

"The thing is, Matt, you *are* doing something. Your hand is in all of the plans. You set this whole operation in place, and with any luck, it will work perfectly. Your team is disciplined, skilled, and they respect you. Go look after Jessie, and let us look after the both of you." Tom started walking. "Let's go, Parker."

"Hell, I guess you're going make me do this, Maxwell."

"You could say I'm pulling rank, and it's an order."

Matt started back toward the Inn with Tom at his side. "Have you made any visual contact with either hitman?"

"No, and I can't figure out why. The Hunter I can understand, but Brewster isn't so careful. He makes no bones about being a tough thug who throws his money and weight around. He's just common muscle for the Murray family."

"Sounds like it would be nice to get him off the streets." Matt's head turned when he heard a sound behind them, and he reached for his gun. "Sorry, I didn't mean to startle you." Dylan looked at both men. "Gary said you had just left, and I wanted to catch you and not risk being heard over the radio.

"What's up?" Matt placed his gun back in the holster.

"We know the Hunter is on the move. They had visual contact but lost it. Gary said that one of the extras called in that they had sighted Brewster coming into the area. It seems your instinct was right. Tonight is the time, and this is definitely the place."

"Damn, I didn't want to be right." He drew a deep breath. "We'll have to keep everybody safe by handling them out here." Tom picked up the pace as Matt lengthened his stride. They were at the back of the Inn when they heard the shot followed by a second. Matt headed left around the house, aware that Dylan was on his heels. Tom had ducked right. Damn. What the hell was coming down?

****

Jessie saw Liam standing alone on the porch as she headed for the restroom—a polite way of taking a breather from the nonstop conversation. What was he doing out there? She squinted through the front window. Who was guarding him? She opened the door and saw a flicker of red light on his white shirt. She leaped forward, shoving him hard with a strength she didn't know she possessed, slamming him to the ground and knocking the wind out of them both as a shot popped.

"Geez, Jessie." He tried to shove her off. "Why'd you push me so hard? I didn't do anything to you."

He sounded drunk. "Keep your head down," she yelled at him shoving his head down and lying flat against him. "You had a laser sight dancing on your chest. Didn't you hear the gun shot? You're lucky I came out the door when I did. You might be a dead man right now. Stay down." She shoved him as he started to sit up. "He still has the Inn in his sights, see?" She pointed to the red light bobbing around the wall and porch. "Let's hope no one opens that door right now. She saw Tom come around the corner. "Tom!" She pointed to the light. He started talking into his radio and took off in the direction the light was coming from. Dylan came around the other side of the house and followed him.

"Jess, are you both okay?" Matt's hissing whisper came from the darkness at the corner of the house where Dylan had appeared.

"I'm fine." She stayed flat. "I think I might have stunned Liam when I shoved him down. I'm not sure he'll get over it."

"I thought she was trying to jump my bones, Parker." Liam laughed shakily. "I don't move in on a friend's girl."

"Yeah, yeah, give it up, Liam. You were mad at me for shoving you." Jessie got a case of the giggles. How ridiculous this was. Liam lay flat on the porch with her on top of him. She used to dream of moments like this.

"Stay down, both of you. I'll tell you when the coast is clear." Matt followed Dylan into the night.

"This isn't exactly how I envisioned us together,

but I'll take what I can get." Liam groaned when she smacked him.

"Behave, or I'll shoot you myself," she whispered. "He's still holding the gun on the porch." She flinched as the red bead of light edged closer. "Good. He doesn't know the guys are closing in on him." *Please keep Matt safe*! She sucked in a quick breath. "We need to scoot back out of the line of fire. Keep low to the ground." The light was coming their way again, and her pulse picked up. "Don't move! Stay down."

"I couldn't move if I wanted to unless you move with me."

She couldn't tell if the light was the same or getting bigger. Was it moving toward them? He had to be using something that gave him night vision, so if the light landed on them, he'd be able to see them. And fire. "We're not out of the woods yet," she whispered. They wouldn't have time to get through the door or around the side of the house if he spotted them.

"You have to know that I never thought that they would find me here," Liam whispered brokenly. "I wouldn't have come. Keep Katie safe, please."

Jessie heard the door. "Don't come out!" she yelled. "There's a shooter." She heard more popping sounds. The door slammed shut, and she heard screams from inside. *Where were they? Was Matt okay?* One side of the porch went dark, and shards of glass fragmented on the chair and the ground beneath it.

"What's taking so long?" Liam lifted his head slightly.

"Keep your head down! It's dark, and they have to find where he's hiding, which isn't easy with all the places to hide around here. Drat. He knows he has us pinned down here now." Another couple of rapid pops sounded, and a potted plant shattered. A bullet grazed the railing beside them embedding itself in the siding. Jessie saw both places it had hit. "Man, that was too close for comfort." Jessie rolled to the side of Liam. The red light was still dancing across the porch. Looking for them.

"What a mess I've made of things." He buried his face in his hands.

"Shh." Jessie strained to hear any sound that would let her know what was going on. It was quiet, but that didn't mean anything. The moon's glow ebbed slowly as a dark cloud moved strategically in front of it, dousing its light. An odd mewing reverberated through the woods, disturbing the eerie silence. "Did you hear that?"

"I didn't hear anything."

Jessie lifted her head slightly, looking at the woods. What was that strange noise? She shivered as she saw them. She could barely make out their forms as they flitted in and out through the trees. She shivered again. This would be no ordinary night! The porch was dark. The red bead of the laser sight had vanished.

"Jessie, are you okay? You're too quiet." Liam turned his head to look at her.

"I don't see the light anymore, but I'm waiting for the all clear."

"What made you come out the door right then? How did you know?"

"I didn't know. I saw you standing out here alone, and you shouldn't have been. Someone was supposed to be watching you. I decided to come out and talk to you. Then I saw the light and the rest is history." She raised herself up a little to look around. "Sorry about shoving you so hard. I must have had a little help because normally I don't think I could have budged you, much less take you down." *Thanks, Gina.* Jessie looked toward the woods, but there was no sign of her now.

"I don't care how you did it, I'm just glad that you did."

Katie opened the door and peeked out at them. "Are you both okay?" Her voice was shaky. "Is it safe now?"

"I'm not sure about okay, but I'm alive, thanks to Jessie, Sis." Liam stood and went to the door. He hugged Katie, and she hugged him back, tears streaming down her face. She glanced at Jessie. "I almost forgot. Matt called and said to tell you that it's all clear. He also told me to ask you where your phone is and why aren't you answering it?" Katie stepped out onto the porch and looked around. "I can't believe he shot out my light." She saw the shattered glass and went to get a broom. A few of the more curious guests came out when Katie did.

"Is everyone okay?" Jessie asked Katie.

"They are in shock, of course, and full of questions."

Jessie looked at the small group standing around Liam. She wanted them off the porch. She had no idea what was going on out there. "Liam why don't you take everyone back inside and answer everyone's questions while we clean up this mess?" She saw him nod.

One by one, the guests filed back into the Inn, and the questions began. Jessie followed them in to get her phone. Liam was great in the spotlight. He could handle it in here. What she needed was to hear Matt's voice. Jessie went back out to help Katie clean up the glass and the broken flowerpot.

Katie sat down on the wicker loveseat. "How did you know? He could have been killed." Katie shivered.

"I saw him standing alone, and he shouldn't have been. I went out when I saw the red laser dot dancing across his shirt."

"My brother." She sighed. "Who would want to hurt him? I don't understand." Katie shook her head. "Why shouldn't he have been alone? Does this have something to do with Tom staying here?"

"I promise you'll have your answers before the night is finished, but right now I need to talk to Matt."

She sat in the chair next to Katie and called Matt. He didn't answer. She sent him a text saying

—He's here—

Jessie shivered. *They* were still out there in the woods. She could still hear their faint whimpering and wailing. Was this the night for settling scores? Jessie was faintly aware of Katie asking if she wanted to go in. She shook her head no. She felt rooted in place. He was watching.

Chapter 41

Matt had followed the sound of the gunshots, the red beam of light, and the others moving through the woods until he found the clearing where Brewster was. He took cover and could see Tom positioned behind a tree across from him. What Matt saw next was something he would never forget. Ian had just got off another round when suddenly he threw down his gun and started screaming and beating the air.

"Get them away from me." He waved his hands around him.

Tom moved first. He grabbed him, pushing Brewster to the ground. "Hold still." He was thrashing and rolling in the dirt.

Matt grabbed one arm, Dylan got the other, and they cuffed him. "You have the right…" Matt yelled his Miranda Rights over his screams.

"Please, put me in the car, get them away from me," he begged, fear etched in the lines on his face.

"Hell, there's nothing here, man. What are you screaming about?" Tom shook his head as they pulled him to his feet.

Brewster whimpered and struggled. "You can see them, can't you?" he asked Matt with terror in his eyes.

Matt shook his head, but then he saw the misty figures swooping around through the trees. He rubbed at his eyes as he saw her floral dress. Matt opened the cruiser door. "Watch your head." He put his hand on the top of Brewster's head when he ducked to get in. Matt couldn't wrap his head around what he'd just seen.

"Keep them away from me. Please, shut the door and keep them away," Brewster whimpered.

"You can take him back to the station and book him," Matt told Kip. "We'll sort this all out later."

"What was that all about? Did you see anything?" Tom asked them.

Dylan shook his head. "I didn't see anything, but something is definitely up."

"I know someone who will understand everything happening out here tonight. I don't think you'll believe it when you hear it, though." Matt heard the faint wailing sound for the first time. It sent chills racing down his spine. He had to get back to Jessie.

****

He had been watching her from the shadows, but he couldn't tell if she was aware of him or not. She stared out into the woods with a strange expression fixed on her face. The night was too quiet. He rubbed his damp hands together and wiped away the sweat dripping down his face. It wasn't warm, so why was he sweating? She had always had a peculiar effect on him. Why was that? Even when they were young, she could turn him into mush when she got near him.

Everything he had done over the years, he had done with her in mind. He measured every other woman by how she compared to Jessie. What luck, after all these years, to find her here! From that moment in the moonlight when she had turned around, he had known that he had to have this dance with her. The thought of it still had the power to steal his breath.

He touched the gun hidden in his pants along with the knife. He moved quietly from his spot and walked up the steps to where she was sitting. He had been born for this moment.

****

"I wondered when you would come out of hiding." She glanced at him. Her pulse quickened, and intense fear raced through her. She had to fight her way through what she was feeling.

He sat down beside her. "You knew I was here?" He saw her nod. "Do you know who I am?"

"I do, I'm sorry to say." She frowned at him as she pushed down her rising panic. He repulsed and scared her at the same time. "Why?" She shook her head in disgust. "How could you destroy all those lives?"

"You wouldn't understand. It has nothing to do with you or this night." He heard the music inside. "We're going to dance and then take a walk."

"We'll see. Don't fancy yourself in control of this night just yet." Her voice didn't sound like hers. She shook her head and took a deep breath. She stood, wanting to get him inside the Inn where maybe she might get someone's attention. When he pulled her into his arms to dance, she felt nauseated. Bobby Angel. He was smooth, handsome with his dark hair and blue eyes. She was indeed dancing with a devil. What a waste of human life.

"What are you thinking about, my lovely Jessie?" His term of endearment made her angry.

Anger was good. Isn't that what Matt had told her? She would be mad. It was better than scared stiff. "That your life is such a waste, and I'm glad that I'm not yours in any way." She felt him tense, and his grip on her arm hurt her.

"Are you trying to provoke me, my dear?" He pulled her close to whisper in her ear. "I wouldn't if I were you. I can be mean if necessary."

"I remember that about you." She glanced around the room for the person who was supposed to be guarding her. She didn't know who he was…what was the signal?

"Do you, my dear? I'm glad that you, at least, thought of me occasionally. You've invaded my mind and senses over the years." He turned her. "If you're looking for your agent friend, he's having a nice nap. I doubt that he will wake up for quite a while." He chuckled. "He looked extremely exhausted to me."

Improvise. "Is that right? I was actually looking for Emma. I saw her earlier tonight." The color drained from his face at those words.

"I hope you're enjoying our little dance. I'm afraid this evening is almost over for you. I can see the wheels turning in your head. I will gladly kill your friends unless you do what I say. None of them means anything to me."

Her mind raced. She was afraid, terrified, but she was also angry. She needed to do something. Scream? Maybe. She had spotted the bulge of a weapon at his waist. And…she had to do something. She didn't want her friends hurt, but she couldn't stand his hands on her either. She needed to get away from him.

Gina, I hope you're here to help. Should she trust them? She had to. Justice was in their hands, and they would keep her safe. "I think your evening might be short-lived or maybe a tad too long depending on what they choose and how you look at it."

"Who are you talking about? The cops?" His lip curled. "They have no say."

"Never mind; it's not important." She tried not to wince as his grip bruised her arm.

"Don't talk in riddles or play games with me. You have no clue who you are dealing with or what I'm capable of." His eyes flashed with anger above his fixed smile.

"I know exactly what you are capable of. I saw what you did to Emma. I'm not impressed." She twisted free of his grip and walked away from him. He was hot on her heels. When she passed Katie on her way out the door, she gave her a look, hoping she'd get it. Katie gave her the perfect opening.

Katie grabbed Bobby's hand. "Gosh, it's been a long time since I've seen you, Bobby. I hope you're having a good time."

"Yeah, it's a nice party." He let go of her hand. "I'm taking Jessie out for a breath of fresh air."

"Katie." Jessie gave her the face that they'd given each other as kids when something was wrong. "Tell Matt I'll be right back and let him know that I'm with Bobby." She felt the gun press into her back.

"I will." Katie's face went white, and she turned away, grabbing for her phone. "See you two in a minute."

Good. She'd let Matt know.

He grabbed her elbow and pushed her through the door. "We are taking a walk, and no one will be able to save you. You know, I actually considered letting you live. You could have been my wife."

She flinched at his touch as he took her arm once more. "Did you ever once think about the women you

301

killed? Emma had a fiancé, did you know that?" The wailing grew louder. "Someone loved her very much, and you stole her from him. She was a wonderful young woman. What right did you have to hurt her family like that?"

"Shut up." He jerked her around to face him and slapped her.

She staggered, then straightened, her palm against her stinging cheek. "You don't like hearing how sick you are."

He grabbed her by her upper arms and shook her hard. "If you say another word, so help me I'll—"

"What? You'll kill me. That's your plan anyway, isn't it?" She slipped off one of her shoes to mark their direction for Matt. She fought him now, as he dragged her along, slowing him down for Matt. But *they* were going to get to him first. *Please*. Beneath the trees, the wailing was stronger and getting closer. He didn't seem able to hear it. She could, and it made her blood turn to ice. He kept dragging her deeper into the woods, panting with each step. Which one of them would die this night? She had to fight. She wanted to live…

He pulled, and she fought him until he was panting with each step. She stumbled when he yanked her hard into a clearing.

"Do you know where we are?" He slapped at the air with his hand.

"I do." She slipped off her remaining shoe. Although she had a feeling that she really didn't need to leave any more markers. She could run if she needed to. She wanted to cover her ears with her hands and block out the wailing that seemed to come from everywhere now.

"Can't you feel the magic? This is where I saw you again. I was stunned when you turned to look for me. What the hell?" He swatted at the air when something flew in front of his face.

He couldn't see them, but she knew he could feel them. She could only see them as wisps of motion, but she knew they were there. "I feel no magic here, only pity for the person you allowed yourself to become. Emma didn't deserve what you did to her." She stood up straight, trying to break free. "If there is any justice, it will all stop right here," she said in a loud, clear voice, "right now in these woods."

He let go of her as if her flesh scorched him and began to dance, thrashing wildly about, not to his own tune but the wailing of the night. Jessie stood still as they came swooping and diving at him. He slapped wildly at them, then grabbed her arm again and dragged her deeper into the woods. "Listen to me, you bitch, I don't know how you're doing this, but I will make you stop." He grabbed at his waist, and a knife blade gleamed in his hand.

The night howled.

****

Matt stared at his phone. Katie's hysterical voice still yammered incoherently through it. Panic hit him like a punch to the gut. He looked at Tom. "That sick bastard has her. I've got to get her."

"Do you have any idea where he might take her?" Tom was already on the radio, alerting everybody.

Matt took several deep breaths. "I have an idea where it might be." He took off running with Tom hard on his heels.

"Where are we headed?" Tom gasped.

"It has to be the place where he first saw her. That's where he snatched Emma." Matt picked up his pace, breathing in ragged gasps. They had just passed the cottage, heading downhill, when he saw her shoe. He stooped to pick it up and then saw the second one a little farther down the hill. "They came this way. She's pointing the way." He was running down the hill on the path when he heard the gunshot. "No," he yelled and charged on. It couldn't end like this. He'd promised her. He pushed himself harder.

"Matt, be careful," Tom yelled. "You can't help her if you're dead. That shot could be our man. Your guy slashes and cuts. He doesn't shoot. Use your head, man." Tom pulled out his Glock.

He was right. Matt forced himself to slow down. Staying in the cover of the trees, he worked his way to the clearing and saw a body on the ground. His heart raced, and he faltered, not able to take the final steps forward to know.

Tom got there first. "Matt, it's not her. I've never seen this guy before." He felt for a pulse. "He's still alive." He checked his pocket for an ID.

Matt radioed for an ambulance. "Who is he?" Matt watched Tom hold up his badge. "Damn. He's one of ours."

"It doesn't look bad. The bullet grazed him, but he's out cold. I wonder why." Matt knelt beside him as his eyes fluttered open. He tried to sit up. "Stay still, medics are on their way." The man grabbed his arm hard.

"Sir, can you tell me what I just saw? I can't believe what I saw." He shook his head.

"What's your name, officer?"

"Chad Roberts, sir. I can't explain it."

"Did you see a man with a girl come this way?" Tom asked him.

"Yes, they went that way." He pointed into the woods. "I was following them when someone shot me. I hope they'll be okay. I saw…I saw…I don't know what I saw. I never saw anything like it before." He rubbed his eyes.

Matt stood up. "I have to go. Tom, you stay with him until the paramedics get here." He charged into the darkness before Tom could stop him.

Chapter 42

He held the blade in front of her face. "I'm going to enjoy this. And sweetheart, it's going to be a slow dance." He placed the sharp point flat against her skin moving it down her cheek like a caress.

Jessie closed her eyes, despair rising to choke her. They couldn't touch him, and Matt wouldn't get here in time. The steel pressed into her skin, and she flinched, felt the trickle of blood flowing.

Unexpectedly the blade lifted from her face. She opened her eyes to see it fly out of his hand, point down to stick into the ground by his foot, narrowly missing it. He swore at her, cowering to avoid the wispy forms that buzzed around his head. He grabbed his gun from his waistband and shot wildly into the air, cursing when it flew out of his hands into the darkness. "We've got to get away from them." He slapped at the shapes with his free hand. "This is you doing this. Stop it!" Spittle sprayed her face as he shrieked at her. He jerked her forward, spinning her around, and she stumbled as he pulled her into the shelter of the trees.

"You'll never get away, you know." She made her voice calm; although her heart was pounding.

He glared at her and shook her again so that her teeth snapped together. "Why aren't these bugs bothering you?" He slapped her, and her head snapped back. She saw stars and tasted blood in her mouth.

Then, a ghostly hand hit him as hard as he had struck her, almost knocking him to the ground. He managed to keep his hold on her arms as he staggered. "How did you do that?" he growled through clenched teeth as he yanked her close.

"It wasn't me." She held his crazed glare, breathing hard. "Are you that stupid that you can't see what's happening?" She tried to twist free, but Bobby held her firm. He let go of her arm and pulled his clenched fist back to punch her. She tried to twist away from the blow, but his fist turned in the air and hit his own jaw, snapping his head back with the force. He sputtered, doubled over, nearly dragging her to her knees as he spit out a tooth. "Are you some kind of damn witch? How did you do it?"

She kicked him in the crotch, and he wailed, even though she was barefooted. Letting go of her, he stumbled backward, cursing. She turned to run, but he had gotten control of himself and rushed at her, his hands curved like claws as he reached for her. A vine snagged her ankle, and she tripped, expecting to feel his hands as she struggled to regain her balance.

He never touched her.

Misty shapes swirled in the air, and something flung him backward. He landed on his back with a hard thud, gasping for air. Struggling to catch his breath, groaning, he tried to sit up. His eyes widened, and he looked around wildly.

He could see them now. Jessie stood still, panting, as Emma and the others hovered above him, taunting him and wailing. A look of terror came over his face as they swirled down onto him. He twisted and rolled, screaming, trying to get away. He slapped at them, beating the air as he tried to get to his feet, but they wouldn't let him. Finally, he crawled, clawing at the undergrowth, cowering, his screams growing weaker as he tried to shield his eyes from their accusing faces. Jessie stood as if turned to stone as he writhed and screamed. He finally died—with the same fear in his eyes that he must have seen in theirs when he had murdered them. It was awful. She covered her eyes and sagged against the tree, gasping for air.

The clouds that had hidden the moon shifted, and the night sky was once again awash in moonlight, mocking the victim that lay motionless on the ground. She looked away.

Gina appeared and shoved her sideways. A bullet splintered the bark of the tree where she had been standing. Jessie ran. She could hear someone crashing through the brush not far behind her. Another bullet missed her, hitting a little to the right, kicking up dirt and leaves on the ground. She ran faster. Up ahead, she could see a branch hanging low, and she did what she had done many times as a kid. She reached out, grabbed it as she ran by, and swung herself up into the tree to hide. She got a foot on a low branch and climbed up further, out of sight, her dress snagging on twigs. Her feet screamed in pain, her palms were slick with blood. Be silent! She crouched, one arm around the main trunk, trying to stifle her breathing. Her heart pumped hard, her ears strained for any sound. She took her gun from the holster, but her hand wouldn't stop shaking. A branch snapped, and she jerked. Quiet! She covered her mouth with her hand. He was still coming, the hunter hunting his prey. He wasn't trying to be quiet. Branches snapped, and she heard the thud of running footsteps.

Jessie clung to the trunk, still as a piece of tree bark.

He charged into the clearing, a small man with a big gun. The leaves and twigs crunched beneath his shoes, and she could see his breath in the cool evening air. Even from her hiding place, she could see the determined look on his face. "Where did she get to?" he said aloud and looked among the low-lying bushes, scanning the area. "She couldn't have gotten far," he mumbled, kicking at the dirt.

He stopped under the tree where she was hiding, and she closed her eyes. *Be a tree.* She heard Matt calling her name. He had heard him, too. Matt was walking into a trap. Think fast, Jessie. He lifted his gun. Quiet and tense, she waited, staring down at him, holding her breath. The man's head moved back and forth, listening. Someone else was calling her name now. Was that Tom? Which way were they coming from? He focused, his gun lifting to rest snugly against his shoulder, his finger on the trigger. Ready. Someone was pushing through the brush on the far side of the clearing. Jessie leaped.

****

Matt burst into the clearing and saw the rifle barrel aimed at his chest. Before he had time to react, something fell from the tree onto the gunman. He yelled and went sprawling, his gun falling to the ground. "Get off me!" he yelled, his voice muffled. Matt charged forward and snatched up the rifle. He started toward the gunman, then stopped to watch him try to buck and roll out from under her. Damn. He started to smile as she got a fistful of his hair, yelled at him to be quiet, and shoved the muzzle of her gun into his back.

She was a beautiful sight.

Tom burst into the clearing, and Matt stepped forward with him. He grabbed one arm, Tom grabbed the other, and when Jessie got off, they cuffed him as he cursed. "Jessie, are you okay?" Tom helped her up as Matt finished snapping the cuffs closed.

"I'm all right now, but I bloody well won't be in the morning." Jessie gave a shaky laugh that filled Matt's heart. "I'll pay for this, but I couldn't let him kill you both."

He took in her torn dress, her shoeless feet, and her hair filled with pine needles. Damn, she was amazing. "Looks like you've had a rough night, sweetheart." He opened his arms. She walked into them and promptly started crying.

"Did you see her drop out of that tree?" Tom shook his head. "I've never seen anything like it. She saved our lives. Damn, what a beautiful sight that was. I would love to have it on film."

Matt felt her shiver. "You're cold. We need to get you warmed up. It's chilly out here, and you have no shoes on." He picked her up gently and carried her up the hill to the waiting ambulance. "Jess, honey, you need to let go," he said when they reached it. "I want them to clean up your feet and hands. We'll talk soon." She just shook her head, her face still buried in his shirt. So he sat with her and held her while they took care of her injuries. They were minor, considering what she had gone through. Matt's heart swelled with pride. "What happened to the chameleon?"

"He's dead." She didn't look at him. "His body is near where you found Emma."

"Do you want to talk about it?" He saw her shake her head and felt her shiver.

"Not yet." Her voice was barely audible. "Soon."

"I can wait, sweetheart." He laced his fingers through hers. "Let's get you away from here."

"I don't know if I want to walk back." She took a shuddering breath. "And I need to change. My dress is ruined, I think."

"I think we can arrange all that." He hugged her. "Your carriage awaits—or golf cart—depending on how you look at it." He grinned and carried her over to a small motorized cart parked next to the ambulance. "The gardener uses this to carry plants around the grounds. It's perfect for getting into those hard to reach places." He set her gently on the seat.

"Thank you." She made a face and rubbed her left foot. "I didn't feel like taking another step out here without some shoes on."

How many women would be in hysterics at this point? He smiled, loving her more than he ever had. "I'm afraid your feet will be hurting for a while, along with that shiner you have."

"What shiner?" She reached for her face.

"The one that's starting to show on the end of a huge welt across your cheek, and may I say, you've never been more beautiful to me than you are right now."

"I think you're trying to tell me in a nice way that I look a mess."

"Not me, sweetheart, not tonight." His breath caught in his throat. "You were amazing." He held her tight, kissing her hair, neck, and face.

Chapter 43

While she changed, Matt talked to several of the officers in the field. The FBI had taken Clarence Schaffer, AKA the Hunter, into custody. He wasn't talking. They had found the body of the chameleon, which Jessie would have to identify, but Katie had said was Bobby Angel. His body was right where Jessie said it would be. The preliminary cause of death was heart failure. Lewis still had to perform an autopsy to be sure. Dylan said the look on his face was terrifying.

Officer Chad Roberts would be fine. He still didn't understand what he had seen attacking the man with Jessie. Matt wasn't sure he believed it even when he explained it to him. Matt had witnessed what had happened to Brewster, and it was hard for him to believe in spite of what he knew. Now, he had to figure out how to write it up in his report. It had been one hell of a night.

He watched her limp out of her room wearing a skirt and sweater. He held her coat so she could put it on and drove the path to the Inn. "I know you're tired, Jess. I wouldn't ask you to do this, but everyone is asking about you. Katie hasn't stopped calling Tom and Dylan since this began. We don't have to stay long, if you don't want to."

"I'll be okay; I need to be with friends for a while." She climbed the steps to the porch at the Inn and promptly sat down on the small wicker loveseat. He sat beside her. "It's hard for me to deal with everything I saw tonight. I need to sit here for a minute and try to wrap my head around it."

"Take all the time you need." He put his arm around her. "I'm in no hurry. They're processing the crime scenes now."

She looked across the property to the woods beyond. "This was one strange night." She shivered.

"I know. I saw a few unusual things myself. You can tell me all about it as soon as you're ready. We can compare notes." He studied her profile and noticed the faraway look in her eyes. He couldn't begin to imagine what she had seen.

"Yes, that'll be good, but I don't think anyone will believe me anyway."

"I will. Remember, I was out there. I saw and heard some weird stuff. It's messing with my whole logical approach to everything." He stood. "Are you hungry? I could eat a little something. Katie has quite a spread in there, or so I've heard." He reached for her hand. "I don't want you to get chilled." He opened the door for her and walked her over to the chair beside Frank. "Why don't you sit here and talk to Frank, and I'll bring you something to eat."

"Sit, Matt. I'll bring your plates to both of you. You both look tired." Katie gave the orders, and several people moved to help. "Jessie, be sure to eat something." Katie patted her hand.

"Where's Radar?" Jessie looked around the room.

"He's in his crate out in the car. He did a lot of walking and found the suspect tonight, and now he's tuckered out."

"I know the feeling." Jessie looked at her feet.

"How are you?"

"I don't know, to tell you the truth. Right now, I'm a little numb. I know that will wear off soon, and it will all come rushing back in. I think this might be the calm before the storm." She smiled at him. "And I think I'll enjoy the calm!"

"I think you're probably right." Frank stretched his leg out.

"Is your knee bothering you?"

"A little," he replied. "You should eat while your food is still hot. Katie is a mighty fine cook, that's for sure. I ate my fair share, believe me. The pulled pork is especially good when you put the coleslaw on top of it. Looks like Matt will be ready for seconds before you even taste yours."

"I'm happy to just sit here. My feet are killing me." She looked again at her feet. "I had some crazy notion I should kick my shoes off so Matt could find the way I went." She pointed at Matt, who was devouring his food. "I didn't account for all the things out there that could hurt my bare feet. Running barefoot didn't seem to hurt when I was a kid." She made a feeble attempt to laugh. "I don't think I'll do any more late night shoeless runs through the woods."

"Sounds like a good lesson to have learned. Personally, I would throw out running through the woods at night altogether and probably running entirely, day or night. I'm not much of a runner, though." He chuckled. "I'm more of a sitter, unless I'm being pulled by my dog over a several mile stretch.

"I would second the no running, Frank." Matt winced when she punched his arm. He thanked Liam for bringing their drinks.

"You run all the time." She started to move the food around on her plate, picking at it. She took a bite of the salad, put her fork down, and sipped her iced tea.

"I wouldn't run at all if I didn't have to do it to keep in shape for my job." Matt watched her but didn't say anything. Katie handed two big pieces of chocolate cake to Jake's wife who was helping her serve. She placed the cake on the table beside them. Another plate of food magically replaced the one he had finished. He was tired but happy to be sitting by her.

"Hey, Jessie, can we talk a minute?" Liam pulled the ottoman over in front of her chair when she nodded. "I wanted to thank you for saving me tonight. It almost sounds trite, but if you hadn't come out when you did…I wouldn't be here."

"I'm glad I was there to see it and do something." She smiled at him.

"I'm glad, too. You're really something, you know it?" He grinned at her.

"So I've been told. No one seems to be able to say what that 'something' exactly is, though." She looked over at Matt, grabbed his hand, and smiled at him.

"Give me enough time, sweetheart, I'll come up with the right words." Matt turned her hand over, touching his lips to each of the scrapes and cuts.

Liam looked down at her feet. "Do they hurt?"

"Right this minute, no, but I'm not walking."

"Does this hurt you?" He gently touched her cheek.

"I'm okay; I think they gave me something in the ambulance. I don't feel anything right now."

"I guess you don't feel like dancing then, do you?" Liam looked at her. "We're about to begin, and I wanted to dance with the woman who saved my life. I still don't know how you did it I'm only happy that you did. I'm in your debt, Jessie." He stood and held out his hand. "Dance with me, please. That is, if Matt is okay with it."

"He's fine with it if she is." Jessie followed Liam to the dance floor, and Matt watched them dance. She had conquered another heart. Liam was doing a little hero worship. Who could blame him? Matt would have to put up with Liam indefinitely. He smiled. Heck, he had felt the same way when he had seen her fly out of the tree to save him. But that was okay. Liam could dream. He watched them dance, still smiling. Matt was sure her heart belonged to him.

Chapter 44

She came back after her dance with Liam and stood beside Matt's chair. "I'm ready to talk. I need to get this out while it is still fresh in my mind."

"Okay, let's do it." He stood up. "I'll call Tom, and we'll meet in the library."

Jessie went to the library to wait and to try to put the events of the night into some kind of order in her mind. She didn't know how any of them would take what she was about to tell them. She found it all hard to believe herself. Matt came in and sat down next to her, taking her hand in his. Well, he'd believe her at least. She smiled to herself. Frank, Tom, Dylan, and several men she didn't know followed in him. Oh great, a bunch of strangers. They'd think she was crazy, for sure.

"We can start whenever you're ready," Tom told her.

She nodded. "It started with the laser sight on Liam. I pushed Liam to the ground, but there is no way I could have done it on my own. The oddity of this night begins there. I had help in saving him." She saw the raised eyebrows and outright doubt on some faces and plowed on. "I'm not sure who helped, but I'm pretty sure that one of the spirits involved was Gina. You all went rushing into the woods. I don't know what happened out there. Only that Liam is still alive, and you got his shooter."

"Remind me to tell you later about that." Matt looked at her and smiled reassuringly.

"Liam told what happened to a few guests who had come out to see the damage after the gunshots. I told him to take them inside so Katie and I could clean up. I wasn't sure if you had both shooters in custody. Afterward, I went to sit on the loveseat. That's when I heard them wailing again and saw them gathering."

"Who did you see, Jessie?" Tom asked. All eyes were on her now.

"The women he had murdered. Emma was there and several others. They were flittering in and out of the trees. I knew this wouldn't be any ordinary night." The room was silent.

"I could feel him watching me. He was hiding in the trees, not far from the Inn, and I wasn't surprised when he came up to sit beside me." She retold some of their conversation. "I maneuvered him inside hoping someone would see and come to my rescue. I looked around for whoever was supposed to be watching me, but he had already got to him. I thought about screaming, but I didn't dare. He had a gun and would have started shooting my friends. My only hope was a secret signal that Katie and I had used as kids when something was wrong. He had a gun on my back, and he was in charge. Bless Katie, she knew exactly what it meant and called you. I was afraid, of course. I knew they were out there, but I didn't know for sure how they could help. But I kept telling him I had seen Emma." She turned to meet Matt's eyes and smiled at him. "I didn't think they would let him hurt me, but how was I to know for sure?"

"What happened next?" Matt spoke softly when she didn't go on.

"I made him angry." She reached up to touch the bruise on her face. Winced. "I wasn't intimidated, which seemed to make him madder. Somewhere, I kicked off my shoes to let Matt know which way we had gone. I realized that he was taking me to the place where he had first recognized me." She took a sip of water from the glass someone had placed near her.

"I'll never forget what happened next." She leaned forward in the chair. "The spirits were following us, and they started swirling in around him. I could just barely make them out, but I could feel their...their rage." She swallowed. "He started slapping at them. He thought they were bugs. They kept striking at his head, one by one. At one point, when he slapped me hard and grabbed my hands, Emma slapped him hard across his face. It hurt him." She shivered seeing his twisted snarling face again. "They were starting to physically affect him," She told them about the punch that went into his face and not hers, and how they threw him to the ground when he charged at her.

"How did he die?" Tom asked.

"He was surrounded by them." She shook her head. "He was screaming, and his screams got fainter as if the life was just draining out of him. I don't...I don't know what actually killed him. They were clawing at him." She swallowed again, remembering the abject terror in his voice, then sat up straight and looked at them all. "He died in fear. The way they had."

"There will be an autopsy, but the ME's first call is heart failure," Tom said quietly.

Her hands trembled. "I thought I was safe. But then

Gina pushed me out of the path of a bullet, and I took off running." She told them the details, up to the place where she had leaped out of the tree onto the hitman.

"I'll never forget her flying out of the tree." Tom shook his head. "He had Matt dead to rights when she dropped down on top of him and knocked the gun to the ground."

"Jess, who was the chameleon? Did you recognize him?" Matt laced his fingers through hers.

"Yes…" She paused to wipe her eyes. "I knew him as Bobby Angel. He later called himself Robert. She shook her head. "He used to pick on me when I was a kid, and he was kind of creepy." Her voice quivered. "He used to pull the wings off flies and laughed at them when they crawled around. I haven't thought about him in years." She wrapped her arms around herself. "I don't know how else to explain what happened in a way that doesn't sound crazy. But, that's what happened out there."

"You might not have thought about him in years, but he had been thinking about you. He kept an extensive record of your life. He had pictures of you from childhood all the way through high school and beyond. There were clippings of your news stories. I would say that you've been undeniably on his mind for some time." Matt put his arm around her when she shivered. "He had written in his journal that he was headed to New York to find you. All that changed the night he saw you on the running path."

"I'm glad it's over," she said softly.

"Yours is not the only strange story tonight, Jessie." Tom put a hand on her shoulder. "Do you remember anything about him from your years growing up?"

"I think his family was extremely religious and strict. Maybe that is why he got so wild when his parents weren't around. I do remember the girls in high school thought he looked like Elvis and that he had dreamy eyes. He was a part of the drama club and loved acting. I heard he took drama in college too." She looked at Matt knowingly. "I think I forgot all about him because he was so mean to me."

"I know we'll need to talk more over the next few days, Jessie." Tom took her hand. "You're free to go home and get some rest." She stood and waited for Matt.

"Matt, I don't think she should be alone tonight," Tom told him as Jessie yawned, rubbing her eyes.

"She won't be. Frank and I will be with her. I'll take care of her."

"Her story collaborates what Chad and Brewster told us. It's beyond strange."

"I guess we don't see half of what goes on, do we? I doubt we are as much in control as we think we are." Matt turned to Jessie. "Can I interest you in a real dance?" Matt asked as they walked out of the library. "Or would you prefer to wait?"

She smiled at the look in his eyes. "If it's a slow one, I'm thinking now would be perfect. I want to get the feel of his hands off me." She squirmed, just thinking about it.

"I know the man playing the tunes, and he owes you big time. I'll put in your request."

A few moments later, the music came to a stop. "This song has come in as a request that I can't turn down," Connor called out. "So grab a partner and dance to this great tune by Percy Sledge." He led Katie out onto the dance floor.

Matt knew Jessie was hurting, so they simply stood still and swayed together. *When a man loves a woman*...the music played. "If I remember, the last time we danced I was the one limping."

"Do you think we'll ever be able to dance without one of us limping?" She gazed into his eyes.

"I think we'll have to give it a try." He chuckled. "It might be nice to move around a dance floor a little more. We might actually be good at it. I know you can leap, and I bet you can turn and dip too." He chuckled again. "I bet our old friend, Clarence the Hunter, didn't know an angel had landed on him."

Jessie laughed. "No, I'm sure he wasn't thinking 'angel' at all when I landed on him."

"I can't imagine why not, that was my first thought...and this was my next one." He lowered his head and kissed her.

Chapter 45

After several rounds of answering questions over the next few days, Jessie was happy to be back in her cottage. She heard the light tap at her door.

"Jessie, it's me." Katie opened the door and walked in.

"Hi, friend, what's up?" Jessie looked up from the couch.

"Are you doing okay?" Katie asked. "I have something for you." She opened the screen door, carried in a box, and placed it on the table.

"I think I'll make it." Jessie watched Katie.

"I thought it was time I stopped to fill you in on what's been happening. I brought you dinner. That's what's in the box. The directions for heating it up are in there, too." She set the box on the table, took out the various containers, and put them in the refrigerator.

"Thanks, that was nice of you. What did you make?"

"How does Chicken Cordon Bleu, wild rice, asparagus with hollandaise sauce, and that lovely chocolate mousse for dessert sound to you?"

"It sounds like I'll need to run extra at the gym tomorrow after I eat all that tonight."

Katie plopped down in the chair across from her. "We haven't had much time together the last few days. I want you to know how thankful I am to you for saving my brother. He can be a pest, but I love him." Katie's eyes teared up.

"I'm just glad to have been at the right place at the right time. I needed a break from Jake Perry, which sent me to the window where I could see Liam right in the nick of time." Jessie shook her head. "It still amazes me that I could push him out of the line of fire. You're both so much a part of my life. My childhood would have been boring without you two." She handed Katie a tissue. "May I get you something to drink?"

"Not me. I can't stay long. I have some new guests coming tonight. How are your aches and pains, by the way?" Katie reached across and grabbed Jessie's hands.

"Almost gone, thankfully." Jessie leaned forward. "My black eye is looking better, as you can see, and with the help of my sweet therapist, Dr. Gilbert, I'm sleeping better at night. Which makes me nicer to be around." Jessie smiled. "What's the latest news?"

"I don't know if you've heard or not, but Liam is moving here to stay. He's going to open a family law practice."

"That's nice. He'll stay away from some of those bad guys in New York, eh?" Jessie grinned. She loved it when Katie was in gossip mode.

"That's not all. Connor is moving here too. They're going to open an Irish pub together."

"Maybe it will keep the two of them out of trouble." Jessie paused. "They will be good for each other. Just think, they could tell their stories and entertain folks all evening long."

"I have to say I'm happy about both of them being here. I like Connor." Katie blushed.

"You like every male." Jessie laughed

"Yes, but I *really* like Connor."

"And Tom, Jeremy, and...ouch." Jessie rubbed her arm where Katie had pinched her.

"Pastor Kevin told me Liam needed a fresh start after his near brush with death." Katie's eyes took on the look that Jessie knew too well.

"Oh, I see. Now you're talking to Pastor Kevin, too." Jessie bit her lip.

"Of course. A girl has to keep all her options open. You never know who might be that right one." Katie fluttered her eyelashes.

"Well, I have a bit of news too." Jessie tried to sound serious, but it wasn't quite working, considering that she'd started giggling.

"You actually know something I don't know?" Katie mimed surprise.

Jessie nodded. "I got a letter from a mutual friend of ours and guess who's coming to Blue Cove for a visit?"

"I don't have a clue."

"Sally Mansfield." Jessie smothered another chuckle.

"You mean running through the graveyard with us, Sally Mansfield?" Katie laughed.

"The exact same one. Only now it's Sally Mansfield Kingman."

"It seems to me I heard that she was married. Wasn't she the first in our group to get married?"

"Yes, we were there. Don't you remember."

Katie smiled. "I wanted to see if you did."

"Of course. Now she will be among the first in our group to be divorced." Jessie stretched out her legs. "She mentioned in the letter that she was thinking about a divorce but wanted to come and talk to us first. It all sounds so mysterious."

"Wow, it's been a long time since I've heard her name. When is she coming?"

"Sometime in the next few months. She said she would call and talk to me soon."

"You and I are changing this town. Only time will tell if they'll love us for it or want us to move on—especially you, with all the weird things you see and do." Katie laughed and dodged the pillow Jessie threw at her. "I need to get back to the Inn. Be sure to let me know when Sally is coming."

"I will, and thanks for the dinner."

"That's dinners. One is for you, and one is for Matt," Katie said wistfully.

"I don't even know if he'll be here. He's been busy the last several days."

"He'll be here, so heat them both up. While you're at it, comb your hair and dress up a little, would you?" Katie laughed and walked out the door.

Jessie spent the afternoon following Katie's suggestion. She was happy to be back standing in her favorite place and looking out at the cove. Everything looked the same as the first day she had moved here. The only thing different was her. Blue Cove had woven its magic around her, changing everything about her. She had come here to acquire a new life, and, boy, the town had delivered on that. She heard the door open, her breath caught, and she knew he was there without turning.

"A penny for your thoughts?" Matt walked up behind her and wrapped his arms around her.

She relaxed against him. "The Cove is beautiful

today. I wonder how long the quiet will last this time." She sighed. "I have to admit that I was pretty scared. How many dangerous moments can one person take?"

"Are you asking me? I don't have an answer, if you are." He rested his chin on the top of her head.

"I'm just thinking aloud, I guess. I don't want to try and test my limits." She gazed out the window. "I was so confident that he wouldn't be able to hurt me, that the spirits wouldn't let him. But there were times when I wasn't sure if I would make it back to you." She snuggled closer into his arms. "Right here with you is where I want to be. I wanted to live so I could be here with you." He was her soul mate in every way. She smiled inwardly as the full revelation hit her.

"That's nice to know, sweetheart, because where you are is home to me," he whispered in her ear. "Truthfully, since we are confessing, I wasn't confident I could get to you in time after I heard the gunshots. When I came into the clearing, I wasn't sure what I would find. I definitely didn't expect to see you leaping from that damn tree. I still feel terrified every time I think about it."

"Really, why? I've been doing that since I was a kid; although, not so much in the last few years." She made a face. "I'm still a little sore from that escapade. If that scared you, I don't think you want to see how I got up in that tree in the first place. Coming down was the easy part." She turned in his arms to face him.

"Jess, you really are something." He pulled her tight against his chest.

"Would you care to explain what that something is?" She smiled against his shirt.

"No, I have something else in mind entirely."

"I see. I could try to read your mind, but I have a few ideas of my own." She pulled back in his arms so she could see his face.

"Would you care to elaborate?" He leaned a little closer to her and grinned.

Oh, how she loved that grin. She traced his lips with her finger. "Well," she said, slightly breathless. "I've meant to give you a small promotion—in honor of a campaign valiantly waged."

"I'm not sure I understand, sweetheart." The vein in his neck pulsated.

She gazed into his eyes. "You told me once you would charm me and win me over. Now, I have to admit I was a little skeptical at first, but you have been masterful, and I am charmed." She heard him take a deep breath." She moved closer to him. "Up to now, I've thought of you as my knight in shining armor, but I find you're more than that." She watched his face and spoke from her heart. "You're my Prince Charming. You're everything thing this girl has ever dreamed of."

"I can live with that." He stared at her lips. She felt herself getting lost in his searing look.

"I'm glad because you've won," She whispered. You see, Mr. Parker, I love you. I love being with you, I love your grin." She touched his lips again. "As a matter of fact, I love everything about you." She pulled his head down and kissed him.

He scooped her up in his arms, kissing her back. "Jess, sweetheart, you really are a mind reader."

A word about the author...

Iona Morrison is the author of *The Harvest Club, Not For Sale,* and *The Game Changer*, the first three books in the Blue Cove Mystery Series.

For this book she brought back Gina the ghost from *The Harvest Club* and a few friends.

~*~

http://www.ionamorrison.com
https://www.facebook.com/Iona-Morrison-Author
https://twitter.com/ionacrv
https://www.goodreads.com/author/show/8605155.Iona
_Morrison